THE GANGSTER'S GOLD

Ellen H. Reed

Copyright © 2016 by Ellen H. Reed

www.ellenhreed.com

ISBN-13 978-1537002675

ISBN-10 153700278

Printed by Create Space Publishing Platform

All rights reserved. No part of this publication may be reproduced, stored in any retrieval system, or transmitted in any form or by any means electronic, mechanical, recording, or otherwise, without prior written permission of the author.

This is a book of fiction. Any references to historical events, real people, or real locales are used fictitiously. Other names, characters, places and incidents are a product of the author's imagination and any resemblance to actual events, locales or persons, living or dead, is entirely coincidental.

Cover Design by Amanda Stacey of Hops Design

Printed in the United States of America

To my parents who always encouraged me to write and to my husband, Tim, who patiently urged me on.

CHAPTER ONE
2002

Saying good-bye to Krista was without a doubt the worst part of this whole ordeal. Who in their right mind chose to move from Washington, D.C., to someplace like *Maine*? Maine, a place known for its never ending winters, giant mountains and bear-infested wilderness. What was there that could possibly replace Krista? Nothing, that's what.

Gwen Andersson sniffed, trying not to cry. She couldn't possibly imagine feeling any worse than she did this very moment. For most of her life, Gwen hadn't had any close friends. Oh sure, she got invited to the occasional birthday party, mostly because all the girls in the class were. To be honest, books had been her only real friends. Then Krista moved in next door two years ago and everything changed. Krista was a lot like Gwen. She was quiet, loved books and making up stories. She didn't like change and was content to spend long hours sitting next to Gwen reading. They had been a perfect pair. They were supposed to start seventh grade together in the fall. But that was all over now, wasn't it? Her parents were dragging her off to the wilds of Maine and now Gwen was totally and utterly alone. Again.

Gwen glared at her parents in the front seat of the family SUV. Her mom had the map open on her lap. She always navigated on family trips. Her father was jabbering on about that stupid bed and breakfast he was going to open. Whoopee. What on earth did he know about running an inn? He'd been a foreign aid worker for crying out loud. Just because some old relative left her dad a house didn't mean they had to live in it, did it? And turning it into a hotel in the middle of nowhere was insane. Besides, wouldn't that mean they'd have to share their house with all kinds of weirdoes and creeps? Gwen shivered at the thought.

She glanced over at her brother. Lance was immersed in a handheld video game. He was fourteen, two years older than Gwen, and if the girls in school were to be believed, incredibly hot. With his shaggy jet black hair and brilliant blue eyes, he was quite a contrast to Gwen with her mousey brown eyes and hair. He was athletic, popular and never had trouble making friends. To Gwen, he was just a pain in the butt, who often made her the victim of his practical jokes. She sighed.

Beyond Lance was her sister, Faye. She was reading some book about Maine. Figures. Faye, at seventeen, was an obnoxious know-it-all. Gwen was sure she only read stuff so she could make everybody else look stupid. It was her favorite indoor sport.

Gwen rolled her eyes and turned her attention back to the scenery. Just more depressing highway. They were on the second day of the two-day trip to Maine, although it felt more like two weeks. She was beyond bored. She was bored *and* miserable. She slumped farther into her seat. She stared at pieces of potato chips mashed into the carpet. "Dad, why did your great-uncle or whoever leave this stupid house to you? I mean, didn't anyone else want it? You know, like one of his kids?"

Dad glanced back at her then shrugged. "Well, I know I'm not his closest relation. I guess his kids didn't want it and, for some reason, he didn't want to pass it on to his only grandson. So, that left me. These big old Victorians aren't cheap to maintain, and I imagine no one wanted the expense."

"Then why not just sell it?" Lance finally separated himself from his game. "If nobody wanted it, why keep it?"

"No doubt it has to do with the missing treasure." Mom glanced back with a smile.

"What missing treasure?" Faye looked up from her book.

Gwen said nothing. She had to admit missing treasure *did* sound interesting, but there was no way she was going to let anyone see she cared. She stared out the window, determined to remain miserable.

Dad laughed. "Well, there's a legend my grandfather's brother, Charlie Andersson, disappeared along with a bag full of gangster loot. The story says he and another kid were transporting money for some local gangster. One night the two of them went out, but only one of them came back. The loss of the money stirred up a lot of trouble with this gangster and bad feelings within the family. I guess it was quite a mess. Some believe Great-Uncle Charlie took off with a quarter of a million dollars and headed west. On the other hand, there are some that believe Charlie was killed by rival gangsters and the money is still around Fishawak someplace, just waiting to be found."

"When did all this happen?" Faye leaned forward. Gwen could almost see the dollar signs in her sister's eyes.

"Oh, sometime in the nineteen twenties."

Gwen chewed her lip as she considered her father's story. Finding lost treasure really would be cool. Then she shrugged. It probably wasn't even true. Just some stupid story for tourists. She glanced again at the others who now excitedly discussed the money. She shook her head with a dismissive sniff. *Let them waste their time chasing fairy tales. I have better things to do.* She opened her book. She couldn't concentrate on the story, though. An image of a bag crammed full of money popped into her head. It really couldn't be still around…could it? If only Krista were here. They could find it together.

Gwen blinked, fighting the urge to cry. She pictured Krista, her friend's face stained with tears, waving good-bye as the Anderssons drove away. Gwen's throat tightened. She rested her head against the cool glass of the window and finally let her tears fall. As far as she was concerned, her life was over.

When there were no more tears to be shed, Gwen leaned back against the seat. Suddenly, she was exhausted. She closed her eyes and let the rhythm of the highway slowly lull her to sleep.

When she awoke, Gwen was surprised they had left the cities behind and were now in the country. Scrubby trees lined both sides of the road and houses were farther apart. Gwen noted several large wooden homes with towers and wrap-around porches. *Those are kind of pretty. Is that what ours is going to look like?* She shook her head, irritated with herself. *Our old house in D.C. was better than any of these dumps.*

She sat up and pulled a soda from the cooler. "How much farther?" She glanced around. Lance was sound asleep and Faye was engrossed in a novel. It was late afternoon now, and the sun was well past its peak.

"About another hour." Her father yawned. "We'll be staying at a motel for a few days until we get things sorted out. No one has lived in the house for years, and I'm sure it'll need some work to make it livable again. I've had an electrician and plumber out to make any repairs, so we should have power and water at least."

"Great." Gwen popped the top of her soda. "Can't wait." *Doesn't that sound fun.* She silently watched the scenery speed by. Lost in thought, she was surprised when her dad pulled up to a small rundown motel. Gwen inwardly groaned when she noticed the sign boasting "Air-Conditioning and Color TV." *At least it didn't mention AM/FM Radio.* She shook her head. These were sure signs the hotel wasn't exactly the Hilton.

"Do we have to stay here?" Gwen whined. She knew she sounded like a brat, but she was tired and just wanted to be back in D.C. with Krista. "This place looks like a real dump."

"Ah, who needs one of those fancy-schmantzy hotels?" Her dad pulled into the parking lot.

Gwen winced as the car dropped into a deep pothole.

"To really get the feel of a place you have to live amongst the natives."

Gwen just rolled her eyes. She hated it when her father talked like that.

Ten minutes later, they'd checked in and pulled the car in front of their rooms. Gwen and Faye shared one, her parents another and Lance had a room to himself. As usual. Gwen glared at her brother. He gave her a jaunty little wave and firmly closed his door in her face.

Muttering under her breath, Gwen stood with her suitcase in hand as Faye opened the door to their room. Stepping inside, Gwen wrinkled her nose in disgust. The room felt damp and smelled musty. It was decorated in depressing shades of dirt brown and muddy gold. This just got worse by the minute. Eyeing the beds warily, she couldn't help but wonder who'd slept there before them. She shuddered, not wanting to think about it. The bathroom wasn't any better. What on earth was Dad thinking? This place made her skin crawl. She dropped her suitcase on the floor and tentatively sat on the edge of the bed nearest the bathroom. At least they were out of that cramped car.

She looked up as her mom opened the door. "We'll be leaving here in about fifteen minutes. Dad wants to go look at the house while it's still light then go to dinner."

Faye and Gwen exchanged weary glances. Despite the grim surroundings, Gwen would have been happy to just hang out in the hotel and watch TV, but she knew arguing with her parents was pointless.

Twenty minutes later, Gwen was back in the car headed to their new home. Despite stories of lost treasure, Gwen was certain nothing about this house would make her happy. As far as she was concerned, this old rutted road led to nothing more than a life of misery and loneliness.

CHAPTER TWO

Fewer trees were visible as they got closer to the shore. Gwen opened her window and inhaled the salty air. She had always loved the smell of the ocean. *Probably the only thing I'll like about Maine.* She twisted a strand of hair. They soon left the main road and turned onto a narrow, pitted track that wound up a bluff overlooking the Atlantic Ocean. Clumps of sea grass and other scrubby brush lined the road and grew through the broken patches in the asphalt.

As they reached the crest of the bluff, the house came into view. It was a massive house that boasted a tall round turret on one corner and a huge wrap-around porch that embraced the entire lower half. Once it must have been quite a show place, but now it was simply a sad, neglected relic of a bygone age. The paint had faded to sickly, mottled beige where it hadn't peeled off entirely. Shutters hung askew from the empty windows and many of those on the lower level were boarded over. Old wasp nests hung from the eaves while grass and other vegetation grew rampant all around the house, further emphasizing its sad deterioration.

"According to my book, this house is in the Queen Anne style." Faye pointed at the house. "The tower and large porch are definite indicators. All that fancy woodwork is called gingerbread…"

Gwen immediately tuned her out. Faye pretty much

considered herself an expert on everything and frankly, Gwen couldn't care less what that fancy woodwork was called. It looked like it should be torn down.

"Uh, Dad," began Lance, "Exactly *how* long has this place been empty?"

"Well, I'm not sure." Dad stared at the house, his voice low. "At least thirty years I think. I was hoping it might be in a little better shape."

"You mean you didn't even check it out first?" Gwen whirled to face her father. "You dragged us all the way up here, and you haven't even *seen* this dump?"

Her father lifted his hands. "Hey, I saw some photos."

Gwen shook her head. This was so typical. Dad probably looked at a few photos taken fifty years ago and decided the house was perfect. Forget coming to look at it in person. *That* would make too much sense. Gwen slumped farther into her seat. This just got worse all the time.

Her father pulled the car in as close to the house as he could and turned off the engine. They sat in silence, staring at the house. Finally, Mom opened the car door and climbed out. Gwen and the others slowly followed in her wake.

Gwen shook her head in disgust as she took a few tentative steps toward the house. The hulking form of the derelict structure towered above them. *Jeez, the thing must have like a hundred rooms.* She looked up toward the windows at the very top. It looked as sad and lonely as she felt.

Suddenly, Gwen froze as a flicker of light in one of the upper windows caught her eye. Had she just detected some kind of movement up there? The rest of her family was talking and climbing up the steps to the porch, but she stood glued to the spot, a tight knot forming in her stomach. She blinked and stared harder at the window in the center of the top floor. There! There *was* somebody up there. She was sure of it. She'd just made out the shadow of a figure before it disappeared. Somebody must be hiding in the house, figuring since it was abandoned no one would care.

"Dad!" Gwen ran toward the house. "Wait!"

Her father turned, his key in the lock. "What's wrong?"

Gwen clambered up the stairs, panting slightly. "There's somebody in the house. In the attic. I saw them!"

Everyone stared at her for a moment then moved back and instinctively looked upwards. Nothing moved.

"Are you sure?" Her mother frowned.

Gwen nodded rapidly. "I saw a face in the upper window–twice. I know there's somebody up there."

Dad's jaw tightened. "Okay, I want all of you to move to the car. I'm going to go in and see what's going on."

"Let me come." Lance stepped forward. He'd played football for years and was powerfully built. Dad hesitated, nodded then cautiously pushed open the door. Her mother herded the two girls closer to the car where they turned to watch and wait. It was a good ten or fifteen minutes before Dad and Lance returned. Lance was laughing.

"Well, Gwennie," Dad approached the car, "I'm not sure what you saw, but we couldn't find any signs that anyone besides the electrician and plumber has been here."

"But Dad! I'm sure I saw somebody. Right in that window up there. I'm not making this up."

Her father shrugged. "The door to the attic level was locked. It took us awhile to even find the key. There wasn't any sign someone was up there. Believe me, there is so much dust on the attic floor that if there had been, I'm sure they would have left tracks. It was probably just a reflection."

"Maybe it was a ghooooosst!" moaned Lance in an eerie voice.

Gwen just glared at him. She'd been so certain she'd seen *something* in that window, but maybe it was just her imagination playing tricks on her. The knot in her stomach said otherwise. She glanced back up at the window. It was a pretty creepy-looking house even in the daylight. She had the feeling it was going to be tough *not* to imagine ghosts around every corner in this dump.

"Okay, that's enough." Dad turned back to the house. "Let's all go inside and take a better look at this place."

Gwen's face burned as she trailed behind the others into the house. She should have just kept her mouth shut. Lance was never going to let her forget this. She still heard him laughing.

Passing through the front door, she shivered slightly as she felt a drop in the temperature. It seemed oddly chilly in the house. She rubbed her arms. It must be all the broken windows. They stood in a large foyer with a ceiling that had to be twenty feet high. An old chandelier draped with dusty cobwebs hung crookedly above. Just in front of them rose a magnificent staircase splitting in two directions at the landing then sweeping up to the upper levels like graceful wings. Gwen's mouth hung open. The focal point of the staircase landing was a huge stained glass window, dulled by years of grime and neglect, depicting what appeared to be the ocean view from the house. *It must be amazing when it's clean.*

"That is *so* cool." Faye stood beside her. "Can you imagine how much that must have cost to make? It's amazing! Maybe it's even a Tiffany. That would be worth a fortune."

Gwen just rolled her eyes and ignored her.

Once Gwen tore her eyes away from the spectacular window, she became more fully aware of just how decrepit the rest of the house really was. The first floor was composed of a kitchen, parlor, dining room, library, conservatory and what Mom said was supposed to be a music room. All Gwen noticed was the rotting, peeling wallpaper, the musty smell of mildew and the dull, encrusted woodwork. Doors hung off their hinges; broken banisters and warped flooring just added to the picture of decay. Gwen rubbed her nose. There was an acrid smell that made it burn.

Lance leaned over and pointed to small dark piles on the floor and grinned. "Mouse poop." Gwen felt sick. She couldn't believe they were going to actually *live* in this disaster.

Fearful the stairs might give way beneath her, Gwen followed the others up the main staircase to a long, dim hallway covered by the remains of moldy, tattered carpet. There were six large bedrooms up here and a couple of bathrooms.

Mom frowned as she peered into the closest bathroom. "I'm thinking the last time these were upgraded Truman was president."

Gwen just shuddered at the mess and turned away. The decay upstairs was no better than below. There was one more level above this. She was sure it would be just as bad.

"Servants lived up in the attic." Dad opened the door. "I believe there was a playroom up there, as well, for the children of the house."

"They had servants here?" asked Faye.

"Everyone had servants back when this house was built." Dad flicked a switch. "It was the only way you could keep a house like this going. Everything had to be done by hand, like laundry, cleaning, cooking and so on. There's no way one person could do it all. Jonas Andersson, my great-grandfather, was pretty wealthy. That was before he lost everything back in the twenties."

They climbed the dark, narrow stairs up to the third

level. A single bulb dimly lit the way. Gwen shuddered as a cobweb trailed across her cheek.

On the top level there were four small bedrooms and one bathroom as well as one larger room with a few shelves built into the walls. Undoubtedly, this was the playroom her father had mentioned. This room looked out to the ocean, and a second tower created a round sitting area with window seats. Gwen wandered over to the sitting area and paused. The seat was covered with dust and dirt, yet she could picture sitting up here reading her books, listening to the relaxing ocean roar. She gave a sniff of disdain. Yeah right. The wood was probably rotten, and she'd just fall through to certain death or get eaten by rats. She turned away.

"We'll convert this level to the family living space," her dad said.

She drifted off to look at the smaller rooms. All the rooms were empty. These must have been for the servants. Two had windows that looked out toward the road. Gwen frowned. She must have seen the mysterious figure in the window of one of these rooms. She stepped into the first chamber and glanced out the window. She quickly decided it was too far off to the side. It must have been the next one.

She turned and walked out of the room to the doorway of the second room and paused. She peered in, ready to run. There was no sign of anyone. Gwen stooped down to examine the floor. Her dad was right. There was so much dust any footsteps would have been obvious, and there were none near the window. All tracks in the dust ended at the doorway. Lance and her father must not have actually entered the room.

Taking a deep breath, Gwen stepped into the room, one hesitant step at a time. Nothing happened. Her shoulders relaxed. She laughed softly. *Gwen, you're such a chicken.* She moved farther into the room and looked out the window. Yes, this was the right place, but she must have imagined the shadowy figure. She'd just been so sure.

Standing there in the late afternoon light, she began to absently rub her arms. A chill rippled over her skin. She shivered and closed her eyes for a moment. There was something very odd about this room. She just couldn't figure out what it was.

Gwen swallowed, surprised her mouth had gone bone dry. The hairs on the back of her neck stood up as the cold knot in her stomach returned. With a shock, she couldn't move a muscle. She couldn't breathe, couldn't think. She desperately wanted to call out to her family yet couldn't make the slightest sound. Her very core was chilled. Out of the corner of her eye there was a flash of light.

Then a voice, no more substantial than the softest whisper, sounded in her mind.

"Help me."

It was the last thing she remembered.

CHAPTER THREE

"Gwen! Come on, Gwennie, wake up. Come on, sweetie, wake up." A voice seemed to be calling from far, far away, and it took her a moment before she realized it was her mother's. Slowly, she opened her eyes and blinked, trying to focus in on the faces hovering above her.

"Gwen! Are you okay? What happened?"

Gwen blinked a few more times then struggled to sit up. Her head spun, but after a few deep breaths, the world settled down. She gratefully took the bottle of water her mother offered. "I… I don't know. I…just suddenly felt really cold, and next thing I know, here I am."

"How do you feel now?" Her dad hunkered down beside her, placing a hand on her arm.

"A little dizzy but okay." She bit her lip and decided not to mention the weird voice she heard. Well, *thought* she heard anyway. She glanced at Lance. He'd just laugh at her again. Really, it was just this creepy house. It made her imagine things.

"Okay." Dad patted her shoulder then stood. "I think we've had enough sightseeing today, and it's way past dinnertime. I think Gwen just needs something to eat and a good night's sleep. Then she'll be fine. Tomorrow we have a lot of work to do, and I think we should go find some food before we head back to the hotel."

Gwen was silent as the family drove back into town to find someplace for dinner. They opted for a local seafood joint. Gwen had little appetite. She felt her parents watching her closely. She'd never fainted before. It made her feel like an idiot as well as a little unnerved. She barely listened as her father described all the plans he had for the house and outlined what they'd be doing the next few days.

Had she really heard a voice up in that little room, or had it just been her imagination…again? Could she have imagined both a voice *and* a person at different times in the exact same place? She frowned as she picked at her popcorn shrimp. She refused to acknowledge that word hovering at the edge of her confused thoughts. She glanced over at Lance who, as usual, shoveled in food as quickly as he could pile it on his fork. He was the one that started it, him and his stupid *ghosts.* Gwen pressed her lips together and shook her head. No! *There are no such things as ghosts.* Sure, the house looked like something out of the *Addam's Family*, but that was no reason to think it was actually haunted. She sighed. Her dad was probably right–it was just a combination of being tired and hungry. Once they got the house all cleaned up, it would be just fine. Maybe.

The next morning was gray and chilly. Gwen sat in the hotel with Faye watching TV, while her parents and Lance scoured the town for the supplies they needed to get started on the house. Although her dad claimed they were going to do a lot of the work themselves, Gwen still hoped he'd eventually cave in and hire some professionals. Her parents had renovated their house back in D.C. They did an amazing job, but what really stuck with Gwen was how their lives were turned into a complete mess for months. She clearly remembered the gritty taste and feel of the sawdust and plaster. It got into everything. She dreaded the thought of going through all that again. Especially with as big as this monstrosity was, it could take *years* for them to finish all the renovations.

Her parents and Lance returned around lunchtime, somewhat discouraged. "We still need to get a bunch more stuff. The local hardware store doesn't have everything we need, so we'll have to look elsewhere," Dad said as they sat down to lunch at the local McDonald's. "I don't think we'll get up to the house until tomorrow." He turned to Gwen. "The public library is just a short walk from the motel if you want to go check it out."

Gwen's eyes brightened. "That would be great!"

"I don't guess there's anything like a mall in this town, is there?" Next to being a know-it-all, Faye loved nothing more than shopping.

"Well, not exactly," said Mom. "However, there is the downtown pedestrian shopping area. They've closed off part of Main Street and opened lots of little boutiques, souvenir shops, restaurants and so on. We drove by, and it looks charming. I don't think they have the same stores you're used to, but I imagine you could find something."

Faye looked doubtful but shrugged and said it would be something to do. She looked at Lance and Gwen. "Why don't we all go? You can go to the library later, Gwennie. It's not going anyplace."

Lance grunted his assent.

Gwen thought about it a minute. As much as she'd love to check out the library, Faye was right; there'd be time enough for that. All summer, in fact. Maybe there'd be a bookstore. That would be worth the trip.

After lunch, her parents dropped the three of them off at the shopping district. They'd be back in a couple of hours.

Gwen had to agree with her mother. She loved the downtown area with its bricked walkways, quaint little stores and plentiful shade trees and benches. *It's like Main Street at Disneyland.* Gwen sat on one of the benches eating frozen custard. In some ways, it didn't seem like a real town. It was just too pretty.

"Oh, look here!" cried Faye a short while later hurrying to a shop window. She hauled Gwen into a little boutique full of funky and unusual clothes.

Gwen groaned and rolled her eyes. She absolutely hated it when Faye did this. Gwen could imagine few things more boring than spending an afternoon watching her sister try on clothing.

Faye *had* to have the weirdest sense of style of anyone Gwen had ever met. Right now she was into a bizarre Renaissance/motorcycle gang look.

Gwen looked around hoping Lance would rescue her, but he'd disappeared into a board shop next door probably to check out their selection of skate boards. That was even worse.

With a sigh of disgust, Gwen wandered over to the entrance of the boutique and spent several minutes gazing at the people that walked by. Suddenly she noticed a sign on a small building across the way. It said Fishawak Historical Society. Gwen glanced back at her sister. Faye was busy piling clothes into the arms of a waiting shop girl. They were both laughing. *She'll never even notice I'm gone.* Gwen turned back to study the small building. Gwen loved history, and perhaps the historical society might have some more information on that legend about the missing gangster money. She grinned as she imagined being able to tell know-it-all Faye a thing or two.

Leaving her sister to immerse herself in gauzy skirts and studded leather jackets, Gwen made her way to the historical society. She pushed open the door and stepped in. She took a deep breath. She loved the familiar musty smell of old books. It took her eyes a minute to adjust to the dim room, but she soon made out shelves of books and several large tables. The place appeared deserted. "Hello?" She searched for anyone who might work there.

"Hullo."

Gwen's heart jumped as she whirled around.

A girl about her age stood next to a desk in the corner. "Can I help you?"

Gwen was speechless for a moment. She'd expected an old gray-haired lady, not some kid.

"Um, we've just moved here and well, I was trying to find out some stuff about the town."

The girl studied her for a few moments before grinning. "I didn't think I recognized you, and I know *everybody* in this boring town. My name is Molly, by the way, and I'm just helping my grandma. She's the one that really runs this place. Where did you move from? What grade are you going into? Where's your house?"

Gwen just blinked at the sudden verbal onslaught.

It was as if once this girl got going, there was no stopping her. She was tall and lanky with wild red hair and freckles. Being shy, Gwen had always felt a bit intimidated by outgoing girls, but Molly reminded Gwen of a happy puppy, all gangly and delighted to meet you.

"Um." Gwen tried to figure out which question to answer first. "My name is Gwen, and we moved here from Washington, D.C. My dad inherited that old house up on the bluff."

Molly's eyes went wide. "The old Carmichael place? Really? That place is haunted, y'know. You're really gonna live *there*? Wow. You couldn't pay me enough to even spend one night there. You must be really brave."

"What do you mean it's haunted?" That knot returned in her stomach. After her recent experiences at the house, she wasn't entirely surprised by this announcement, but it creeped her out nonetheless.

Molly shrugged as she leaned against the desk. "It's just what everybody says. People say you can sometimes see lights moving around, and my cousin claims he saw a face in one of the windows. Other people say you can hear screams and gunshots. Gangsters lived there y'know."

Gwen bit her lip. "Do you know anything about missing gangster money? My dad was telling us a story about some guy that ran off with a bunch of gangster loot and was never heard from again."

"*Everybody* knows about the missing gangster money." Molly tossed her hair. "Every year we get a bunch of stupid tourists who've read the story and just know *they'll* be the ones to figure out the mystery. I think every kid since nineteen twenty-three has tried to find that money, but no one ever has. There's never been any sign of Charlie Andersson since he disappeared that night."

"So, what really happened?"

"Well," Molly leaned forward, her voice low. "Back in nineteen twenty-three, Charlie Andersson and his partner, Bertie Carmichael, worked as bagmen for a big-time gangster, Jimmy "The Blade" Houlihan. That means they collected money from people and delivered it to Jimmy. Anyway, one night Charlie disappeared with a quarter of a million dollars and was never heard from again. Bertie claimed they were chased and the two separated. There were all kinds of rumors at the time, but most people believe Charlie saw an opportunity and took it. They figure he stole the money and headed out west where no one would ever find him. It absolutely ruined the Andersson family. They lost everything. There's a book here that tells all about it. Ever since my grandpa was little, kids have tried to find the missing money. It's the biggest mystery in Fishawak!"

"Wow." Gwen's head spun. "So, do you think the money is still here?"

Molly shrugged. "Nah. I think somebody would have found it by now. I mean it's been like eighty years."

"Yeah, but lots of treasures have been hidden for hundreds, even thousands of years. Maybe Charlie Andersson hid it really well, and it's still here."

Molly shrugged again. "Maybe." Then she grinned. "Wouldn't it be really cool to be the ones to find it? It'd be like winning the lottery."

Gwen nodded. Finding that missing money could really make a difference. Her father had worked for an organization that helped third world countries. Last year he was shot and almost killed during an uprising in central Africa and forced to retire. That's why he was so keen to open this bed and breakfast. If they found the money, maybe they wouldn't have to open a stupid hotel. They could take the money and move back to D.C. And Krista. Gwen smiled. That was reason enough to find the missing money.

The front door opened, and a tall woman with short, red hair heavily streaked with gray entered carrying a couple of sodas. She stopped in surprise when she noticed Gwen. "Well, hello there." She turned to Molly. "Would you like to introduce me to your friend?"

"Oh, we just met, Grandma. She came looking for information on the gangster gold. Her family is moving into the old Carmichael place!"

"Ah!" Molly's grandmother eyes lit up. "Welcome to Fishawak. My name is Janet Berger. I'd be happy to tell you anything you'd like to know. That is a very historic house your family has purchased. It was built by Jonas Andersson in 1890. It was considered to be one of the finest homes in town back in the day."

Gwen nodded. "My name is Gwen Andersson. I think Jonas Andersson was like my great-great-grandfather. The house was left to my dad. He wants to fix it up and turn it into a bed and breakfast."

"What a marvelous idea!" Mrs. Berger beamed. "It's certainly large enough for such an enterprise and has a stunning location up there on the bluff. It would be wonderful to see it returned to its former glory."

"Too bad it's haunted," muttered Molly.

Mrs. Berger scowled at her granddaughter then turned again to Gwen. "Don't listen to Molly. There are always rumors of ghosts with any old, empty house like that. Although…" She grinned a bit mischievously. "I've always heard ghosts in hotels can really bring in the customers. There are some people who specifically seek out haunted hotels. So, who knows? You might want to put that in your brochure."

Gwen wasn't so sure that was a good idea but laughed anyway. She was worried there was more to the ghost stories than simply rumors.

The door opened again, and Faye looked in, her dark, curly hair blowing in a wild tangle around her face. She had an impatient scowl on her face. "Finally! I've been looking all over for you. It looks like a storm is coming up, and Mom's waiting. C'mon, let's go."

"Hold on, Gwen." Mrs. Berger went to a rack and pulled out a pamphlet. It was titled *The Legend of the Gangster's Gold.* She shook her head a little as she handed it to Gwen. "The title is rather misleading since it would have been cash, not actual gold, but 'Gangster's Cash' doesn't quite have the same ring to it, does it? Anyway, this tells the whole story or at least as much as is known, so perhaps it will answer some of your questions. Feel free to come back anytime."

Molly stepped forward and handed Gwen a piece of paper. "Here's my phone number. Call me when you get settled, or else you can always find me here. I love history, so it would be nice to have somebody else that understands that. Most of the girls here don't care about anything but boys, clothes, makeup and the latest reality show. It's really boring."

Gwen took the paper and smiled. She followed Faye out the door. She'd actually made a friend. Maybe things were beginning to look up.

CHAPTER FOUR

Early the next morning, the Anderssons headed out to the house armed with a full arsenal of cleaning supplies, ladders and tools piled into a rented trailer. Dad was determined they move into the house as soon as possible.

"This is going to be so much fun," he exclaimed as they drove along.

Gwen and Lance exchanged knowing glances. Fun was hardly the word Gwen would use. She saw it as nothing more than months and months of inconvenience, sawdust and noise.

"Okay." Dad pulled up to the house. "First of all, your mother and I will take the big master bedroom at the front of the house, but you guys can each pick out your own room from the other five bedrooms. It will be your responsibility to clean up that room and start making it livable. I want to get the main level restored first, then I'll convert the attic level to family living quarters, and we'll all move up there. Then the bedrooms will be redone, and we'll be ready for business!"

Gwen shook her head. Dad made it all sound so simple, but she knew perfectly well they were all in for months, maybe even years, of misery.

Once inside the house, Gwen, Faye and Lance roamed through the five bedrooms, carefully inspecting each. Faye decided she wanted one of the front bedrooms because, not only was it closest to the bathroom, but it also had the largest closet. Lance chose one that had a small separate sitting area. He said it would be a great place to store all his athletic equipment. Gwen wandered into the one at the end of the hall. It was near the back stairs that led both up to the attic and downstairs to the back of the house. She was delighted to find the outer wall was part of the tower and created a cozy little sitting area identical to the one in the attic. This was perfect, and she knew it was meant to be hers.

She went back downstairs. Her parents were in the kitchen where they discussed all that would need to be done in order to update it into a more commercial facility.

"Mom, I picked out my room. Now what?"

Mom glanced at her. "Oh, we'll be unloading the trailer in just a few minutes, but you can explore until then."

Gwen nodded and trudged back upstairs. She looked at the flight leading to the attic and shivered. It had been pretty creepy up there, yet something pulled at her, urging her to venture back. She chewed on her lower lip as she considered whether or not she should go. *Gwen Andersson, there are no ghosts in this house. You're just being stupid. It's broad daylight, and even if there were ghosts, they don't come out until dark. Just go!*

She took a deep breath, pulled open the attic door and quickly hurried up the narrow stairs to the hallway at the top. Bright light poured in through the windows from the rooms on either side of the hall. Gwen hesitated then turned and entered the large playroom.

She paused in the doorway and looked around. The room was empty, except for dust and cobwebs. She sneezed. There was a stone fireplace at one end and the remains of shelves lined one wall. She imagined it was a very cheerful place in better days. Broad windows lined the wall facing the ocean and, of course, there was the curved sitting area in the tower. As she slowly made her way around the room, Gwen noticed a door that opened onto a wide outdoor balcony. She walked over and turned the knob. It wasn't locked, but the door was stuck.

Using her shoulder, Gwen shoved until the door finally popped open. Peering out, she frowned doubtfully at the balcony. Was it safe? She tentatively put a foot out on the weathered red tiles. It seemed sturdy enough. She stepped out and laughed as the fresh sea breeze whipped around her and the roar of the ocean filled her ears. She had to admit, it was beautiful here. She gazed out toward the rolling waves of the sea and relaxed in the warm embrace of the sun.

Suddenly, a tremendous bang sent a vibration through the balcony. Gwen whirled about, her hand flying to her mouth. The balcony door was now closed. Her heart beat wildly as she stared at the door for several long seconds. When nothing more happened, she released her breath with a whoosh. Of course. The breeze must have blown it shut. It was really windy up here after all. Her knees went weak as she gave a little laugh. Well, it was time to go in anyway.

She stepped over to the door and pulled on the knob. It wouldn't budge. Frowning, Gwen pulled harder.

Nothing.

An uncomfortable tightness grew in her stomach. *Okay, don't panic. It's just an old door and it's stuck.* She pushed her blowing hair out of her face. What should she do? She peered through the beveled glass panes in the door and froze.

There, standing near the doorway of the room was the shadowy figure of a person. The hair rose on her neck. Then she shook herself. *Lance!* It had to be. He must have come up to find her. She banged on the door and called her brother's name. She struggled to get a better view through the windows, but they were so covered with salt residue and grime, it was hard to see anything clearly. She tried to scrape away some of the filth. She looked through the beveled glass again. The figure was still there, unmoving. She called again then stopped, the words caught in her throat. The figure simply dissolved. One second it was there and the next…it was gone.

Unable to breathe, Gwen slowly backed away from the door. Her body was like lead; each movement took all her strength. Surely she hadn't just seen that? People didn't just *dissolve!* As she backed away from the door, everything went silent. It was if the world had been put on mute. She stopped only when she came up against the wrought iron railing encircling the balcony. She stumbled and felt the railing start to give way.

With a scream, she scrabbled to get a grip on another section of the railing. She was one step from going over the edge and plummeting onto the rocky bluff below. She cried out again as her fingers slipped off the slick metal. Her body continued to tumble backwards. She grabbed for the railing again. The rusted metal simply dissolved in her grasp. Fighting to breathe, Gwen flailed about trying to anchor herself to something, anything, but there was nothing.

Gwen tightly closed her eyes. She was going over, and she was helpless to prevent it. As she began to tip over the side, someone or something grabbed her by the wrist and hauled her roughly back to the safety of the balcony. For the briefest moment, Gwen thought a young man with blond hair stood over her before she collapsed onto the balcony. Gasping for air, Gwen lay there for several long moments trying to convince her heart to start again.

"Gwen?" Lance hovered over her, frowning. "You okay?"

Gwen gaped at him, his dark hair ruffling in the breeze, then laughed shakily. "Yeah, I…I…just tripped and the railing came loose. Thanks." *Of course.* She put the image of the blond-haired boy from her mind. *It must have been Lance in the playroom after all.* She'd been *so* stupid to think there was some kind of ghostly presence in the room. That was just crazy. *There are no such things as ghosts.* She could never admit to Lance she'd thought he was a ghost. He'd never let her live *that* down.

Lance studied the broken railing then glanced at his sister again. "You better stay off this balcony. I don't think it's safe. I'll tell Dad. Listen, Mom wants us all downstairs. I just came up to tell you." He paused, his eyes narrowed. "You *sure* you're okay?"

"I'm fine," Gwen assured him as she sat up. Lance nodded although he still looked uncertain.

Finally he shrugged, turned and left. The loud thump of his footsteps faded down the stairs.

Shaken, Gwen got to her feet and stumbled to the balcony door. The door was wide open now. She turned and glanced back at the broken railing, swallowing hard. She couldn't remember ever being so scared. Her heart still raced. She shuddered to think of what could have happened if Lance hadn't arrived in time to pull her back onto the balcony. That really was lucky.

Gwen frowned as she replayed the scene in her mind. It had happened so quickly. The image of the strange young man came back to her. She shook her head again, attempting to dismiss the thought her rescuer could have been anyone but Lance. There simply couldn't be any other logical explanation. Right?

As she started for the stairs, a bright ray of sunlight cutting through the filthy windows caught her attention. *How weird.* She paused to follow the path of the beam. It seemed to spotlight the closet door as if inviting Gwen to come and investigate.

Gwen stared at the door, her brow furrowed. Did this mean something? She glanced around uncertainly, still feeling a little shaken. For a brief moment, she pictured the mysterious figure disappearing before her eyes.

"Come on, Gwen, get out of here," she muttered as she headed toward the stairs once more. She paused by the doorway and looked back. The sun still shone on the closet. She pushed her hair from her face as she glanced around the room. She was drawn, as if the closet called to her. Brows knitted, Gwen struggled between the urge to get out of that creepy attic as quickly as possible and the strange call of the closet. She took a deep breath and took a step back into the playroom, then a second and a third.

Slowly, she moved toward the closet door. Standing a few feet away, she examined it closely. The door, painted a dingy white, hung partially open. Gwen tried to see inside, but the darkness held her back. Holding her breath, Gwen very slowly, very cautiously pulled the door open wide. She immediately jumped back as if expecting a boogieman to leap out. There was nothing. With a nervous laugh, she pulled out the little keychain penlight she always carried and peered in. Carefully, she shone her light all around the interior of the closet. It was quite deep and completely empty.

Gwen sighed, disappointed. She wasn't sure what she'd expected, but something more than an empty closet. She was about to close the door when her attention was caught by odd marks on the door frame. She frowned as she tried to make them out in the shadows. She shone her light on the frame.

There were numerous pencil marks all labeled with a name and date. One said "Tom, 6 yrs. June 4, 1918," another, "Charlie, 13 yrs. July 9, 1920" and so on. The marks started with those of William in 1903, followed by Louise in 1905, Charlie in 1911 and Tom in 1913. It took her a moment to realize these must be height marks of children who lived in the house over eighty years before.

A jolt of surprise ran through her as she spotted her own name. "Gwen, 11 yrs., May 15, 1922." Gwen stared at the name for a long moment, trying to picture this unknown girl with her name. It seemed like such an incredible coincidence. She glanced at the other dates and noticed the last were in 1924. Suddenly Gwen's eyes grew round as she looked at the names again and focused on Charlie. Could this be *the* Charlie? The Charlie Andersson who stole the money from Jimmy "The Blade" Houlihan? She knew her father's grandfather's name was Bill, and that was short for William, wasn't it? He was Charlie's brother so these must be the names of all the Andersson kids. Her heartbeat quickened.

Who was this Gwen? The girl didn't show up until she was eleven, so it wasn't likely she was one of the Andersson children. A relative maybe? How strange to think this girl with her name and close to her age was measured in this very spot so many years ago. She shivered.

"Gwen!" Mom called. "Come on. It's time to get started on your room. Quit dawdling."

Gwen sighed. She would have liked to examine the dates and closet some more, but she knew if she didn't show up soon, her mom would send Lance back here to fetch her. For some reason, Gwen didn't want him to know about the marks. She carefully closed the closet door, giving it a long, pensive look then smiled. This was one mystery she thought she might be able to figure out.

CHAPTER FIVE

The Anderssons spent the rest of the day cleaning the bedrooms. Gwen stared in disgust at the growing pile of dirt and debris in her room. This job had been even worse than she imagined. "Ugh." She looked down at her filthy clothes. "So much for this shirt."

As Gwen grimly yanked off another strip of tattered wallpaper, she stopped to study the faded pattern. "Do you think this is the original paper?" She looked at her mother.

"I wouldn't be surprised." Mom came over and examined the wallpaper. "It certainly looks like it could be from the Victorian age."

Gwen frowned a little as she looked around her new room. "Mom, if Jonas Andersson built this house, why is it called the Carmichael place?"

Her mom raised her eyebrows. "How did you know that?"

Gwen shrugged. "That's what the girl at the historical society called it."

"Well," Mom's brow furrowed. "If I can remember what your dad told me, after Charlie Andersson disappeared with the money, the gangster…"

"Jimmy 'The Blade' Houlihan."

"Uh, right, Jimmy 'The Blade' Houlihan demanded the family pay it all back. I'm not sure of all the details, but Jonas' business partner, some guy named Carmichael, got hold of the house. Then his son ended up marrying Charlie's sister, so technically the house stayed in the family."

"And there aren't any Carmichaels that wanted this place?"

Mom hesitated a moment. "Actually, there is. A guy named Bob Carmichael. He lives here in Fishawak. He really wanted the house, but his grandfather, the one who left the house to your dad, apparently didn't think he should have it and left it to us instead."

"Why wouldn't he let his own grandson have the house? Especially if he wanted it?"

Mom shrugged. "Beats me. We've never met any of these people. I'm not sure how Mr. Carmichael tracked down your dad. The families haven't had any contact for years and years."

Gwen absently twisted the piece of wall paper. "Was there ever another Gwen Andersson? You know, like a sister of Charlie or something?"

"I have no idea." Mom laughed. "What makes you think there might have been?"

Gwen hesitated. She felt like the height marks in the attic were a secret just for her and that telling her family about it might ruin it somehow. "Oh, no reason." She tossed the wallpaper on the pile. "I thought I heard the lady at the historical society say something about a Gwen."

"Well, maybe you need to spend some time researching our family history. I don't think your dad knows any more than the story of Charlie and the missing money." Her mother turned and resumed scraping off the old wallpaper. "Next time you go to the library, you should ask the librarian to help you. Maybe they have census information from the turn of the century. You might be able to get all the names of the family members from that. You might also ask that lady at the historical society. She could probably help you."

Gwen nodded happily. Yes, she'd do just that, and then she could see Molly again.

Gwen had little time to think about her mysteries over the next week as the family worked to get the house livable. Gwen looked with some satisfaction at her new room. It had been transformed by a coat of pale yellow paint with white woodwork. The hardwood floors still needed to be refinished, but that would have to wait until they renovated this level of the house. To cover the rough, discolored floor, her mom let Gwen pick out a colorful, braided rug. That gave the room a cozy feel. Mom also covered the window seat in the alcove with cheery yellow and red cushions. When the movers finally arrived with their furniture, Gwen was surprised she felt more at home in her new room than she ever thought possible.

Despite that, the first night in their new home felt odd to Gwen. She was a little apprehensive about moving into a derelict house so long empty, and her thoughts kept straying to the odd happenings in the attic. As she lay alone in her large room, she couldn't help picturing that eerie figure in the doorway. Irritably she shook her head. *There isn't any ghost. It must have been Lance. I'm sure of it.* Still, it was a long time before she finally fell asleep.

Gwen sat up abruptly in the dark, the only light coming from the full moon outside her window. Her heart pounded as if something had startled her awake. The windows were open to let in the sea breeze, and the only sound was the roar of the surf. She picked up her watch and pushed the little button that lit up the face. It was two in the morning on May fifteenth.

She frowned. May fifteenth. Why did that date seem important? She leaned back against her pillows and thought hard. Wait, wasn't that the first date Gwen appeared on the height chart? Suddenly, Gwen was overwhelmed with a burning desire to know for sure. She started to climb out of bed then paused.

What am I doing? I don't want to go up there, especially alone in the middle of the night. Am I nuts? Maybe she was nuts, but the need to check that date was stronger than the urge to stay safely in bed. She grabbed her penlight and padded to her bedroom door, pushed it open and stepped out into the hallway.

Silently, she opened the attic door and climbed the stairs to the playroom above.

The room was flooded with silvery moonlight. Gwen's mind was fuzzy, as if she were in some kind of trance. She couldn't imagine why she'd come up here alone in the middle of the night, but she forged ahead to the closet and pulled open the door. No light penetrated the solid blackness of the small space. Gwen stood uncertainly, trying to see what was inside before she finally switched on her penlight. She quickly flashed the small light around the interior of the empty closet.

She shivered hard now, as if a blanket of frigid air had settled over her. Rubbing her arms, she looked around one once more then shone the dim light onto the door frame. Yes! There it was:

"Gwen, 11 yrs., May 15, 1922"

A chill ran down her spine. The girl was only one year younger than she was, and to think it was eighty years ago this very day she was measured. On a whim, Gwen turned, backed up against the door frame and put her hand on the top of her head to mark her height. As her hand touched the door frame, she felt an odd electric shock. Jumping back in surprise, Gwen turned to look at the frame. There was nothing there. She shook her head, her hand tingling. She felt an odd attachment to this mysterious girl with whom she shared a name.

Gwen stood there for a moment longer. She again had the feeling of being watched; the hairs on the back of her neck prickled. Slowly she turned and flashed her small light around the playroom. With a gasp of terror, Gwen froze. A shadowy figure stood in the hallway. She dropped her penlight and heard it roll into the closet.

Falling to her knees, Gwen fumbled around on the floor frantically trying to locate her small light. She couldn't find it anywhere. She crawled farther into the closet, running her hands across the dusty floorboards. She cried out again as the closet slammed behind her.

Whirling around and scrambling to her feet, she tried to turn the knob. It wouldn't budge. *How can that be?* She fought down her panic. *It doesn't even have a lock!* It was obvious. She was trapped.

Breathing heavily and trying to think, Gwen stared at the solid shape of the door. *This doesn't make any sense. Doors don't close and lock themselves for no reason.* She *had* to find her penlight. Yes, that was the first thing. She needed some light. Then she could figure out what was going on.

She dropped back down to the floor and started to search again. Her hand grabbed hold of something solid and much larger than a penlight. With a startled yelp she dropped it before her brain registered what it was–a shoe.

Tentatively, she felt around some more and was taken aback to find a number of shoes on the floor. They certainly weren't there earlier. She then became aware of things hanging around her. She reached up and felt what seemed to be a dress. What was going on here? Gwen was so bewildered by the sudden appearance of clothing in what had been a previously empty closet that, for a moment, she forgot to be frightened. As she pondered what to do next, a faint light flickered under the closet door. She froze as the door swung open to reveal the completely unexpected figure of a young boy holding a candle.

"Gwen!" hissed the boy, "What are doing up here? Get out of there before somebody catches you!"

Gwen stared at him for a few minutes before

slowly obeying. She crawled out from under the hanging clothes. She stepped out into the room and looked down in surprise. Rather than the T-shirt and flannel pants she usually slept in, she wore a long cotton nightgown. She blinked and looked at the boy again, who watched her impatiently.

He was about ten years old with fair hair parted down the middle and round wire-rimmed glasses. He was barefoot and wore an old fashioned nightshirt.

"Who are you?" she finally managed to blurt out.

The boy frowned. "Not that again. I'm your cousin, Tom. Don't you remember? You've been sick with scarlet fever. Sometimes it makes you forget stuff. You shouldn't even be out of bed. Mama will kill me if she thinks I let you come up here."

Scarlet fever? Gwen shook her head. She certainly didn't remember being ill, but suddenly her head spun. She staggered and might have fallen if Tom hadn't reached over and steadied her.

"Come on, Gwen," he said softly, "Let's get you back to bed. You must have been sleepwalking. You'll be right as rain tomorrow."

Gwen, in her confusion, allowed Tom to lead her through the playroom. She dimly noticed it was furnished now as they headed toward the stairs. The hallway to the bedrooms was richly carpeted and the gentle glow of the gaslights softly illuminated the papered walls.

This must be some kind of dream. Gwen fought back her panic. *I can't really be here.*

Tom led her down the hallway to her room. She was relieved to see it was the same room she had chosen. At least some of this weird dream made sense. Tom's flickering candle threw shadows across the darkened room, but enough moonlight shone in for her to make out a large bed against one wall and what looked to be a dresser and mirror on another. A set of shelves stood nearby.

Tom led her to the bed and stood aside as she climbed in. "You'll feel better tomorrow, Gwen." Then he grinned. "Besides, it's really boring when you can't play. So you better get well or else!" He waved then turned and disappeared into the hallway, quietly closing the door behind him.

Gwen sat silently on the bed as the shock of this unexpected situation slowly began to subside. She ran her hands across the bedding. The texture of the pillows and the blanket was soft. The ocean noises and its salty tang were familiar.

If this is a dream, she gazed around the dark room, *it's the most detailed dream I've ever had.*

Her eyes became unbearably heavy, as she lay back against the soft pillows with a sigh. *Surely,* her weary mind mumbled as she drifted off to sleep, *everything will be back to normal in the morning.*

CHAPTER SIX

Gwen woke slowly the next morning to the sounds of someone quietly moving around her room. *Mom.* She sleepily opened her eyes. With a cry, she sat up quickly and stared at the strange woman. Definitely *not* Mom! This woman was short with bobbed red hair and wore an old-fashioned pale yellow drop-waist dress.

Her heart racing, Gwen looked around the room. It was covered with pink floral wallpaper and had a large braided rag rug in the center. There was a small white dresser with an oval mirror against the far wall, bookshelves full of books and a couple of dolls. In the tower seat was a soft pink cushion. Gwen blinked then rubbed her eyes. Could she still be dreaming?

"Gwen, honey." The woman spoke with a soft lilt. There was the touch of an Irish brogue in her words. "You're awake at last. How do you feel?" She smiled as she approached the bed, but her brows quickly knitted in worry at Gwen's look of confusion. "It's me, darlin', your aunt Katherine." She reached over and placed a cool hand against Gwen's forehead. "You don't feel warm." She sighed. "I'd hoped we were past this. Well, no matter. It'll all come back to you soon enough. I'll be bringing up your breakfast in a bit." She gently smoothed back Gwen's hair, adjusted the covers and, with a last worried look, walked out of the room, her heels clicking on the polished wood floor.

Gwen jumped out of bed, but an unexpected wave of dizziness forced her to grab onto the tall bedpost. Odd. She felt as if she'd been sick for a long time. Breathing quickly, she looked around the room, trying to make sense of the situation. It was the same room, of that she was certain, but this definitely wasn't her stuff. The furniture was old-fashioned, like something she remembered seeing in her great-aunt's home years ago. Very weird. The bedpost felt solid enough so maybe it really wasn't a hallucination. If it wasn't a dream or a hallucination, then what on earth was going on?

She staggered over to the dresser and looked in the mirror. She frowned as she carefully studied her reflection. She still saw the same round face and long brown hair and eyes, but there was something *different* almost as if she were seeing a copy of her face, not exactly identical but very close. She couldn't quite put her finger on it.

She looked pale, and the dark circles under her eyes made it appear as if she truly had been ill. How could that be? She turned and looked at the room again. Yes, it was definitely the same room she remembered cleaning and painting, but it lacked that feeling of neglect that had been so strong in the house when they moved in. It looked exactly as if she'd gone back in time.

Gwen felt her legs go weak as this idea hit her, and she collapsed in the little rocking chair near the windows. *Back in time?* She laughed softly at this crazy idea. That made about as much sense as the house being haunted. But then, who were these people, and why did they seem to recognize her? All this confusion made her head throb. She closed her eyes, rested her head against the back of the chair and gently rocked as she tried to make sense of everything. *Okay, what am I going to do? These people seem to think they know me.* If she started asking them about her "real" family, would they think she was crazy? Frankly, she began think she was.

She considered what little she knew thus far. Tom said he was her cousin, and that lady called herself Aunt Katherine. Gwen frowned. There *had* been a Tom among the names on the closet door. Could he be *that* Tom? *Of course not.* She shook her head. How could he be? That Tom would be like a hundred years old or something, not a little kid.

But, what if he was? What if, somehow, she really had managed to go back in time when she entered that closet? Her eyes widened as she remembered the odd tingling sensation when she touched the doorframe. Her stomach swooped. If that boy really was the Tom from back in the 1920s, then they must think *she* was the mysterious Gwen from the closet door.

Gwen sat up anxiously as she tried to work it out. Maybe the 1920s Gwen came to live with the Andersson family because she was their relative. Perhaps something awful happened to her family, forcing her relatives to take her in.

Why do they seem to think I'm her?

She didn't feel as if she were in any immediate

danger, but who knew? Maybe they were all crazy, and she was the only sane one. She turned as the door opened once more.

Tom peeked around the corner of the doorway. He grinned.

"Hey, Gwen." He came in the rest of the way. "Do you know who I am today?" He looked a little worried.

Gwen stared at him for a moment, trying to decide what to do. She still couldn't really believe she'd traveled back in time but, for the moment, maybe it'd be best if she just played along until she knew exactly what was going on.

"You're Tom…my cousin."

Tom's face brightened. "You remember! That's swell." He jumped up on the bed and crossed his legs under him. "So, do you remember everything now?"

Gwen grimaced slightly. It occurred to her if she continued to say she couldn't remember anything because she'd been sick, then that would explain why she didn't know what was going on. She smiled as she imagined trying to explain to these people she really wasn't the Gwen they knew but a girl from eighty years in the future. They'd lock her up for sure.

"Well," she rubbed her hands along the arms of the rocking chair. "Not really. I mean, I know where I am, but I don't remember anything beyond that. I only know you're my cousin, because you told me last night. How long have I been sick?"

Tom looked down. "We thought you were gonna die. You were really sick for about two weeks. The doc didn't think you'd live, but you're tough." He grinned briefly then became solemn once more. "When you finally woke up two days ago, you couldn't remember nothin'. Just bits and pieces. The doc said you might never remember stuff and would hafta relearn everything."

Gwen slowly digested this information. Could any of this be true? If only she knew exactly where and *when* she was. "Okay." Gwen turned to her cousin, hoping to gain more information. "Tell me what's going on. I guess Aunt Katherine is your mom?"

Tom nodded. "Yep, and my dad is your uncle Jonas. I have a brother William who's off at Harvard and a sister Louisa and another brother Charlie. They're all older'n us."

Gwen bit her lip. "Where is my family? Why do I live here?"

Now Tom hesitated and glanced toward the door, as if hoping someone would come rescue him. He stared down at the floor and began to fidget with a thread on his shirt. "They…they were killed in an automobile crash six months ago. Your mom and dad, I mean. Your mom was my mom's sister, so my parents took you in. You're sure you don't remember any of this?" He peered at her, his eyes begging her to remember.

Gwen shook her head. The information interested her, but it really wasn't her family. These people were all strangers. As far as she knew, her family was safe and sound back wherever it was she was supposed to be.

Still, she needed to know everything she could. The door opened again, and Aunt Katherine entered carrying a tray. Behind her was a tall, thin man with a stiff, high-collared shirt. With his graying blond hair plastered down and parted down the center, he looked like a grown-up version of Tom. He smiled, but there was a touch of worry in his eyes.

"Here's your breakfast, Gwennie," smiled her aunt. "Your uncle Jonas came to see how you're feeling."

"Good morning, Gwen." Uncle Jonas gently patted her on the head. "Still having some trouble remembering things?"

Gwen liked his kind eyes.

"I'm helping her remember." Tom leaped from the bed. "Pretty soon she'll know everything from before."

His father smiled at him fondly. "I'm sure you're doing a fine job, Thomas. Now, Miss Gwen, you come and eat your breakfast. The doctor will be here in a little while and maybe, if you're good, he'll let you sit outside on the veranda for some fresh air." He reached down, gently helped her to her feet and guided her back to bed where Aunt Katherine stood waiting with the breakfast tray.

Gwen sighed as she settled back in bed. Aunt Katherine placed the tray over her lap. Gwen's mouth watered at the sweet smoky smell of the bacon as she stared at the assortment of food with interest. *At least breakfast looks good.* With surprising speed, she cleared her plate, much to her aunt's delight. Gwen felt decidedly better.

Dr. Knowlton, a large, harried man with a thick mustache bustled into the room sometime later. He popped a glass thermometer into her mouth. The one her mom used was electronic and beeped when it was done. This one seemed to take forever. He then placed the cold end of his stethoscope against her chest. "Breathe in, young lady." Gwen quickly obeyed.

Dr. Knowlton took the thermometer from her mouth, examined it briefly then nodded in satisfaction. "Young lady," he put away his equipment. "You are most definitely on the mend. What you need now is plenty of rest, good food and fresh air."

"What about her memory, Doctor?" asked Aunt Katherine. "She still can't seem to remember much."

Dr. Knowlton nodded and glanced at Gwen. "Scarlet fever is a funny disease. It can do strange things to a person. It may be that she'll wake up tomorrow and recall everything, but it's also possible she won't. Only time will tell. Just don't push her. She'll do it in her own time. In the meantime, you can simply tell her things she needs to know."

Gwen tried to pretend like she wasn't listening. She hadn't lost her memory yet couldn't help but wonder if the "other" Gwen would remember any of this. She winced briefly as the doctor patted her on the head and strode from the room. She rather liked him.

"Well, sweetheart," soothed her aunt. "Don't you worry. You're young, and you'll learn things quickly. We'll all help. Now, you rest for a bit. In a little while we'll take you outside to the veranda. You're finally starting to look a bit better. It won't be long before you and Tommy'll be running about like wild Indians again."

Later that afternoon, her uncle carried her downstairs and onto the large wrap-around porch. Gwen's breath caught in her throat. Instead of the dilapidated wreck she knew, the house was now a thing of beauty. The pale-yellow paint shone warmly under the sun and the intricately carved gingerbread woodwork was painted a rich forest green. Uncle Jonas set her on a chaise lounge that faced the ocean. The breeze was cool, and her aunt wrapped her in a blanket, just in case, but Gwen relished the warmth of the sun on her face.

Tom came and sat beside her, a checkers game beneath his arm. "I thought you might be bored." He set the game up on the small side table. "I know *I* am."

Gwen just smiled faintly and helped him arrange the game pieces. As Tom contemplated his first move, Gwen thought about her situation. She still had no idea where this would lead. Would her family miss her? Did they even know she was gone? If she was traveling in time, did time move the same here as it did at home? She rubbed her head. Even worse, she didn't have a clue as to how to get back to her family. *Can I be stuck here forever?* Tears burned at the thought of never seeing her mom or dad again. Even stupid Lance would be a welcome sight.

"Your turn." Tom watched her expectantly.

She nodded and turned her attention to the board but her mind kept working. *I came here through the closet, maybe I can go back the same way.* Her heart skipped a beat. Yes, that was it! The closet. That was the key. Maybe she could try it out this very night. She glanced at Tom. She would have liked to know him better, but she couldn't risk getting stuck here forever.

CHAPTER SEVEN

It seemed the house teemed with people. Later in the day, a couple of teenagers came to join Gwen and Tom on the porch. Tom introduced them as Louisa and Charlie. Gwen's eyes widened as she took in Charlie. Was this *the* Charlie? The one that stole all that money? The fifteen year old was tall and gangly with freckles and a shock of blond hair. Something seemed vaguely familiar about him, but Gwen couldn't quite place him.

Charlie grinned at Gwen. "Well, it's about time you got out of bed and started pulling your weight around here. Never met anybody so lazy in my entire life."

Louisa rolled her eyes and punched her brother in the arm. She was seventeen and petite. She wore her reddish blonde hair fashionably short, and her pale blue dress hugged her slim figure.

Gwen felt a twinge of envy. She couldn't imagine wearing a dress like that.

"Really, Gwen darling," said Louisa with an air of teenaged superiority. "We're delighted you're nearly recovered and look forward to you rejoining the family."

Gwen stifled a laugh as the two boys made faces at Louisa's airs. With a huff of annoyance, Louisa slammed a wide-brimmed straw hat on her head and flounced off toward the beach.

The boys laughed. "Well, kiddos," said Charlie. "Gotta run. Pop's expecting to see me workin' in the warehouse this afternoon, and I better skedaddle." With a wave of his hand, Charlie strode off down the gravel drive.

Gwen absently twirled a checker in her hand as Charlie disappeared around the corner of the house. She simply couldn't imagine this friendly boy running off with a bag full of stolen loot. He just didn't seem the type, but then what did she know? She was silent for a minute and then turned to Tom. "Are there any gangsters around here?"

Tom's eyebrows shot up, his hand poised to move his checker. "Gangsters? Why are you askin' about gangsters?"

Gwen frowned and pretended to study the board. "Well, no reason, really. I just seem to remember something about gangsters being here in Fishawak. It's probably nothing important. Just my brain not working right, you know." She cringed. Boy, did *that* sound lame. Still, she had to find out if there were any gangsters around. It was the only way she could know for sure if this was *the* Charlie.

Tom looked around as if to make sure no one was listening and leaned in closer. "Everybody knows about Jimmy 'The Blade' Houlihan," he whispered. "He's the big cheese around these parts. Bootlegging and everything. Least that's what Charlie says."

Gwen nodded her eyes still on the board. That certainly matched what she'd read in Mrs. Berger's brochure, as well as what her dad told her about the missing money. She wondered exactly who this Jimmy 'The Blade' Houlihan was and how dangerous he was?

That night, Gwen tossed restlessly in her bed, listening as the sounds of the house gradually stilled. She was determined to find out if she could go home. She was going to test the closet, no matter what. Finally, when all was quiet, she took a deep breath and slid out of her bed. She opened her door a crack and peeked out. The coast was clear. As quickly as she dared, she hurried to the attic door. She paused a few moments to catch her breath. She hated feeling so weak. She pulled the attic door open just enough to allow her to slip through then climbed the stairs, cringing at every creak of the stairs.

When Gwen reached the top, she stood still for a moment, listening for any sound from the maids' rooms nearby. All was still. Slowly, she walked into the playroom and approached the closet. The door was ajar. Licking her lips, Gwen reached out and lightly touched the frame. There was no tingling or electric jolt. She frowned, her throat tight.

I have to try this. Squaring her shoulders, she opened the door, stepped in and firmly closed the door behind her. Holding her breath, she waited.

She waited several long moments then slowly released her breath and pushed the door open. She stepped out and knew immediately she'd failed. Nothing had changed. The playroom was exactly as she'd left it just a few moments ago. Gwen leaned against the wall and fought back hot tears. *I can't go home.* Defeated, she turned and returned to her bedroom. Maybe everything would be okay in the morning.

Gwen was awakened by the warmth of the morning sun. As she lay in bed, she remained very still, her eyes shut tight. *Okay, that has to have been the weirdest dream I've ever had.* Slowly, she opened one eye then the other and immediately her stomach dropped. She was still in the 1920s. She groaned as she buried her face in her hands. *What am I going to do now?*

Every morning, it was the same routine. Instead of waking up safe at home with her family, she continued to be in what she eventually learned was 1922. She fretted about what her parents must think, but she had no idea how to get back to them. She had to trust she'd eventually find a way. How long would that take? Deep down she was terrified she'd be stuck here forever. She just had to find a way home.

She grew a bit stronger each day and soon was able to go down to the ocean with Tom. She really enjoyed spending time with him.

Tom, being the youngest, often found himself the butt of his older siblings' jokes, but he and Gwen supported each other more and more. He had a great sense of humor, which Gwen appreciated, but he also had an adventurous streak, which she did not. He constantly searched for pirate gold or tried to convince Gwen to come out with him at night to watch for rumrunners off the coast. She told him she just wasn't up to it yet, and he seemed to accept it. Disappointment shone in his eyes.

One of these days, she frowned as he ran off toward the beach, *he's not going to take no for an answer*. She didn't want to lose him as her friend. He was her only ally in this weird world. Yet, she'd still rather read than explore caves.

Her uncle Jonas, along with his business partner, George Carmichael, owned an import/export company of some sort and worked out of a large warehouse in town. One evening after Gwen had been there for about two weeks, Mr. Carmichael came by the house with his son, Bertie.

Bertie was short, rat-faced boy a little older than Charlie. He looked Gwen up and down with obvious distaste. "So, this your abandoned cousin? Dumped on your doorstep with no money or nuthin'. Just your luck. My old man woulda packed her off to the orphanage straight off."

"I'm surprised your old man didn't dump *you* in one," snapped Tom. "There's nuthin' wrong with Gwen. She's swell and a lot better to have around here than you. What are you doin' here anyway?"

Bertie shrugged. "Waitin' for Charlie." He picked at his teeth.

"Ha! You're waitin' for Louisa. Everybody knows you're stuck on her."

Bertie flushed bright red. "Like you'd know, you little squirt. You just better stay out of my way if you know what's good for you." He roughly shoved Tom to the side, glared at Gwen and swaggered back into the house.

"He's a real dope." Tom got back to his feet. "I wish Pop didn't work with his dad. Bertie's always causin' trouble. I don't know what Louisa sees in him. What a jerk."

Gwen barely heard him as she stared after Bertie. Bertie was with Charlie the night the money disappeared. She thought about how Bertie supposedly told everyone he and Charlie were chased by thugs and that was why they split up. Frankly, she could easily picture the little weasel stealing the money. "What does he do, anyway?"

Tom shrugged and started tossing a baseball into the air and catching it. "He and Charlie help down at Dad's warehouse moving boxes around and stuff. I've been a couple of times but it's really boring. They won't let me do anything but watch. It's huge. You could get lost in there for a week."

"What kind of stuff does your dad import?"

Again Tom shrugged. "I dunno. All kinds of stuff, I guess. Food from Italy, cloth from China, stuff like that. Why d'you care?"

Gwen rubbed her head. She really didn't know if any of this was important, but if she was ever going to solve the mystery of the missing money, she needed to gather as much information as possible. The theft and Charlie's disappearance was still a year away, but sometimes Gwen felt downright spooked looking at Charlie, knowing what was going to happen.

She glanced up as Charlie and Bertie came out the

front door onto the porch. She wished she could go demand to know what happened to him and the cash. She shook her head. In this world, it hadn't happened yet. He'd think she was totally nuts. As she listened to Charlie's laugh across the soft evening air, her heart felt heavy. *What happened to you, Charlie?*

She turned back to Tom. "I'm just trying to learn as much as I can since I don't remember anything. It's just so frustrating!"

It *was* frustrating not knowing even the simplest things about 1920s life. Everything was so different, starting with having to always wear a dress. She couldn't remember the last time she'd worn a dress in her own time. No girls she knew wore dresses every day; most just wore them for special occasions. The underwear was different too. There just seemed to be more of everything to put on. The lack of technology was especially disconcerting. Gwen's life had revolved around television, the Internet and talking to Krista on the phone.

She was appalled when Tom mentioned many of their neighbors still used outhouses and had no electricity or telephone service. He was proud of the fact his father was the first to have a phone in his house. Gwen couldn't help but wonder what Tom would think of cell phones. Life was so much slower here, and when her aunt bemoaned how quickly things changed these days, Gwen had to fight the temptation to laugh. Aunt Katherine had no idea.

On rainy days, the children spent their time up in

the attic playroom. Gwen couldn't get over how homey the place felt now. She didn't experience any of that spooky chill or the feeling of someone watching her. It felt like a real home. *Will her family ever achieve that with this house?* For now, it was her sanctuary.

Tonight was a special evening. The sun had set long ago, and Gwen and Tom should have been shooed off to bed, but Tom's father had invited a number of business associates over for dinner. She and Tom had been sent off to the playroom for the evening. Aunt Katherine had even given them permission to sleep up there.

While Tom wandered over to the bookshelves, Gwen was drawn to the closet, as she so often did. She carefully examined the measurement marks on the doorframe. They were there, but unlike in her time, they only went up to 1922, the current year. It still seemed so odd to see her name there. A slight chill ran through her body as she remembered the night she'd appeared here. Again, she felt a pang of homesickness as she pictured her parents finding her gone. Would they call the police? There'd be no clue to as where she'd gone. She fought back the tears. She gently touched her name but nothing happened. No tingle. Nothing.

Tom joined her. "It's dumb how Ma always wants to see how much we've grown." His mouth was full of apple. Gwen blinked back the tears and focused on her young cousin. Gwen noticed he had a book in his hand. It was H.G. Wells' *The Time Machine.* She smiled as the irony of the situation struck her. Tom frowned, looking from Gwen to the book.

"What's so funny? You don't think we could ever travel through time?"

Gwen almost laughed again. She wished she could tell him: "Oh, definitely. In fact, I come from eighty years in the future."

She resisted the urge and instead studied him thoughtfully. "Would you want to?"

Tom's eyes shone. "You bet I would! Just think. We could go back and see Robin Hood or dinosaurs or maybe see what the future is like. Mr. Wells thinks people will even go to the moon someday. Wouldn't that be somethin' to see?"

Gwen simply nodded. If Tom lived long enough, he'd get his wish. "I think it'd be wonderful to see knights and ancient Egypt. I think it'd also be cool to go back and find out what happened to Amelia Earhart."

Tom frowned. "Amelia Earhart?"

"That lady pilot who tried to be the first person to fly all around the world. You know, she disappeared over the Pacific Ocean in nineteen thirty-seven..." She'd read about Earhart for a school project. She was fascinated by the woman pilot's mysterious disappearance, but Gwen had forgotten that, even though it was in the distant past for her, it was still in the future for Tom.

Tom stared at her. "Nineteen *thirty-seven*? What, you can see in the future now? Maybe we better go find Harry Houdini. He's always lookin' for people who can talk to dead people. I bet he'd pay big money for someone who can see into the future."

Laughing, Tom lay back on the carpet, resting his head on one of the large floor cushions. "Maybe someday I'll invent a time machine, then you an' me can go back and see whatever we want. Or maybe I'll build a rocket and go to the moon or, better yet, Mars. I wonder what the Martians are like."

Face burning from her near-disastrous mistake, Gwen let him prattle on as she wandered around the room looking at the toys and books. There were several books by Charles Dickens as well as many authors she didn't recognize. She'd read a couple of the books and that had been more than enough for her. The books for children in the 1920s seemed bound and determined to ram some lesson down their throats–be honest, be helpful, stay away from bad company and on and on. It was pretty nauseating. No wonder Tom avoided them. She looked over. His nose was buried back in his time travel book.

She skimmed over the titles again then moved on. She picked up a toy horse, examined it for a moment then set it back down. With a sigh, she made her way out onto the balcony. She inhaled the fresh salty smell. As she approached the railing, she paused, remembering the day she had almost flown over the edge. She wondered again who'd saved her. Had it really been Lance? He'd seemed confused when she thanked him for saving her. Or perhaps it had been someone or some*thing* else. The brief image of a young man popped into her head. He seemed so familiar. She sighed. In the moonlight, the ocean looked as gray and restless as she felt. She rested her head on her hands and again wondered what was going to happen to her.

It was late. The maids had come up to bed a short while ago. They couldn't go to bed until the dinner was finished and everything cleared away, so Gwen figured it must be close to midnight. She continued to listen to the sounds of the ocean surf then gave a little jump when she heard a door below open and bang shut. It sounded like one of the doors to the veranda. A moment later a figure moved in the dark toward the shore, the beam from his flashlight illuminating the way. The air was cool and damp from the day's rain, but the moon frequently broke through the gaps in the clouds scudding across the night sky.

Who is that? She leaned forward, trying to get a better look. Her stomach clenched when a light blinked on and off some distance from the shore. Could it be a rumrunner?

She hurried to the balcony door and flung it open, looking for her cousin. "Tom!" she hissed urgently. "Come quick. I think there might be rumrunners out there!"

Tom stared at her open-mouthed for just a minute. He then scrambled to his feet and joined her out on the balcony.

"I saw someone leave the house and head that way." She pointed toward the path that led from the bluff down to the ocean. "He had a flashlight. Then a light blinked on and off out there on the water."

The two stood watching breathlessly out into the inky darkness. "There!" Tom cried softly as the lights again flashed on and off three more times. "Come on. Let's go!"

"Go?" Gwen stared at him, aghast. "What do you mean *go*?"

Tom rolled his eyes. "To go see the rumrunners, of course. They must be bringing in a shipment of booze to be picked up by some bootleggers. Wow, this is so amazing!" He turned and headed for the door.

"Tom!" Gwen grabbed his arm. "These people are dangerous. They're *gangsters*. They carry guns. They *kill* people. Are you nuts?"

Tom whirled to face her. "Quit being such a nervous Nellie. If you don't wanna go, *fine*. Stay here and read your stupid books. I don't care. I'm gonna go see what's going on!"

He ran out the door.

Her heart raced. What should she do? She glanced back at the balcony and then to the door. She blew out her breath then hurried to the door. She ran after Tom. "Tom Andersson, if you get us killed, I'll never talk to you again."

CHAPTER EIGHT

Gwen found Tom in his room gathering up his small flashlight and an old pair of binoculars. He turned and stared at Gwen for a moment then grinned. "I knew you'd come."

Gwen was anything but sure about this, but she couldn't let Tom go off on his own. What if he got hurt? "I still don't think this is a good idea."

"It's as safe as houses." He checked his penknife before slipping it into his pocket. "We won't let them see us. There are plenty of big rocks down there. We're just gonna watch and see who it is." He paused and looked serious now. "Remember, we can't tell anybody about what we see. It could be dangerous."

Gwen glared at him, her hands on her hips. "Isn't that what I just *said*?"

Tom grabbed his jacket and handed her one. "It's gonna be chilly out there so take this. Ma'll kill me if you get sick again. Here." He thrust a small flashlight into her hand. "This is William's. I don't think he'll miss it. Now, c'mon!" With another excited grin, he grabbed her hand and dragged her out the door.

Gwen hovered behind her cousin as they silently waited for a few moments to make sure no one else was up. Holding her breath, she tiptoed down the hallway to the back stairs where she followed Tom down into the kitchen. All was still as they opened the kitchen door and slipped out into the damp, windy night. Tom looked left and right then started running toward the path down to the beach. Gwen watched for a moment, her heart pounding rapidly, then dashed after him.

Tom nimbly descended the steep slope like a young mountain goat. Gwen followed more slowly, grumbling about her cousin's crazy ideas. The moon provided just enough light she avoided killing herself. She looked longingly at the flashlight clutched in her hand. Tom had said not to turn it on in case they were spotted. "If I fall down this stupid cliff and break my neck, I don't think being spotted is going to be my biggest problem." She bit back a cry as she slipped on some loose stones.

Breathing hard, Gwen finally joined Tom at the bottom of the hill. They slowed to a creep, straining to hear anything over the roar of the ocean. When they reached the beach, Gwen followed Tom to the cover of several large boulders. She cautiously peeked out from behind a rock. Where had that man gone? Gwen was startled by the deep rumble of an engine. A small boat slowly glided from the beach out to sea. She grabbed Tom's hand and pointed out across the ocean to a blinking light in the distance.

"I bet they're making a pickup." Tom bounced with obvious excitement.

"On our beach?" Gwen struggled to spot either of the boats. "Does your father know, do you think?"

Tom sank down beside her, his face worried. "I…I dunno. A lot of people are mixed up with sellin' booze. Good people, too. My dad says this whole Prohibition thing is just wrong. I heard him tellin' Ma Congress has its own giant store of liquor in the basement, and they're the ones that passed the law."

Gwen didn't know much about Prohibition other than people weren't allowed to buy or sell alcohol during the 1920s. She didn't know why or when it ended, but it resulted in lots of crime and gangsters. *Something else I need to learn about.* Living in a different time was more difficult than she would have thought. *It could be worse. I could have ended up in the Middle Ages and gotten the Black Plague or had my head chopped off or something. At least here I have indoor plumbing.* She smiled.

Time seemed to crawl as they crouched in the damp night. Gwen shivered as she fought to keep her eyes open. "How long are we gonna wait here?" She wasn't impressed with this adventure stuff so far and would much prefer to be in her warm bed.

"Until we see who's picking up the booze." Tom scanned the ocean with his binoculars. "Wait! I think I see something. The boat's coming back. Come on. Let's move closer." Without waiting for a reply, Tom scurried forward, darting from one jumbled pile of rocks to the next, his dark form barely visible.

Gwen hurried after him, not wanting to be left behind.

Gwen joined Tom behind some boulders nearer to the beach and waited, her body tense with anxiety. She could barely breathe. Spying on rumrunners wasn't a good idea, but she wasn't going to let Tom do something really stupid if she could stop him. They could now hear the thrum of the boat engine as it moved closer. It would land near the cliff face, about twenty yards from where they hid. The butterflies in Gwen's stomach fluttered more strongly than ever. Yet, despite her fear, she was curious to know what was going on.

As the boat neared the beach, one man jumped out into the surf and helped pull the craft up onto the shore. A second smaller man got out and pushed until the small boat was firmly beached. The two conferred for a moment then began lifting sacks out of the boat and disappeared into the deep shadows of the bluff. Tom raised his binoculars and watched for several minutes. He gasped.

"What?" Gwen leaned forward.

Without a word, Tom passed her the binoculars.

It took Gwen a few moments to focus in on the men, but when she managed to zoom in on their faces, she too gasped in shock. "Mr. Carmichael and Bertie!" She turned to her cousin.

Tom's face was dark with anger. "I always knew those two were no good. I bet they're working for Jimmy Houlihan."

Gwen glanced back to where the men worked. "Why would they be doing this here? I mean, what if your dad found out? You don't really think he's in on this too, do you?"

Tom was silent for a few moments. "I sure hope not." He sounded worried.

"So, what do we do now?" Gwen lifted the

binoculars once more. "Do we tell your dad?" Mr. Carmichael lifted another bundle out of the boat and waded through the sand back to the bluff. "What are they doing with that stuff anyway? Is there a cave or something?"

She handed the binoculars back to Tom who studied the scene across the beach. He scratched his head. "There might be. There are all kinds of little caves along here. I don't remember one right there, but that doesn't mean there isn't one. Ma doesn't like me playing around down here." He put the strap of the binoculars around his neck and pushed his glasses back up his nose. "Come on. We gotta find out."

Gwen grabbed his arm. "Are you nuts? Not while they're here! We've got to wait until they leave."

Tom turned and glared at her.

"Listen," whispered Gwen, "if we go now, Bertie and his dad will spot us. Then what would happen? They might turn us over to Jimmy 'The Blade' or worse."

"All right." Tom flopped back onto the sand and scowled.

It took the Carmichaels another forty-five minutes to unload the boat. Mr. Carmichael said something to Bertie, patted him on the shoulder then helped his son push the boat back into the water. Bertie leaped in, revved up the engine and headed back out to sea, disappearing behind the curve of the shoreline. Mr. Carmichael watched a few moments longer then turned and made his way back to the house.

Tom and Gwen crouched low and held their breath as he strode by. He hummed as he passed.

With a soft whoosh, Gwen resumed breathing and relaxed slightly, but she didn't move until they were sure enough time had elapsed to allow him to reach the house.

When it seemed safe, Tom crept out of their hiding place with Gwen right behind. The two then rose and, with one last look around, sprinted across the sand to where they'd seen the men working.

"Look here." Tom pointed to tracks leading from the edge of the water toward the bluff. He hurried forward, following the trail, while Gwen struggled to keep up.

When they reached the face of the cliff, they followed the tracks behind a large boulder. Gwen felt a thrill of excitement as she spied a narrow cleft in the wall. The cave was well hidden, and if it hadn't been for the bootleggers' trail, they never would have noticed it. Gwen inspected the small opening. How had anyone ever found this place to begin with? Hidden behind the large rock, the cleft was barely wide enough for a grown man to squeeze through.

Tom pulled out his flashlight and shone it into the black opening. He took a step inside then stopped. He glanced uncomfortably at Gwen. "I…hate closed places." He then glared at her as if daring her to laugh.

Gwen stared at him and fought the impulse to do just that. That was the last thing she expected to hear from her daring cousin. Fighting the instinct to turn around and go home, Gwen swallowed and pulled out her light. "I'll go. You keep watch."

Tom smiled weakly in relief and stepped back.

She'd surprised herself.

She flicked on the light, but its dim beam quickly failed. Tom silently offered her his. With a trembling hand, she accepted his as she pushed the dead light back into her jacket pocket. Taking a deep breath, she gave Tom a nervous grin and then slipped into the cleft.

The opening led into a narrow, winding passageway not much taller than Gwen. How did Mr. Carmichael possibly fit? Maybe he hadn't. He'd probably handed the bundles to the smaller Bertie, who then carried them in. The air in the tunnel was cold and dank and smelled of rotting seaweed. Gwen wrinkled her nose in disgust.

After climbing about twenty feet, the passage opened into a much larger cave, about the size of her bedroom, although maybe not as high. Unlike the entrance to the passageway, it was quite dry. *Smells different, too.* Gwen inhaled deeply. *Like Uncle Josh's tavern back home.*

Gwen's eyes widened as she flashed her light around the cave. It was packed tight with stacks of crates and mounds of burlap-wrapped bundles. She reached down and gingerly felt one, making out the distinctive shape of a glass liquor bottle. There was no doubt about it. She and Tom had stumbled on the cache of liquor undoubtedly belonging to some gangster, and she was pretty sure that gangster was Jimmy Houlihan. She needed to get back and tell Tom right away. If Mr.

Carmichael returned and found them here, they'd be in big trouble. Did gangsters kill kids? She didn't want to be the one to find out.

She made her way down the passageway as quickly as she dared, her feet slipping on loose stones. As she approached the last turn before the tunnel opening, she paused. *Is that someone talking?* Inhaling sharply, she flicked off her light and listened.

"What are you doing here, kid?" demanded an angry voice. Was that Bertie? The voice was deeper, older. It must be someone else.

"I…uh…nuthin." Tom's loud voice trembled. Was he trying to warn her? "I just like to play on the beach at night."

"Well this ain't no place for kids. If you know what's good for you, you'll get outa here and never tell anybody you saw me. Understand?"

"Y….yes sir," gulped Tom. "I won't, sir. I won't tell nobody. I'll *get out right now*!"

He *was* sending her a message. Gwen's mouth was painfully dry as she tried to swallow, her heart pounding in her ears. How could she escape?

Silently, she retreated farther up the passageway, her flashlight off but held as a possible weapon. Just what good her little flashlight would be against a gangster's gun, she had no idea, but it made her feel a little better. She just made out the sound of Tom running off. A moment later someone entered the passageway.

Her heart in her throat, Gwen turned and scurried

back into the cave, trying not to alert the man to her presence. Flicking on her light, she looked wildly for a place to hide. Finally, she darted behind a large stack of crates in the farthest corner from the opening. There was a small space in the rock that allowed her to push farther in. It wouldn't take the gangsters long to find her if they really looked.

She huddled in her small niche. A quiet clink. The dead flashlight had fallen from her pocket, disappearing somewhere in the darkness. She froze. Did anyone hear that? She turned off Tom's light, held her breath and waited in the suffocating darkness.

CHAPTER NINE

Terror held Gwen tightly in its grip. She could barely breathe and every nerve seemed to be tingling. *Please don't look over here*, she silently prayed over and over.

A few moments later, a bright light illuminated the interior of the cavern. She tried to see, but her view was completely blocked by the crates around her. Someone walked around muttering to himself.

It sounded like he was counting. Then a second voice came from the passageway. "How many we got?"

"Looks like Carmichael brought in another fifty crates' worth," replied the first voice.

"Great. He say any more about how he's gonna get rid of Andersson? That guy's gettin' too nosey for his own good."

Gwen went cold, fear for her safety momentarily forgotten. Mr. Carmichael planned on getting rid of Uncle Jonas? She must have heard wrong. She bit her lip.

"I know the boss said if Carmichael didn't do sumthin' soon, I was to take dear Mr. Andersson for a ride, but Bertie told me his dad is working on setting Andersson up to take the fall for that jewelry store heist we pulled last week. That would get him out of our hair."

Gwen pressed her hand to her mouth to keep from

crying out. This was horrible! She had to get back to the house and warn her uncle. At least now she knew he wasn't involved with the smugglers.

"Well, Jimmy says to bring in ten crates of whiskey tonight. They need it for that new joint he's opening in the old bakery on Fifth Avenue."

"Okay," replied the other man. The men lifted cases and carried them off down the passageway. For a moment, Gwen thought she might throw up. She could barely think straight. What was she going to do? She had to get out of here as soon as possible. She couldn't let anything happen to Uncle Jonas.

As she thought about the situation, her anger grew, pushing her fear aside. How dare George Carmichael threaten Uncle Jonas? Charlie had told her how much Uncle Jonas helped Carmichael after Carmichael's wife died. Uncle Jonas had even taken George on as a full partner in the business and hired Bertie to help in the warehouse. This is how that jerk repaid Uncle Jonas' kindness? If only she could escape and warn her uncle.

A short while later the men returned for more crates. It took them about fifteen minutes before they finally grabbed the last ones and left for good. Gwen waited and waited, scared to leave too soon in case she ran into someone, either in the passageway or on the beach.

Finally, when it appeared certain the men weren't coming back, Gwen stood and stretched her stiff limbs. Turning on her flashlight, she slipped out from behind the crates and moved warily down the passageway. She paused frequently, alert to any sounds. When she approached the opening, she again turned off her light so as not to warn anyone that might still be there. She peered out into the darkness and listened hard. All she could hear was the pounding of the surf against the rocks. She gave a little sigh of relief then hurried across the sandy beach toward the house.

Once she reached the path to the house, Gwen began to run as fast as she could. There wasn't a moment to lose. She had to find Tom and tell him what had happened. As she approached the house, she slowed. *Where is Tom?* Surely he would have waited for her, wouldn't he? She began to feel a little uneasy. She silently climbed the veranda steps.

"Tom?" she whispered urgently. "Are you there?" No response. Maybe he went back to the playroom.

Soundlessly, Gwen opened the door and slipped inside. Except for the ticking of the grandfather clock in the front hallway, the house was still. "Tom?" The butterflies in her stomach were back as her thoughts raced. She couldn't believe Tom would abandon her. Something must have happened. But what? She crept a little farther into the parlor.

Roughly, a hand clapped over her face. Gwen tried to scream as someone grabbed her, pulling her close. The hand pressed even more firmly over her mouth.

"Shut up!" a voice hissed and gave her a shake.

Gwen struggled wildly, finally loosening the grip on her mouth. She bit down hard. The man cursed and released her. Gwen darted away, knocking over a small table with a loud crash.

Gwen looked back and gasped. George Carmichael lumbered toward her, his face dark with menace. "Just where do you think you're going, girlie? You been snoopin' around where you don't belong."

"Where's Tom?" Breathing hard, Gwen slowly backed away, her eyes never leaving Carmichael. "You better not have hurt him!" She trembled but refused to back down.

"Oh, I haven't hurt him." Carmichael watched her closely, ready to pounce. "Just put him to sleep for a little while. Just like I did everyone else in this house. That way I can do business without worryin' about being bothered. Come morning, they won't remember a thing. Just like you."

"I know all about you, Mr. Carmichael." Gwen's anger overrode her fear and good sense. "I heard those men in the cave saying how you're gonna frame Uncle Jonas for some jewelry store robbery or maybe even kill him!"

Carmichael went very still as his eyes narrowed dangerously. "I'm really sorry you heard that, missy." His voice was low and so cold Gwen's knees went weak. "That means I might just have to do something more permanent with you."

Realizing her blunder, Gwen gave a small gasp, turned and fled through the house crying for help. If Carmichael was telling the truth, he'd drugged everyone. There was no one to save her. She knew Charlie and Louisa were staying with friends that night so at least they were safe. She darted down the hallway toward the kitchen, turned and fled up the stairs to the bedrooms. Carmichael yelled for her to stop. His heavy feet pounded on the stairs behind her.

Spurred on by her growing panic, she soon outpaced him. She flew up the second flight of stairs to the attic. As she burst into the playroom, she spun wildly about, searching for a hiding place. Without thinking, she yanked open the closet door, dove in and buried herself deeply in the back of the closet behind the coats and dresses. Curling up as small as she could, she prayed fervently Carmichael wouldn't find her. She was the only one who could save Uncle Jonas. She couldn't let Carmichael stop her.

The man stormed into the playroom shouting her name. There was a loud crash as he began knocking things over.

"Please don't let him find me!" she whispered. "Please don't let him find me." She repeated this over and over as if it saying it enough times would make it true.

The commotion in the playroom faded. Finally, Gwen no longer heard Carmichael at all. Could he have given up already? It was pitch black in the closet, and as she uncurled her body, she set her hand on the floor reaching for her flashlight. Her hand landed on something small and cylindrical. She froze. It felt too small for Tom's flashlight. She picked it up and realized with a shock that it was her penlight.

Quickly, she flicked it on and found herself in a

closet empty of all but dust. Blinking in confusion, Gwen scrambled to her feet and flung the door open to a dark, empty playroom. She slowly spun in a circle, taking in the expanse of the dark, lifeless room. She was back--back with her own family, her own time, her own life and safe from the murderous George Carmichael. Her heart leaped with joy and relief. *I'm home!*

Then it hit her like a punch to the stomach. *Uncle Jonas!* Gwen whirled and stared at the closet, her heart pounding. She was the only one who knew what George Carmichael was planning. She couldn't come back now. She *had* to save her uncle.

Gwen leaped back into the closet, slamming the door behind her. Breathing heavily, she willed herself back to 1922. No use. She knew it wouldn't work the minute she stepped inside. There had been a different feel in the closet before. It had almost felt alive. Gwen then recalled the odd shock she'd gotten when she touched Gwen's height mark on that night she went back. Almost reluctantly, Gwen reached out and rested her fingers on the small pencil mark. Nothing happened.

Her shoulders slumped in defeat. Gwen pushed opened the door and stepped out into the moonlit playroom. Whether she wanted to be or not, she was home. No one could help Uncle Jonas now.

CHAPTER TEN

Gwen fought back the tears that threatened to erupt. How could this have happened *now*? What would happen to her uncle? No one else knew what George Carmichael was planning. That horrible man would ruin everything. Sobs now wracked her body as she gave in to the wave of helplessness that washed over her. Finally, when she had shed every last tear, she took a long quivering breath and looked up.

The playroom looked so different now; so bleak and lonely especially now she'd seen it brimming full of life. Even its dusty smell added to the feel of abandonment. In her mind's eye she pictured the shelves full of books and toys, the big rocking chair by the windows and the small sofa that had been positioned in front of the now cold, desolate fireplace. It had been such a warm, wonderful place all those years ago. She sniffed and wiped her nose and eyes with the sleeve of her pajamas. She looked down. She was back in her usual nightwear. She rubbed her arms as she became aware of just how cold it was in the room. Funny. She never remembered it being so cold when she spent time there with Tom.

She stood and dusted off her pajamas. She was slightly woozy with exhaustion. *How long have I been gone?* A stab of fear made her catch her breath. Had her family been searching for her? What day was it? She turned to hurry downstairs, but was brought up sharply by a form in the doorway.

Gwen gasped and took a step back. "Lance?" she called hesitantly.

The form moved in a little closer.

Gwen went cold. It was a person, but he wasn't fully formed and seemed to glow. As Gwen watched in horrified fascination, the form took the shape of someone she recognized–Charlie Andersson.

Gwen couldn't move, couldn't breathe; every muscle in her body was frozen in place by overwhelming terror.

Charlie turned and looked directly at her, his pale translucent face a study in misery. He held his hand out as if begging her to help him. What was he trying to tell her? He took another step closer. Gwen gave a small whimper of fear, her eyes wide. "Charlie?" she finally managed to whisper.

The apparition stopped and studied her, his eyes full of grief.

Gwen's heart went out to him as her terror began to fade.

He stood there for a moment longer. He was trying to say something, but a moment later, he slowly sank through the floor and was gone.

Gwen's knees gave way then, and she collapsed onto the dusty playroom floor. Had she really seen Charlie Andersson's *ghost*? She hugged herself, her thoughts whirling. She was dimly aware the room was much warmer than it had been. What had he been trying to say? She closed her eyes and tried to imagine his face just before he disappeared. He'd mouthed two words. She thought hard. Help. Me. Yes! That's what he'd said. Her eyes popped open: *Help me!*

Gwen rose and began to drag her weary body to the stairs. She laughed softly as she considered her situation. Not only did she need to figure out how to return to the 1920s to save her uncle, but now she had a ghost wanting her to help him to… what? Move on to Heaven? No…she stopped as the thought hit her hard–Charlie wanted her to prove his innocence! All these years everyone accused him of running off with the money, and now it seemed he wanted Gwen to prove that hadn't been the case at all. She shook her head. Maybe this was all just some weird and elaborate dream and in the morning everything would be back to normal.

When she got to her room, Gwen frowned as she realized it was exactly the way she left it when she went up to the attic to check the dates. In her mind that had been weeks ago, but had that been the case here? Maybe she hadn't been gone at all? Well, she was simply too exhausted to think about this any longer so, collapsing into bed, she quickly sank into a deep, dreamless sleep.

She awoke the next morning to the sound of her brother banging down the stairs demanding his breakfast. Gwen snuggled deeper down into the covers before she realized where she was. Sitting up, she quickly took in the nearly empty bedroom, the smell of fresh paint still heavy in the air. She really was back. Had she actually been anywhere? There was a knock on the door.

Her dad stuck his head in. He grinned at her as he tried to smooth his tousled hair. "Breakfast is ready, Gwennie. Better come down before Sir Lancelot eats it all." He gave her a little wave and disappeared, closing the door behind him.

Gwen sat there for a few moments before slowly climbing out of bed. Could it have really been a dream then? Tom? Bertie? Mr. Carmichael? The cave? She thought about this as she pulled on her shorts and T-shirt. *Well, if I really was gone*, she looked in her mirror to see if she could detect any changes, *I wasn't gone long enough for anybody to notice.*

She turned away from the mirror, brow wrinkled in thought. How could she prove to herself it had all been real or not? Her eyes lit up as the answer came to her. "I just need to find that cave!" There was no way she could know about that cave if she hadn't really been there. She'd go look at the first opportunity. She finished dressing and hurried downstairs.

Her family was gathered around the table eating pancakes. Lance had at least ten piled up in front of him and, as usual, shoveled the food in as quickly as he could get it on his fork. Faye sat beside her brother and stared at him in disgusted fascination. Gwen shivered as she realized how much they reminded her of Charlie and Louisa. She slipped into a chair next to her father, who worked on his own stack.

"Good morning, Gwen," smiled Mom, setting a plate on the table before Gwen. "Hope you're hungry."

Surprisingly, Gwen was famished and began to attack the pancakes on her plate.

"Well," Dad finished the last of his coffee. "I have to go into town today to talk to an architect about the plans for finishing the attic. It's such a nice day, you guys can all take the day off."

Gwen looked up, her heart thudding. This could be her chance to check out the cave.

"Oh, Gwen," her mother finally sat down to her breakfast. "I met Janet Berger the other day. I thought I'd stop in at the historical society to see if they had any photos or drawings of this house in its heyday. It would help when we really get into restoring it. Anyway, she called last night and was going to stop by today with some things she found, and she's bringing her granddaughter, Molly. I believe you two met when you were in town?"

Gwen nodded. She wasn't sure if she was excited or annoyed Molly was coming over. Then she gave a little shrug. Maybe Molly could help her find the cave. It would probably be more fun to go exploring with someone else anyway. "Great, Mom. Molly seemed really nice."

Her mom smiled. "Well, it'll be good for you to make some friends during the summer. It'll make school easier in the fall."

"Thanks for reminding us, Mom." Lance grimaced with a roll of his eyes. "I hope you don't plan on doing that every day for the next three months." He sat up straight and turned to his father. "Can I come into town with you? I wanna talk to that guy in the board shop again. He said they were getting in a new shipment of skateboards and I wanna see what he's got."

"Sure. No problem. What are your plans, Faye?" Dad started to clear the plates.

"I want to start designing a mural to paint on my bedroom wall." Faye handed him her plate. "That one wall is so big and empty. I thought it would be cool to paint a big medieval scene. This is the first time I've had such a big space to work with."

Shortly after the breakfast dishes were cleaned and put away, Dad and Lance left for town. Faye retired to her room to begin designing her mural.

Gwen hurried to her room to make her bed and brush her teeth. She was oddly nervous about having someone come over. She decided to take a book outside and wait on the veranda for Molly and her grandmother. She was reading one of her favorites, *A Wrinkle in Time,* for the fifth or sixth time and was totally lost in the story of Meg's journey through the universe when she became aware of the crunch of tires on gravel. A dark blue minivan came slowly into view. Gwen stood up, opened the front door and called to her mother, who appeared a few moments later and joined her on the veranda.

Molly practically leaped out of the passenger side door as the car barely came to a halt. "Hi, Gwen!" She hurried up to the veranda. Her grandmother remained in the vehicle as she gathered some things together.

"Hi, Molly," grinned Gwen. "Mom, this is Molly."

Mom laughed. "So I gathered. Welcome to our disaster area, Molly. Hi, Janet." she greeted the older woman as Mrs. Berger hurried over, trying to catch up to her granddaughter. She held a large folder in her hands.

"Hello, Heather. I see you've met Molly already."

Mom laughed. "Come on in. Be careful though. The house is in need of a lot of work and we haven't even started on this floor." Mom and Janet led the way into the house as Molly and Gwen followed.

"Did you actually sleep here last night?" gasped Molly, gaping at the grim interior of the foyer and parlor. "Boy, is it creepy in here. It really looks like a haunted house."

Gwen bit her lip and then whispered, "Can you keep a secret?"

Molly's eyes went wide as she nodded eagerly.

"It *is* haunted." Gwen leaned closer. "I haven't told anybody else, and I don't think anyone else can see him, but I saw a ghost last night."

Molly stopped in her tracks and turned to stare at Gwen in awe. "You actually saw a ghost? *A real ghost?* Oh my gosh, what did it look like? Weren't you scared?" Molly's face had gone pale. She peered about nervously as if expecting a ghost to appear any minute.

Gwen wanted to hit herself in the head. Why had she told Molly about the ghost? What had she been thinking? Well, there was no going back. "I saw him last night up in the attic. I think it was the ghost of Charlie Andersson."

Molly was speechless for a few minutes then took on a look of incredulous disbelief. "You're just making that up. You're just trying to scare me. I don't believe in ghosts." She didn't sound entirely sure about that last statement.

"Well, it sure looked real to me." They stood in an awkward silence for a few moments. "You want to see the rest of the house?"

Molly shrugged then nodded.

As the two girls made their way through the house, Gwen pointed out all the different rooms and explained what her parents planned for the inn. Molly studied each room and nodded thoughtfully. "My grandma showed me the pictures of this place from before, and it looked really nice. Not like it is now. I'm just trying to remember how it should look."

Gwen wished she could tell Molly about her experience traveling back in time, but if Molly thought the ghost story was crazy, who knew what she'd think of Gwen going back to 1922.

After the tour of the house, Gwen and Molly wandered into the dining room where Mom and Mrs. Berger had spread out some antique photos. The two women were in kitchen.

Gwen hurried to the table to look at the photos, hoping to find something she recognized. Her breath caught as she picked up a photo of a group of people standing in front of the house. She looked at the back and read the caption: "Jonas Andersson Family, 1920." She turned it back over and carefully studied the photo.

Yes! She could just make out Uncle Jonas and Aunt Katherine. Beside Jonas was a tall young man whom Gwen didn't recognize. She assumed it must be their oldest son, William, and next to him stood Charlie, smaller than Gwen remembered. On the other side of Katherine was Louisa and in front stood young Tom.

Gwen felt an odd pang of homesickness. What happened after she left? There was no sign of the other Gwen, but then there wouldn't be. She didn't show up until 1922.

She shuffled through the photos and found another family portrait in front of the house. She frowned as she studied this one. She turned it over and read the date: 1923. She again looked at the photo. William was there, to the right of his mother, looking grim. Charlie stood on her other side also looking unhappy, as did Louisa. Tom and a plump, dark-haired girl about eleven or twelve stood beside him. Her face was cast downward, so Gwen couldn't quite make it out. Her stomach dropped. Uncle Jonas was missing. She gripped the photo tightly, trying not to cry out. *What had happened to him?*

"Are you okay?" Molly stepped closer as she peered at the photo. "You look like you just saw a ghost. Or…maybe I should say *another* ghost?"

Gwen pressed her lips tightly together so as not to snap at the girl. There was no way Molly could possibly understand why she was upset about someone missing from a photo taken eighty years ago. *I have just got to find a way to get back there!* She glanced at Molly who now stared at her.

"Um…" Gwen fumbled for an answer. Then it came to her. She held out the photo and pointed to Charlie. "That's the ghost I saw. He looked just like him."

Wide eyed, Molly blinked then looked down at the photo. "You're sure?"

Gwen nodded, relieved she was actually able to tell the truth.

"Wow," whispered Molly, her face pale. Gwen could tell her friend was finally beginning to believe her.

Carefully Molly placed the photo on the table. "Well…" her voice quavered, "maybe we should go look around outside for a while. It's such a pretty day."

This was just the opening Gwen was looking for. "Great idea. I haven't gotten down to the beach yet. Want to go explore down there?"

Molly smiled in relief. "Yeah, sure. That'd be great."

"Okay. Let's go get some food, and we can have a picnic. How does that sound?"

Molly agreed and they headed off for the kitchen.

"You girls be careful down there, okay?" called her mother as they packed a cooler with lunch.

"Sure, Mom." Gwen quickly stuffed a couple of flashlights into the cooler. Now they were prepared to go explore, and Gwen prayed she'd find what she was searching for.

CHAPTER ELEVEN

Gwen and Molly stepped through the French doors in the parlor onto the broad veranda overlooking the sea. Again, Gwen was almost overwhelmed with memories of how the house should look. The veranda had been one of her favorite places in the 1920s and she remembered clearly recovering from her illness right in this spot. It was just so bizarre. Molly glanced at her, frowning at Gwen's hesitation.

"Is this the way?"

Gwen gave herself a little shake and nodded. "Oh, yeah. There should be an old path that leads down to the beach. It's probably pretty overgrown, though, so we better be careful."

Slinging the strap of the cooler over her shoulder, Gwen led the way across the yard, which was little more than scrubby grasses and weeds. It took a while, but finally they discovered the remains of an old trail leading down the side of the bluff. Gwen knew her father and Lance had been down it a couple of times, so it was just clear enough for them to follow its path down to the narrow, rocky beach below.

The day was sunny and warm, and for a few moments the two girls just stood and basked in the bright sun. Molly wandered up to the water's edge watching the surf roll in and out with that peculiar mesmerized look so common among beach-goers. The gray-green water foamed as it slid across the narrow beach. Gwen set down the cooler and scoured the sand for interesting shells, her quest to find the cave forgotten for the moment. Molly took off her shoes and waded into the water

"Ahh!" Molly shrieked. "It's *freezing*!"

Laughing, Gwen kicked off her sandals and joined her, tentatively testing the water. Her eyes went wide. "How can you stand it? It's like ice!" She turned to Molly. "Whose stupid idea was this anyway?"

Molly just laughed and waded in deeper.

Gritting her teeth, Gwen followed her. "I can't feel my feet. I think they're frozen." At that moment, a large wave surged forward, knocking her over. Gwen floundered and sat up sputtering in the cold, salty water. Laughing wildly, she dragged herself up onto the beach and collapsed in a shivering heap.

Molly, also laughing, dropped down beside her.

"How can anyone swim in *this*?" Gwen searched the cooler for the blanket she'd packed to sit on. Gwen was used to the warm beaches of Virginia. There the ocean could seem as comfortable as a bath. It was nothing like this ice water. The two girls crawled onto the blanket, vainly trying to brush off some of the sand that was stuck to them.

"I don't think anyone does." Molly stretched out on her back in the warm rays of the sun. "Not without a wetsuit anyway."

Gwen stretched out on her stomach and sighed contentedly as she began to relax under the sun's heat.

Between the warmth and the rhythmic roar of the waves, she quickly grew drowsy.

"Do you really think you saw a ghost?" asked Molly.

Gwen blinked, startled out of her doze. "Yeah." She gathered her thoughts. "I'm sure of it. He looked right at me and said 'Help me.' Or at least I think that's what he said. He just moved his mouth. I couldn't hear any words."

Molly was silent for a few moments. She turned on her side to face Gwen. "Help him do what, do you think?"

"I think he wants me to prove he didn't take that money." Gwen stared at the clouds. "I mean, the ghost looked like the kid in the picture. I think that must mean he died as a kid. If he died as a grown-up, wouldn't he look like grown-up as a ghost?"

Molly frowned as she considered this. "I guess." Suddenly she sat up and stared at Gwen excitedly. "Wait! If he died as a kid, that means he must have been killed that night when he was escaping with the money. It could still be here someplace!" Molly's eyes shone. "Maybe he could tell you where it is."

Gwen sat up as the idea took hold. Molly was right. He must have died that night in 1923, but where and how? What happened to his body? She shuddered. She didn't want to be the one to find his remains if they were still around. That was just too gruesome. Finding the money, now that was something else altogether. Gwen knew, even though her parents never said anything, that with her father no longer working, money was tight, especially with all the house renovations.

"I don't know if he *can* tell me. I mean, he couldn't even say 'help me.' He just mouthed the words."

Molly gave a little laugh. "What, he's like a second-rate ghost? I thought ghosts were always saying 'Boo' and scary things like that. Well, if he can't tell you, couldn't he at least point to where the money is?"

Gwen shrugged. "I don't know. Maybe." She twirled a shell thoughtfully in her hand. "If we can find the money, wouldn't that prove he really hadn't run off with it? That he was innocent?"

"Sure. Maybe somebody was chasing him and he hid the money, but they killed him, and nobody knew what he did with it. Stupid gangsters."

"Well," sighed Gwen as she reached for the cooler, "I can't ask him anything unless he decides to show up again and, to be honest, I'm not sure I want him to." She rummaged around and handed Molly a peanut butter and jelly sandwich and a soda. She pulled out some for herself.

As the girls ate, Molly told Gwen about the school, the other kids in town and all the other important things kids needed to know in a new place.

Gwen absorbed it all. Running into Molly that day was one of the best things to happen to her since she moved here. Her mother was right; it would make things so much easier to have a friend when school started in the fall.

After they had eaten, Gwen decided it was time to

explore the end of the bluff where she hoped to find the bootlegger's cave. She pulled out the flashlights and handed one to Molly. "I've heard that sometimes smugglers hid stuff in caves around here. I want to see if we can find one."

Molly shrugged and threw her trash in the cooler. "Okay."

"Come on."

The sun had dried them, although their shorts and T-shirts felt stiff with salt. They grabbed their sandals, slipped them on and headed down the beach to the bluff face. Gwen almost expected to see the marks from the rumrunners' boat still etched in the sand, but there was nothing. They worked their way around the piles of rocks and driftwood until they reached the spot Gwen remembered from …when? In her mind, it was just hours ago, but in reality, it was much, much longer. She carefully examined the area and then noticed the tall rock that hid the entrance to the cave.

She wanted to walk directly there but decided it might look really odd since she'd told Molly she'd never been to the beach before. So, the girls spent time meandering around looking at the cliffs and rocks. They found one shallow cave Gwen hadn't seen before.

"Oh wow," Molly looked inside. "You know, according to my grandmother, this is just the kind of cave bootleggers used to hide the whiskey they brought in from Canada."

Gwen wrinkled her nose against the dank smell as she picked her way around the rotting strands of seaweed strewn along the bottom of the cave. "I doubt they used this one." She examined the damp walls. "I bet it floods when the tide comes in. Wouldn't do them much good if all their whiskey floated away."

Molly laughed as they continued on.

Finally, Gwen felt enough time had passed, and she wandered over to the rock and peered behind it. At first she thought there was nothing there, but pulling out her flashlight, she shone it in the shadowy recesses. There it was. Exactly as she remembered–a narrow cleft just barely visible. She moved in closer and shone her light inside. The passageway wound off into the darkness.

She stepped forward and, without a thought for Molly, entered the passageway. Again, she was taken back to the night when she was trapped here by the smugglers. Her mouth went dry. Silently, she climbed until the passage opened into the large empty space. All she could do was stare. The cave *was* there.

"It wasn't a dream," she whispered, feeling a chill run up her spine. "I really did go back in time." For a moment, her knees felt weak. Closing her eyes, she took a deep breath. Opening them once more, Gwen flashed her light around, picturing the cave crammed full of crates. There were a few empty whiskey bottles strewn about the cave floor but nothing else to show it had once been a storage place for illegal liquor.

"Gwen?" Gwen turned as Molly called from outside.

Gwen hesitated. Suddenly, she wasn't sure she wanted Molly to know about the cave. Would it ruin the almost magical atmosphere of the cave to have others know about it? She bit her lip in indecision but, in the end, the choice was made for her.

It was only a few moments later when Molly made her way up the passage. "Gwen? Are you in here?"

Gwen sighed. "Yeah. I'm here." She waited until Molly appeared in the entrance before moving deeper into the cave, now drawn to the far wall.

"Wow!" cried Molly a little breathlessly, now shining her light around the cave. "This is so cool!" She picked up an old bottle and examined it closely. "Look at this. It's an old whiskey bottle. I bet you're right, Gwen. I bet smugglers hid whiskey and stuff in here."

"Yeah, I guess." Gwen was more interested in the little alcove in the back wall. On her hands and knees, she focused her light in the small area. There! In a small crevasse she spied a dark green object. She reached down and, with fingers stiff with cold, pried it up from its resting place, its weight familiar in her hand. She shone her light on it as her breath caught in her throat.

It was an old, old flashlight and carefully etched on its chipped surface was "W. Andersson". Gwen could barely breathe as she stared at the name. *William Andersson.* It was William's flashlight. There was absolutely no doubt in her mind that this was the light Tom had given her. The very one she'd dropped in her haste to escape the smugglers. It was still here after all this time. This truly confirmed she *had* been in this cave all those years ago.

"What's that?" Molly looked over Gwen's shoulder.

"Oh, it's just an old flashlight. I wonder how long it's been here?"

"Since nineteen twenty-two," whispered Gwen still staring at it.

"What?" Molly's eyes narrowed. "What do you mean since nineteen twenty-two? How on earth would you know that?"

Gwen blinked, coming out of her reverie. "Oh, I don't know. It was just a guess."

Molly continued to stare at her. "Awfully exact for a guess."

Gwen thought fast. Obviously she couldn't tell Molly she dropped the flashlight in this very cave eighty years ago. How crazy would *that* sound? "Well, it was my dad's grandfather's. He told me about the smuggler's caves and how he lost his flashlight in one around here when he was a kid in nineteen twenty-two." Not exactly true, but Molly would never know.

Molly studied Gwen a few more moments before giving a shrug. "Okay, if you say so."

"No, really!" Gwen desperately wanted Molly to believe her. "How else would I know there might be caves here and my dad's grandfather's name *was* William Andersson. That's the name on the flashlight." Gwen almost laughed. For all she knew, this William *had* been her great-grandfather. She'd need to ask her dad about that. Didn't he say his grandfather was Charlie's brother? She couldn't remember.

"Okay, okay!" Molly rolled her eyes. "I believe you. Pretty amazing you managed to find just the right cave where he lost his flashlight, though."

"Well," Gwen moved away from the alcove, "I doubt there are that many caves around here." She looked around the cave. You know, this would make a really cool hideout. We could bring stuff in here and make it our secret place."

"Yeah!" Molly shined her light around again. "That would be so awesome. We've got a bunch of camping junk we don't use any more, like lanterns and stuff I bet my dad would let us use."

Gwen appraised the space like an interior decorator. "I haven't been in there yet but my mom said there is a whole bunch of old furniture and junk in the carriage house. I bet we could find some stuff we could use." For the next half hour, the girls excitedly discussed their plans for the cave and how they'd manage to get stuff down to it.

"As long as it's not too big, it should be pretty easy," said Molly as the girls headed back to the house.

"Well, we'll have to tell my mom what we're doing so she'll let us take the stuff, but we don't have to tell her where it is exactly. Knowing her, she'll think it's really cool. I know my dad will. He's just like a big kid sometimes."

When they finally reached the house, Molly's grandmother and Gwen's mom were sitting on the veranda drinking iced tea. "Ah, there you are," smiled Mom, waving to them. "I was wondering if we were going to have to send the dogs out after you."

"Mom," cried Gwen, breathless after their climb up

the bluff. "We found a really amazing secret cave down near the beach. We want to make it into our hideout, so can we take some stuff from the old carriage house? Please?"

Mom and Mrs. Berger laughed. "Well, I don't know." Mom had a slight tilt to her head. "Just how safe is this cave? I mean, do you need mountain climbing gear to get to it?"

"No." Molly shook her head. "It's got a little path that leads up to it so it stays dry, but it's not high or anything. It would be perfect." She held out the old whiskey bottle she'd picked up in the cave. "We think smugglers used it."

Mom and Mrs. Berger exchanged glances. "Drunken teenagers more like it." Mom examined the bottle. "'Old Log Cabin,'" she read the old faded label. "Isn't that pancake syrup?"

Mrs. Berger laughed. "Well, before that, it was a well-known brand of whisky favored by bootleggers in these parts. I'd say the girls have indeed stumbled on an old rumrunner's cache from Prohibition times. Is there more liquor there, Molly?"

Molly shook her head again. "Nah, just a few more of these bottles. They're all empty. So, can we use the cave for our hideout?"

Mom shrugged. "I don't see why not. You can go look in the carriage house for stuff to use, but be careful. I don't what all is in that disaster area. I think there are probably some old wooden chairs and small bookshelves, junk like that that might work."

"Thanks, Mom!"

The two girls ran off to the carriage house. This was going to be fun.

CHAPTER TWELVE

The carriage house was a large, dilapidated building situated behind the main house. Originally built to house the owner's horses and carriages, it had been redesigned to hold cars after the turn of the twentieth century. Now it served simply to hold junk.

Gwen and Molly entered from one of the small side doors and flicked on the lights.

Molly whistled. As far as the eye could see, both the main garage level and the upper loft appeared crammed full of boxes and old furniture. "I wonder if there's anything really valuable in here? Just think of the stuff you could take to one of those antiques shows where people find out how valuable their old junk is. I bet you could make some real money."

Gwen nodded. She rubbed her nose. The smell of mildew was strong. However, there did appear to be some amazing things. As she examined the contents more carefully, she realized, with a pang, some of the items were things she remembered seeing in the house; like the old wooden rocking horse from the playroom and the gilt edge mirror that had hung in the front hall. She blinked and looked away. Tears stung the backs of her eyes. She really needed to get a grip. Now she laughed weakly. "Boy, if my parents want to furnish the house with the original stuff, I don't think they'll have any trouble finding what they need out here."

The girls began to search the periphery of the mass of junk and pulled out an old rocking chair. They also found a small table, a plain wooden chair and a small set of bookshelves. All were coated with decades of grime, but the girls were certain they could clean each up nicely. Gwen thought they were just small enough to fit through the narrow passage. She also managed to dig out a small rolled up carpet that would fit perfectly in their new hideout.

As they made their way through the towering piles of old furniture, yard equipment and boxes, Gwen noticed an old wardrobe pushed against the back wall of the carriage house. She frowned. It seemed to almost glow, making it stand out in the shadows. She looked around. There was no light from the windows or overhead light bulbs that would explain the odd effect. Her curiosity piqued, she moved closer to the wardrobe and studied it. It looked familiar. She closed her eyes and tried to picture it standing in the house and, with a shock, she remembered it had been in Charlie's room. She blinked and stared at it again, wondering if there were any clothes or toys still in it. Even better, maybe there was some clue as to where Charlie hid the money. It was worth opening and taking a look.

Gwen gently ran her hand along the smooth wood. The wardrobe was at least seven feet tall and constructed dark wood. Gwen thought it might be lighter if it weren't so coated with grime. In fact, she thought critically, cleaned up, it would probably look really nice. She reached out and pulled on the small handle on one of the two doors. Nothing happened. After decades of sitting in a damp garage, the wood had warped and the door was firmly stuck. Gwen got a firmer hold and, with a grunt, gave the door a good strong yank. No better result. She frowned in frustration.

"What are you looking at? Whoa, that thing's huge!" Molly now stared open-mouthed at the large wardrobe.

"I was trying to open it." Gwen gave the door another yank. "The door is stuck. Maybe if we both try…"

Molly nodded and both firmly gripped the door and pulled hard. With a groan, the door reluctantly gave way and swung open, causing the girls to stumble backwards. Regaining her balance, Gwen rushed to the open door and peered in.

One side of the wardrobe was made up of shelves and a few drawers while there was a space for hanging clothes on the other. The wardrobe was empty save for a bulky canvas bag hanging from the bar. The girls studied the bag. Gwen wasn't sure she wanted to touch it.

"What do you think that is?" Molly eyed it suspiciously. "You don't think it's, like, a body or something do you?"

Gwen hesitated. "I kind of doubt it. I think if it was a body, it would really stink and would be a lot bigger."

As they stood studying the bag trying to get up the

nerve to reach in and retrieve it, Gwen's brother Lance called her name. A few moments later he appeared in the doorway.

"Hey, snotface, whatcha looking at?" Lance joined her and looked in. "Hey! What's that?" He slowly turned toward Gwen, eyes wide and said in a low spooky voice, "Maybe it's a bodeeeeee! Oooooooo!"

"Shut up, Lance." Gwen reigned in an urge to smack him. "It looks like a bag for hanging clothes."

Lance stared at it a moment longer then stepped into the wardrobe and grabbed the bag, bringing it out into the light. The canvas bag was heavily encrusted with dust and dirt. Carefully Lance lifted the bag up off the hanger and laughed in delight at his find. "It's an old raccoon coat."

Gwen and Molly exchanged confused glances. A *raccoon* coat? "Since when have they made coats out of raccoons?" Gwen frowned at the musty bundle of fur in his hand.

It looked quite old and patches of its brown and black fur had fallen out.

"They were all the rage in like the twenties or thirties." Lance turned the coat around to examine it from all sides. "Here," he handed her the hanger and slipped on the coat. It came down to his knees and its furry bulk seemed to swallow even his substantial frame. "How do I look?" He grinned.

"Like you should have a beanie and a ukulele," laughed a voice from the doorway. Gwen's dad watched them. "Where on earth did you find that relic?"

"It was in this old wardrobe." Lance tried to get a look at his reflection in the window. "I think it's pretty cool. Maybe I could start a new fad." He twirled around but stopped at the soft clatter of something falling onto the cement floor. He raised his eyebrows as he reached down to pick up a small silver item. He blinked and turned to the others. "It's a bullet!"

They all gathered closer as Lance held out the small mishapen bullet for them to examine.

"Where did that come from?" asked Molly.

Gwen felt a chill run down her back as she stared at the small piece of metal. Something about it unnerved her.

"I think it came out of the coat," said Gwen's father.

Eyes wide, Gwen watched as Lance quickly stripped off the heavy garment and handed it to his father.

Dad examined it closely. He finally found a hole in the bottom of the lining where the bullet must have come through. He methodically felt around the rest of the coat and froze as he poked his finger through a hole in the pelt just below the left arm.

"Whoa," gasped Lance. "Was somebody *shot* in that coat?"

Gwen turned and stared at her brother as the same thought occurred to her. Could Charlie have been wearing that coat?

"I don't see any blood stains." Dad examined the bullet again. "It's obviously been fired, but perhaps somebody just shot the coat. Maybe some crazed fashion critic." He searched a little more and pulled out a tarnished silver whiskey flask and an old piece of yellowed newspaper, studying them for a moment before replacing them.

Gwen's father put the coat back on its hanger, carefully replaced the cover and returned it to the wardrobe. "I think we'll just leave it here for the time being. Just another mystery for us to solve." He firmly closed the wardrobe door and turned to the girls. "You must be Molly." He smiled and shook her hand. "It was really nice of you and your grandmother to come by. I took a quick look at the pictures your grandmother brought. Some of them are really amazing."

"Thanks, Mr. Andersson." Molly turned and looked around the carriage house. "I gotta say, this place is so awesome."

Dad laughed. "Well, I hope it will be one day. Now, Gwen, what's this about a secret cave you guys found?"

Gwen quickly glanced over to make sure Lance was out of earshot then described the cave and how they'd found it. "Mom said it's okay if we use it as a hideout, so we're looking for stuff in here to use."

Dad nodded. "Well, after dinner, I suggest you show me this secret cave so I can make sure it's safe. I don't want you girls getting stuck in some cave because it fills with water at high tide. If it looks okay, then I have no problem with you guys using it."

After Lance and Dad had left, Molly and Gwen reopened the wardrobe door and stared solemnly at the hanging coat.

"Wow, a bullet." Molly shook her head. "Why would there be a coat with a bullet in it hanging in here? I wonder who shot it?"

Gwen continued to stare at the coat. "More importantly, was anybody wearing it at the time?" She had such a strong feeling this coat held some important clue to what happened to Charlie, but she couldn't figure out how. Whose coat was it? She sighed. Like her father said: Yet another mystery to add to the growing list.

A few moments later, Gwen's mother called them, and they made their way out of the carriage house to where the adults waited by Mrs. Berger's car.

"Thank you so much, Janet, for bringing those pictures," Mom said as the girls approached. "They will make such a difference when we start painting and doing the interior. We'd like it to look as close to its original appearance as possible."

"Grandma!" Molly ran up to the car, brushing her red hair from her face. "Can I come back tomorrow? It's so much fun here."

Mrs. Berger eyed her granddaughter, a smile playing at the corners of her mouth. "I thought you were the one who said it was going to be really creepy."

Molly glanced at Gwen flushing slightly. Then she laughed. "Well, it is creepy, but we gotta work on our hideout and there's a lot more to explore in that old carriage house and coats with bullet holes and…and…"

"Hold on," laughed Mrs. Berger. "As far as I'm

concerned, you can come up whenever the Anderssons are willing to have you, as long as you don't wear out your welcome."

"Mom?" Gwen turned to her mother. "Can she come back tomorrow? Please?" Gwen knew there was so much work to be done in the house, but she also knew her mom always worried Gwen didn't make enough friends.

Mom hesitated. "Oh, all right, but not till after lunch. We still need to finish painting the woodwork in your room." The girls whooped in delight and arranged a time for Molly to come back the next day. Gwen waved as Molly and her grandmother drove off then followed her mother into the house to help with dinner.

At the table, Dad went over the ideas he and the architect had come up with for turning the third floor into family living quarters, but Gwen barely listened. Her mind whirled with thoughts of ghosts, time travel, smugglers and missing money.

"A raccoon coat?" Gwen looked up at the sound of her sister's voice. Faye stared at Lance in disbelief. "You found some ancient raccoon coat with a bullet hole in it? That's horrible! Maybe somebody *died* in that coat."

"Nah." Lance paused to take a bite of his hamburger. He then glanced at Dad who was deep in conversation with their mother. "Dad says it doesn't look like there's any blood, but who knows? Maybe they got it cleaned? All I know is there is a hole in it, and there was an actual bullet that fell out of the lining. See? Look." He reached into his pocket and pulled out the bullet. Faye's mouth fell open as she gingerly picked up the small metal cylinder and studied it wide-eyed.

"If those coats were around in the twenties, maybe it belonged to some gangster. Hey! Maybe it belonged to the guy who ran off with the money. That bullet could prove he was murdered."

Lance snorted. "Listen, moron, if he was killed wearing the coat, it wouldn't be here, would it? It'd be wherever the body ended up. If it was his, then he wasn't wearing it when he disappeared."

Faye glared at her brother and dumped the bullet on the table. "Whatever." She stalked from the room. Lance just shook his head and resumed eating.

Gwen reached out and picked up the bullet. She gasped as she felt a slight tingle run through her hand like a gentle electrical shock. She blinked and studied it more carefully. This just had to be a clue to who killed Charlie. Deep in her heart, she had no doubt he was murdered. She just *had* to get back to the 1920s. But how?

"Gwennie?"

Gwen looked up.

Her dad watched her. "Something wrong?"

"Oh, uh, no, Dad." She slipped the bullet into her pocket. She glanced over.

Lance watched her, but he said nothing about the bullet. Just a slight tilt of his eyebrow let her know he knew she had it.

"I was thinking you could show me that cave before it gets dark." Dad rolled up the blueprints he had pulled out earlier.

"What cave?" asked Lance through a mouthful of food. Now he looked interested.

"It's my secret cave. Molly and I found it. We're going to make it into a hideout, and we don't want you bugging us." She scowled at him.

Lance made a face, shrugged and returned to his food.

Gwen wasn't fooled. She knew her brother all too well. He wouldn't rest until he found out where her cave was. She'd have to be very careful he didn't.

After the dishes had been cleared away, Gwen led her father down the path and to the hidden entrance to the cave.

Dad shone his flashlight around the opening, studying the narrow confines of the passageway. "I'm not sure I'll fit through there."

"Sure you can, Dad." Gwen smiled. She pictured the two smugglers who managed to make it in, and she knew her dad wasn't any bigger than either of them. "It'll be a little tight at the beginning, but it gets better. You'll see."

He glanced at her doubtfully, but with a shrug followed her in, grunting every so often as he was forced to stoop to avoid hitting his head or work to get his broad shoulders through some of the narrower turns. When the cave opened before them, he gave a low whistle of appreciation.

"Wow, Gwennie. This is incredible!" He shone his light around and, like Molly before him, picked up one of the empty whiskey bottles. "You're right," he nodded, studying the old bottle. "This must have been a smuggler's cave."

"I found this in here." Gwen held out the old flashlight. "It has 'W. Andersson' written on it. Was he related to us, do you think?"

Dad sat down on a rock and carefully examined the old flashlight. "W. Andersson." His eyes lit up as he laughed. "Of course he was. William Andersson! That was my grandfather, but everyone just called him Old Bill." He paused. "Grandpa would have been a kid when he lived here, so I bet he knew about these caves. Wow, this is just so amazing. It's like a real connection to the past." He smiled faintly as he stared down at the flashlight, but his eyes were distant. "I never thought we'd end up with the old homestead." Gwen watched him silently begging him to say more.

"You know, Charlie ran off with the money, the family lost everything, including this house. I'm not exactly sure what happened. My grandfather would never talk about it, but he's always blamed Charlie for the family's downfall. For many years I never even knew he had a brother named Charlie. I'll admit, I'm not big into family history, but it was as if there was an unspoken agreement among the family never to mention Charlie's name again."

Gwen frowned. "You talk like your grandpa is still alive."

Dad nodded, still looking at the old flashlight. "He is, but he's always been such an angry, bitter old coot, nobody could stand to be around him. I've only met him a few times. He's well into his nineties by now and lives in a nursing home in New York. The older he got, the more bitter he became about that money. You see, Grandpa Bill was in college when all this happened. He planned on going to medical school, but when the money disappeared, he had to come home, and he never fulfilled his dream of becoming a doctor. Or even finishing college, for that matter." He shook his head. "My dad had a truly miserable childhood. After he grew up and his mother passed away, Dad rarely saw his father." Dad sighed. "A lot happened during that time in the twenties. Grandpa Bill is the last of that generation, and he won't talk about life before Charlie took off. As far as he's concerned, nothing happened before nineteen twenty-three. Weird."

Gwen nodded, thinking about what she knew of the Anderssons in the 1920s. She hadn't met William and wondered what he would have been like as a young man. Had he been anything like Charlie? From Dad's description, she rather doubted it, but disappointment could change a person a lot, couldn't it? *Maybe one day I'll find out what he was really like.*

Dad stood up and stretched, shining his light around one more time. "Well, kiddo, I don't see any reason why you and your friend can't use this place. Doesn't look like anyone has been here in a long time, and it seems dry. I don't think it's prone to flooding, so full steam ahead."

Gwen grinned broadly. "Thanks, Dad." As they

worked their way out of the cavern and up to the house, Gwen continued to ponder her father's story. Just one more piece to an ever more confusing puzzle.

That night, as Gwen got ready for bed, she thought about how she was going to get back to 1922. To get there in the first place, she simply went into the closet that night she'd gone to check the date. She sat upright in bed–the date! She'd gone into the closet the night it turned May 15, right? She'd felt that strange tingle when she touched Gwen's measurement for that date. That had to be it! To go back in time, you had to go in on the right date. She considered this. It hadn't worked when she tried to go back after she escaped from Carmichael because there was no measurement for that date. Would it work for any of the dates, no matter whose measurement it was? She frowned. She hadn't felt the shock when she touched the other names, just Gwen's. Perhaps that was the real key. There must be some weird connection between herself and the other girl. That meant she could only go back on the dates connected with the other Gwen. She tried to remember those other dates but came up with a blank.

Gwen considered going up to check right now but was simply too exhausted. One thing she was sure of, none of the dates had been May 16 or 17, so if her theory was right, she couldn't go tonight. Plus, she thought sleepily, *I'm really not too keen on meeting up with Charlie's ghost again.* She'd had enough adventures for one day.

CHAPTER THIRTEEN

The next morning promised another clear and sunny summer day. Gwen got up early and, after breakfast, helped her mother finish painting the wood trim in her bedroom. Lance grumbled about how unfair it was Gwen had help doing her room, while he was stuck doing all his own work, but Gwen had no problem ignoring him. She knew Lance would be busy painting all afternoon, so she and Molly wouldn't have to worry about her stupid brother bothering them while they made their plans.

Molly arrived shortly after lunch, eager to get started on furnishing their new hideout. She'd brought a couple of battery lanterns her father let her take. "These will be better than flashlights." She demonstrated how they worked. Gwen was impressed.

The two girls headed to the carriage house and examined their pile of furnishings. "We really need to clean some of this stuff before we lug it down to the cave." Gwen sighed. "It's pretty grimy."

Molly nodded. "Maybe we could repaint these old shelves. That would help make them look better."

Gwen went off to ask her mother and came back with a can of yellow paint left over from her room.

"Mom said we could use this." She put down the can and a couple of brushes. "We probably ought to try to get off some of the dirt so the paint sticks better."

It took a couple of hours for them to finish scrubbing and painting, but Gwen had to admit, it was worth the effort. Once cleaned, the two chairs looked much better and the paint made the shelves look like new.

"We'll have to leave the shelves here to dry." Gwen replaced the top on the paint can. "We can start taking some of this other stuff down."

It only took a couple of trips lugging chairs and rugs down the bluff to exhaust the girls, They collapsed on the veranda, wiping the sweat from their faces.

"Boy, that path seems really long when you're carrying furniture." Molly groaned. "I think I can safely cross off moving man from my list of possible careers."

"Looks like you girls could use something to drink," Mom came out with a couple of cans of soda. "I've been watching you take stuff down. That's some job. Maybe you should ask Lance to help."

Gwen scowled at her mother. "No way! Then he'd come bugging us all the time. We can do it. It might kill us, but we'll do it."

Mom just laughed and returned to the house.

"What do we have left?" Molly took a long swig of her soda. "I don't think I can cart too much more down there."

Gwen thought. "I think just the shelves for now. Also that box of books and stuff to decorate with."

"Okay. That doesn't sound too bad."

After they'd rested, they went to check on the last of their pile. The paint on the shelves was still tacky in a few places, but Gwen figured they were dry enough to carry down. The box of miscellaneous items wasn't too heavy, so Gwen went and got their small cooler and filled it with a couple of sodas and some snacks to take with them. She didn't want to have to make an extra trip if she could avoid it.

Lugging the shelves down was awkward; even though they weren't heavy, they were hard to maneuver down the steep, rocky path, so it took considerably longer than their previous trips. When they reached the opening to the passageway, Gwen set the cooler and box down on the sand and rubbed her aching shoulder.

"Are you sure these shelves are going to fit?" Molly eyed the narrow opening. It couldn't be much more than a couple of feet wide.

Gwen chewed her lip as she considered this. "I think so." She looked back and forth between the shelves and the cleft. "If we can get it past the first part of the tunnel, we should be okay."

Molly shrugged and grabbed one end while Gwen lifted the other and together they slowly made their way into the tunnel.

It was a tight fit. Gwen scraped her arms against the rough rocks several times as they manhandled the shelves up the narrow passageway. "Ouch!" She'd smacked her head against a low hanging rock. "Are you sure we really need these stupid shelves?"

"As I recall," Molly tried to free a corner of the shelves from where it had gotten wedged, "this was your idea."

Despite the cool interior of the tunnel, sweat dripped down Gwen's dirt-streaked face. Molly looked just as bad. Finally they maneuvered the shelves into the cave where they promptly dropped them. Gwen rubbed her sore head and collapsed on a rock to rest.

"Okay." Molly flopped into one of the chairs. "Next time we decide to build a secret hideout, let's make it a lot easier to get to, like in your closet. I'm beat."

Gwen nodded. "We still need to go back out and get the box and cooler we left on the beach." She rose stiffly to her feet. "I better go get them before somebody sees them. Like my stupid brother. I don't want him finding our cave."

"I'll come," Molly groaned dramatically. "Otherwise you'll sit out there and eat all the good stuff."

Gwen punched her arm good-naturedly as they started their descent. As they exited the passageway and made their way around the rock that helped hide the entrance, they were brought up short by a man examining their box and cooler.

The man looked up and attempted what Gwen supposed was a smile. He was an exceptionally large man, well over six feet and heavy. He had small piggy eyes, dark thinning hair and ears that stuck out from either side of his head, reminding Gwen of Dumbo the elephant. He gave her the creeps. The girls glanced at each other nervously and took a step back.

"Hello there, ladies." The man's voice was

surprisingly high. "Didn't mean to scare you. I just was walking here on the beach and saw this pile of stuff and wondered who it belonged to. I don't see many people in these parts."

The girls continued to stare at him for several more moments before Gwen finally spoke up. "My family just moved into the big house on the bluff."

The man's eyes narrowed briefly before he resumed his friendly manner. "Is that so? Then you must be the Anderssons. You know, that house used to be in *my* family. Name's Bob Carmichael. Yep, my great-grandfather first lived here. The house was in my family a real long time."

"How come you don't own it, then?" asked Molly.

Gwen elbowed her in the side and glared.

Again came that odd change in expression in Bob Carmichael's face. He shrugged. "Not exactly sure why Granddad decided to leave it to your dad. Maybe thought he could fix it up better'n me." He gave a hearty laugh. It made Gwen's skin crawl. "That's probably true. I never really wanted that old dinosaur anyhow. It'd cost a fortune to fix it up so's somebody could live in it. To be honest, I ain't thought about it much in years."

Gwen and Molly exchanged glances. For someone who claimed not to care, this weird man seemed *very* interested in the house. With his shifty eyes and all-too-friendly grin, Gwen's gut feeling said he wasn't a man to be trusted. She wanted to him to go away.

"Well, it…it was very nice to meet you, Mr.

Carmichael." Gwen edged away. She glanced at the box and cooler sitting on the sand. "We need to get our stuff and get going."

"Yeah, that was a great old house in its day." It was as if Carmichael hadn't heard her. "Lots of mysteries in that house." He leaned closer toward them and said in a hushed voice, "I bet you girls have heard all about the missing gangster's gold, huh?"

"Yeah, sure. But really…" This guy was seriously creeping her out. All she wanted to do was get away from him and back up to the house.

"You know, if you find that money, it really belongs to the Carmichaels." He stared up at the house. There was a threatening undercurrent to his words. "Some think it's hid in the house someplace."

"That's dumb." Molly sounded as if she'd had enough of this weirdo. "Everyone knows Charlie Andersson ran off with the money. He wouldn't have brought it here. Besides, if it was here, somebody woulda found it by now."

"Maybe." Carmichael turned his cold piggy eyes on her. "But maybe nobody's really looked in the house either."

A cold shiver ran down Gwen's back. She reached over and grabbed Molly's hand. "Really, mister, we need to go. My mom is expecting us back."

Bob Carmichael smiled again and stepped back. "Well then, you ladies don't wanna go leavin' your stuff out here in the open. Somebody might come along and walk off with it." He reached down and handed Molly the box and Gwen the cooler.

Smiling weakly, they both said thanks then, skirting around the strange man, they scurried up the path to the house as quickly as they could. Gwen glanced down as they approached the top of the bluff. Carmichael still stood there watching them. She shivered and ran a little faster. When they reached the safety of the veranda, they dumped their stuff and collapsed on the steps gasping for breath.

"That guy was *so* creepy!" Molly she grabbed Gwen's arm. "Where did he come from?"

Gwen shook her head, still trying to catch her breath. She was thinking hard. George Carmichael had been Jonas Andersson's business partner. This guy must be a descendant of his. Seemed creepiness ran in the family.

"I think he believes that money is hidden here someplace." Gwen wiped the sweat from her brow with her sleeve. "I bet he's really ticked off he didn't get the house so he could tear it apart and find the money."

"Yeah." Molly looked back the way they'd come as if worried Carmichael might suddenly pop up again. "That's probably why they didn't give him the house. They figured he'd destroy it." She noticed the box and cooler where they'd dropped them and scowled. "Dang. Now we're gonna have to carry this stuff back down again."

Gwen sighed. Would that weird guy show up every time they wanted to go to their secret hideout? She shook her head. "Well, I think he's too big to fit inside our cave at least."

Molly laughed. "Yeah, that's for sure. I guess we should wait awhile before we go back down and make sure he's gone. You better tell your dad about that guy. I sure wouldn't want him sneakin' around *my* house." She sat silent for a few minutes. "I know, why don't you show me where you saw the ghost? That'll kill some time."

Gwen hesitated then shrugged. It would give her a chance to check the next date on the door and maybe, if Molly was there, the ghost wouldn't appear. She felt sorry for him, but she really preferred it when he wasn't around. The two girls got up and headed into the house.

"Hey, Dad." Gwen walked into the master suite where her father worked. "Can we talk to you for a second?"

Dad looked up from where he'd just scraped a section of yellowed wallpaper off the wall. He wiped his forehead and set down his tool. "Sure. I could use a break. What's going on?"

"Do you know a guy named Bob Carmichael?"

Dad thought for a moment. "Yeah, well, I know who he is, but I've never actually met him. He was supposedly next in line to inherit this house. He's like some kind of distant cousin. Why?"

"We just met him on the beach." Gwen glanced at Molly who nodded. "He's this really big, creepy guy. He kept talking about the house and the missing money. He acted like he didn't care about any of it, but you could tell he did."

"Yeah," Molly chimed in. "He kept talking about how maybe the money was hidden in this house someplace."

"Wait a minute," frowned Dad. "You guys say you met Bob Carmichael? On our beach?"

The girls both nodded together.

"He was really seriously creepy," repeated Molly.

Dad's frown grew deeper. "I don't like the sound of this. I've never met the man, but he has no right to be wandering around this property scaring kids. I don't know why the house wasn't left to him, but it's ours now, and we don't need him snooping around."

"I bet he wants to tear down the house and look for the money," said Gwen. "That's probably why his grandpa wouldn't give it to him. He was going to wreck it."

"Hmm." Dad stood up and peered out the window toward the beach. He turned back to the girls. "I think you guys better stay off the beach for today. I'll have to have a talk with Mr. Carmichael soon and get some things straight. In the meantime, if you see him again, just stay away from him. Don't talk to him or anything. Just come straight home. You understand?"

They nodded.

"Okay. Thanks for telling me, girls. We'll get this straightened out." He smiled and went back to scraping off the wallpaper.

Gwen touched Molly's arm and the two of them left the room and headed out into the hallway. A short while later, they were up in the playroom. Gwen glanced around then breathed a sigh of relief when she detected no sign of the ghost. While Molly wandered about, Gwen moved to the closet and peered at the dates.

With a pang of sadness, she thought back to the night she'd gone back in time. *Oh, Uncle Jonas, what happened to you?* She gently touched Gwen's second date, May 20, 1923, penciled onto the wall. That was only three days away. She frowned slightly as she noticed an almost imperceptible tingling. She touched several of the other dates belonging to Tom and Louisa, but there was nothing. She touched Gwen's mark again and felt the same odd tingling sensation.

It reminded her of the shock she received when she touched Gwen's first date on that fateful night. Her heart sped up. Did that tingling mean she *could* go back? Would that mean if she did, it would then be 1923? That would mean she couldn't do anything to save her uncle. Her excitement faded to sorrow.

"What're those?" Molly peered at the door frame. "Dates?"

"I think they're measuring marks for kids who used to live here." Gwen had hoped Molly wouldn't notice them, although she should have realized Molly noticed *everything.*

"Really?" Molly looked more closely at the marks. "Gwen, I gotta tell you. This place is so cool. It's never ever boring. Hey look! There's *your* name."

"Yeah, I know. I think she was some kind of cousin to the Anderssons." Gwen hesitated then glanced at her friend. "Do you feel anything when you touch any of the names? Like a tingling or something?"

Molly's eyebrows shot up in surprise but she reached over and gently touched all the names. She shook her head. "Nope. Not a thing. Why? Do you feel something?"

Gwen shrugged. "I thought maybe I did, but I guess it was nothing." Part of her really wished she could tell Molly about what happened to her that night in the closet, but even to her it sounded nuts. Perhaps the fact Molly couldn't feel anything meant it would only work if your name was there.

Molly studied the dates closely. "It's kinda eerie. It's proof these kids were really here. I mean, we know they lived here and all, but this makes them more real."

Gwen said nothing. She knew exactly what Molly meant. Those weren't just names to her–they were real flesh and blood people, and she was worried about all of them.

Molly stepped away from the closet and looked around again. "So, you say you saw the ghost of Charlie Andersson up here?"

Gwen nodded. "I've seen him a couple of times now. At first I didn't know who he was, because I couldn't really see him very well. The last time, he was almost as clear as you are now." She shivered. "I know he wants help, but I don't like seeing him."

Molly frowned. "Is there any kind of sign that he's here?"

"Well, it gets really cold, and I get this feeling like somebody's watching me." Gwen shrugged. "That's about it. He doesn't go 'boo' or move things around. Not that I've noticed, anyway. I know he wouldn't hurt me, but it's still scary."

"So, he's not here now?"

Gwen turned and studied the room around her. "Nope. At least I can't see him if he is."

Molly glanced around again then looked at her watch. "My grandma will be here pretty soon to pick me up. Maybe we better just move that stuff back into the carriage house until I come back." She looked at Gwen. "Now don't you go fixing things up until I get back. It won't be any fun if you've already done everything." Then she grinned.

Gwen gave a little laugh. "Don't worry. I won't. It wouldn't be any fun without you to help. Besides, with that weirdo hanging around, I'm not so sure I want to go down there by myself."

She scowled thinking how much creepy Carmichael had put a damper on their fun. Well, hopefully, after her dad talked to him, he wouldn't come around again.

As the girls started downstairs, Gwen couldn't help but think of the second date on the wall. Butterflies fluttered in her stomach as she thought about the possibility of going back in time again. She was so worried about her uncle and wondered if she could go back, would she still be able to help him in some way? What about George Carmichael? A shiver ran down her back as she remembered him chasing her through the dark house. Would he have caught the 1920s Gwen there in the playroom? She stopped for a moment and then decided with relief that Gwen's other dates proved that even if he caught her, she was okay. Or at least Gwen hoped so.

May 20 -Only three more days.

CHAPTER FOURTEEN

It rained over the next couple of days, and Gwen spent most of her time cleaning and helping to make the house more livable. It was still very forlorn, but the bedroom level looked better all the time. Mrs. Berger needed her granddaughter's help as she sorted some materials at the historical society, so Molly couldn't come over. After so much initial excitement, Gwen rather enjoyed the mundane routine of working on the house. However, in the back of her mind was a growing excitement knowing that soon she'd be able to try to return to Tom and the others. She worried constantly that something terrible had happened to Uncle Jonas.

The night of the nineteenth Gwen was almost sick with anxiety. It felt like the longest day of her life. She could swear the clock never moved.

"What are you so antsy about?" asked Lance irritably as they sat watching TV. "You've been checking the time like every twenty seconds. You got someplace to go?"

Gwen made a face. "No. I don't have any place to go. I just wondered what time it was. That's all." She glanced at the clock again.

Lance grunted. "Whatever. Just knock it off, will ya? You're getting on my nerves."

Gwen sighed and headed up to her room. She

picked up her flashlight and wondered if there was anything she could take with her. Last time nothing she'd had with her when she entered the closet had carried over into the past. She had also decided that very little time passed here while she was there. That was one less worry. At least she hoped that was always the case.

She opened her little jewelry box and pulled out the bullet they'd found in the coat. She studied it for a long time, wishing she knew its secrets. Finally, with a sigh, she dropped it back in the box and returned the box to its place on her dresser.

Around ten, her mother came in and told her it was time for bed. "Oh, and your dad finally talked to Mr. Carmichael." She put away some of Gwen's clean laundry. "He's assured your dad he meant no harm and won't trespass in the future."

"Did he ever actually live in this house?" Gwen climbed into her bed.

"No. No one has lived in this house since sometime in the fifties. I think his grandfather was the last one to actually live here." She turned to look at Gwen. "Mr. Carmichael told your dad his family moved overseas when he was really little and lived there for many years. I'm not sure Bob even realized this house was still in the family until recently. Okay, kiddo. Enough of that. It's time for bed. We've got a lot more work lined up for tomorrow, but if you're good, maybe Molly can come over for a while in the afternoon."

"Thanks, Mom." Gwen settled back against the pillows. Her mother tucked her in, gave her a kiss and was gone.

So that's why Creepy Bob wants in here so badly. She pulled a book out from under her pillow. *He's never had a chance to look through the house before. I bet he'll try and sneak in here some day when we're gone and start going through everything.* Gwen pulled the covers up higher then opened her book and was soon immersed in the land of Narnia.

Gwen woke with a start confused as to what had awakened her. She blinked and realized she had dropped her book onto the floor. The soft glow of her lamp created dark shadows in the corners of her room. She rubbed her eyes and peered at the clock. It was a few minutes before midnight. Her stomach gave a flip. Time to go.

She slid out of bed and picked up her book, setting it on the bedside table, reached for her robe. She tied her it around her then cautiously opened her bedroom door and peeked out. Seeing no one about, she padded down the hallway to the attic stairs. Her penlight firmly clutched in her hand, she crept up the stairs with only the occasional creak of the old wood to announce her passage.

It was a velvety black in the playroom, despite the large windows. The overcast skies of the past few days obliterated any moonlight that might have provided some illumination. Gwen slowly made her way toward the closet. A cold drop of sweat trickled down her back. As she neared the closet door, she paused. The temperature in the room seemed to drop. Her heart pounded in her chest. Gwen gave a small gasp and stepped back as a form glowed in the doorway. She bit her lip to keep from crying out. The glow began to solidify into a shape–that of a young man. Charlie Andersson.

Gwen couldn't take a breath. Her body froze as Charlie took a few steps toward her. His brows were knitted, his mouth a tight line. He closed his eyes for a moment as if in concentration. Gwen just stared silently until suddenly he spoke, his voice very soft but recognizable all the same.

"Gwen, be careful." That was all. Then he faded away.

Gwen continued to stare at the place where Charlie had stood. *Be careful.* That's all he said. *What did he mean?* She stood trembling for a few moments longer as she let her heart slow back to normal. When she could breathe again, she gave herself a little shake and inhaled deeply. Then she turned back toward the closet, her jaw set. She wouldn't let even a ghost stop her from attempting this.

She directed the small beam of her penlight onto the doorframe and checked the dates. Yes. There it was, May 20, 1923. She looked again at the other dates and with a start realized that, although Tom continued to have measurement marks up until 1925, about the time they must have lost the house, Charlie disappeared after 1923 and Gwen's last measurement was in 1924. Not a good sign. Gwen frowned.

Charlie was killed sometime in 1923, but what happened to Gwen? She shivered again then, taking a deep breath, switched off her penlight and reached out to gently touch the May 20, 1923, date. She gasped as she again felt the jolt run up her arm. Swallowing hard, she stepped into the closet and closed the door. She stood silently for several long moments. Nothing seemed to happen. Could she have been wrong? Maybe she couldn't go back after all. She reached for her penlight and discovered she no longer wore her robe and pajamas but a long nightgown. With a grin of triumph, she knew it had worked. She had returned.

Gently, she pushed opened the door and peered out into the playroom. It was just as she remembered it–shelves full of toys and books, the old wooden rocking horse in the corner and the rocking chair by the window. A surge of happiness flooded through her. Maybe she wasn't too late. As she stepped out into the playroom, a wave of dizziness threatened to overwhelm her. She might have fallen had she not grabbed onto the bookshelves nearby. She blinked and rubbed her head. She had a throbbing headache. Funny, she didn't remember feeling this way before she stepped into the closet. Gwen scowled. She didn't have time to be sick. She had to find out what happened to Uncle Jonas.

She took a deep breath and took a step toward the door. The room seemed to spin around her, making her feel nauseous. She sank into a small chair near the door and rested her head on her hands.

"Miss Gwen?"

Gwen slowly raised her head and focused on a figure in white standing in the doorway. She blinked as the figure moved closer. With relief, she realized it was Nina, one of the young maids who worked for the family.

She looked down at Gwen with concern as she pulled her robe closer around her. "Oh dear, Miss Gwen," she whispered laying her hand on Gwen's shoulder. "Looks like you've been walkin' in your sleep again. I can't tell you the scare you gave me when I woke up and found you gone. Are you awake?"

Gwen nodded and immediately regretted it as the pounding in her head increased. This was *not* the way it was supposed to be.

Nina shook her head then gently took Gwen's arm. "C'mon, sweetheart." She helped Gwen to her feet. "It's just the fever again. Let's get you back to bed." Gwen staggered but, with Nina's help, regained her balance. She allowed the maid to assist her down the stairs and back to her room. "Why you keep going up to that closet when you walk in your sleep is a mystery." Nina tucked Gwen into her bed. "Three times now we've found you up there in the middle of the night, but you never say why."

Gwen swallowed. "Um, have I been sick long?"

Nina laughed a little sadly. "Oh, honey, when *aren't* you sick? Ever since you had the scarlet fever last year, I swear you've spent more time in this bed than out of it. Don't you worry. Dr. Knowlton says it's just a phase. You'll grow out of it and be just fine. Now, get some sleep and stay put." With a smile she caressed Gwen's cheek then turned to lie down on a cot nearby, but not before Gwen noticed the sadness in her eyes. A twinge of apprehension went through her. What would happen if she died while she was here? Would she simply disappear? What would her parents think? With these dismal thoughts floating in her brain, she soon fell into a deep sleep.

The next morning was very reminiscent of her first arrival in the past, although at least this time she knew who everyone was. She just wasn't sure what day–or more importantly, what year–it was. She assumed it was 1923, but she needed to be sure. Gwen noticed the cot where Nina slept was empty and neatly made. *She must have watched over me last night.* It made her feel strange. She wasn't used to people watching her sleep. A short time later, Aunt Katherine came in carrying a tray. With a pang, Gwen noticed how worn down she looked. Aunt Katherine gave Gwen a tired smile.

"Nina told me you awakened at last." She set the tray down on the bedside table and placed a cool hand on Gwen's brow. She nodded. "Yes, your fever is down. Thank God." She looked at Gwen with obvious relief but turned hastily as she wiped her hand across her eyes. Gwen quickly understood during the 1920s Gwen had been very ill.

"I feel much better, Aunt Katherine." Her voice sounded weak though.

Her aunt turned back to her with the tray now in her hands. "That's wonderful, darlin'. Here, I brought you some breakfast. Nothing much, but you need to start getting your strength back, Gwennie." The nickname gave Gwen a start. Only her family ever called that. Her aunt helped her sit up then fed Gwen her breakfast of beef broth and toast as if she were a baby. Gwen's frustration grew as she realized just how weak and helpless she seemed to be. She had to get out of this stupid bed. Where was Tom? He had to help her. When she was done, Aunt Katherine bathed her and helped her put on a fresh nightgown.

"There." Her aunt picked up the tray. She smiled again. "Dr. Knowlton will be here soon for his daily visit, and I'm sure he'll be pleased with your improvement."

The doctor was indeed impressed as he checked Gwen over. "Young lady, I honestly thought we might lose you this time, but look at you. Sitting up, eating–it's like a miracle. You're like a whole new girl." He gave her a warm smile as he put away his thermometer. "You keep going like this, and you'll be up and around in no time." He met Aunt Katherine by the door. They kept their voices low so she couldn't make out what they said. She sighed and hoped Tom would come soon.

She didn't have to wait long for her young cousin to stick his head in the doorway. He peered shyly at her. "Tom!" She struggled to sit up a bit more. She refused to act like she was sick even if her body wouldn't cooperate.

With a grin and whoop of delight, Tom galloped into the room and leaped onto her bed. "Gwen! You're not dead! I told 'em you'd lick this."

Gwen grinned. She suddenly realized how

important Tom had become to her. Then she grew serious. "Tom, it's happened again. I don't know the date or anything. How long have I been sick?"

Tom's grin faded, and he looked away for a few moments. "It's May twenty-third, nineteen twenty-three, and you've been sick for three days." He tilted his head. "It was weird," he said slowly. "You got sick right after Ma measured us in the playroom. Just like last year."

Gwen was confused. How could there be a difference of three days? She entered the closet on the 20th. Had she actually been here for three days? She shook her aching head. She had no answer for this and sighed. She turned again to Tom. "Where's Uncle Jonas?" She feared his response.

Tom's face darkened. "You know where he is, Gwen. He's in jail! Somebody framed him for that jewelry store robbery. It was all a setup."

"Oh no." Gwen buried her face in her hands. It was just as she'd feared. Tears filled her eyes and slowly trickled down her flushed cheeks. Then she looked up at Tom as anger colored her words. "George Carmichael set him up!"

Tom stared at her, his mouth open. "What? How do you know? Are you sure? Why didn't you say something before?" He shook her arm angrily.

"I…I just remembered," whispered Gwen weakly. How on earth could she possibly explain this to Tom without sounding crazy?

"Just remembered?" Tom's eyes were wide with fury. "My father is accused of robbing a jewelry store, and a year later you just happen to remember *he was set up*? That's not something you just *happen* to remember, Gwen!"

Gwen closed her eyes, feeling more miserable than she thought possible. Her headache was worse. "You remember when we saw George and Bertie smuggling liquor last ni…year and I got trapped in the cave by those two goons? I heard them talking. They said George was going to try and set it up to look like Uncle Jonas was responsible for robbing a jewelry store. If that didn't work, they said they were going kill him." She looked pleadingly at her cousin. "I'm so sorry, Tom. I don't know why I couldn't remember it before. I came back up to the house and Mr. Carmichael was here waiting for me. He said he'd drugged you and your parents, and that you wouldn't remember anything. He chased me up into the playroom, and…and that's the last thing I remember."

Tom stared at her in silence. "We saw George and Bertie smuggling whiskey?" He frowned as if trying to grasp this elusive memory. "We saw George and Bertie smuggling whiskey," he repeated more slowly, his frown deepening then his eyes went wide. "We saw George and Bertie smuggling whiskey! How could I have forgotten that?" He shook his head as he tried to make sense of this. "You say Mr. Carmichael drugged me?" He paused. "I do seem to remember seeing him that night after I got back to the house but that's all. If only we had remembered this before. We coulda saved Pop." His thin shoulders slumped in despair.

"Can't we still?" Gwen leaned forward. "I mean, it's not too late, is it?"

Tom looked away. "Who would believe that after a year we *suddenly* remembered Mr. Carmichael and Bertie are rumrunners and they set Pop up for a jewelry store heist? Pretty convenient, wouldn't you think?"

Gwen sagged against her pillows, feeling drained. She was too late after all, and now Uncle Jonas was in jail for who knew how long. What should she do now?

CHAPTER FIFTEEN

Gwen worked hard to get back on her feet, amazing both the doctor and the rest of her family. All of them said they'd never seen her bounce back so quickly from one of her fevers. Gwen ate and walked as much as she could, even when Dr. Knowlton told her to ease up or she could have a relapse.

"A lot he knows." Gwen scowled as she and Tom played checkers in her room. "He probably still uses leeches. I think the more I move around, the stronger I'll get. I just can't stand sitting around in this room. If I don't get out of here soon, I'll go nuts!" She moved one of her pieces. "Have you checked out that cave again? Are the rumrunners still using it?"

Tom shook his head. "I dunno. I've been too scared to go back. I told Charlie about it after you and I talked the other day, and he told me I'd better mind my own business." He took off his glasses and rubbed his eyes. "I think Charlie might be doing some work for Jimmy Houlihan."

Gwen stared at him. "Charlie? Why? Why would he work for a gangster?"

Tom looked at her strangely. "You know why. Ever since Pop went to jail, money's been really tight. Mr. Carmichael claims business is down, so there's less money."

Gwen had almost forgotten George Carmichael

was Uncle Jonas' business partner. She chewed on her lip thoughtfully. "Do you believe him?"

Tom shrugged. "Doesn't matter what I believe. He showed Ma the books and claimed they prove there's not much money comin' in. William was gonna come home from college, but Ma told him not to. If he can become a doctor, everything'll be okay. She wants that more than anything. So Charlie said he'd get a job, and Mr. Carmichael said he could help him. I didn't think nuthin' about it until we remembered about the rumrunning. Now we know Carmichael's in with the gangsters, I'm pretty sure he's got Charlie doin' something for them. Charlie says he just runs errands but won't say nuthin' more."

Gwen nodded. That made sense. Gwen knew Charlie eventually became Jimmy's bagman, but he most likely started out doing something simple like running errands.

"Tom, what are we going to do?" Gwen picked up a red checker and absently turned it over and over. "Your dad is in jail, and his partner is probably robbing him blind. Who's going to believe a couple of kids?"

Tom sighed. "I don't think telling at this point would help. Jimmy the Blade runs everything in these parts. I bet even the police do what he wants. They won't do anything to help. If Mr. Carmichael is in with Jimmy, they won't touch him either."

Gwen slammed the checker down on the board, causing the rest to jump. "Well, it's just not fair! Uncle Jonas is a good man. He helped that jerk Carmichael when he needed it, and what does Carmichael do? He stabs your dad in the back. It's not right."

"What's not right?"

Tom and Gwen looked up.

Charlie sauntered in.

Gwen was shocked by his appearance. He had grown considerably over the past year and seemed to have acquired a cocky swagger. His eyes, however, had a distant, guarded look.

"It's not right your dad should be in jail while criminals like Mr. Carmichael and Jimmy Houlihan go free!" Gwen crossed her arms and glared at her cousin.

Charlie stood silent for a moment, his eyes hooded. He slowly grinned, but his serious tone belied his expression. "Now, now, Gwen. I wouldn't go accusing people of stuff you can't prove. Especially people like Jimmy and Mr. Carmichael. Bad things happen to people that start mouthin' off like that."

Gwen stared at him in angry disbelief. "You think your dad should be in jail? You think he actually organized that jewelry store robbery?"

Charlie looked away quickly then shrugged. "That's what Mr. Carmichael said. He even found the jewelry in Dad's safe at the warehouse. The two guys the cops nabbed for robbing the store identified Dad as the one who organized the heist. Claimed they'd done a few other jobs for him in the past." He narrowed his eyes warningly. "Like I said, there's nuthin' you can do about it, so keep your nose out of business that don't concern you. This ain't some stupid kids' game. You could get seriously hurt if you start messin' around where you don't belong. *Do you understand me?"*

Gwen and Tom exchanged shocked glances then nodded meekly. Gwen had never seen Charlie like this and he scared her. He was so unlike the happy-go-lucky Charlie of just a year ago. Charlie glared at them for a few seconds longer then turned on his heel and stalked out. Gwen stared after him, trying to understand what was going on.

Tom sighed. He looked down at the checker in his hand. "Charlie used to be lots of fun. Now he's a real wet blanket."

Gwen could only agree.

Several days later, as Gwen and Tom sat dejectedly on the veranda watching the sunset, a large, bright yellow car pulled up. They stared in open-mouthed admiration. It was a real beauty–a Stutz-Bearcat. Louisa had shown Gwen a picture of one in one of her magazines, bragging about the one Bertie had bought. The Stutz was a beautiful automobile with its sleek black fenders and gleaming chrome details. Gwen and Tom hurried down to get a closer look but stumbled to a halt. The driver's door opened and out swaggered Bertie Carmichael. Swathed in a luxurious raccoon coat, he smirked at the two children as they gaped at him.

"Hey, squirt." He strolled over toward Tom. "Where's your sister? Louisa 'n me are going out on the town tonight." He gave them a wink as he pulled a small silver flask from his voluminous pocket, unscrewed the top and took a long swig. He closed his eyes for a moment then smacked his lips as he slipped the flask back into his pocket. He grinned.

They all turned as the front door opened, and Louisa appeared skipping lightly down the veranda steps. She wore a short, drop-waist skirt with long strings of beads draped around her slender neck. Her short hair was covered by a stylish hat and her shoulders draped with a colorful cashmere wrap. Gwen was amazed by her cousin's transformation. She'd seen pictures of stylish women in magazines called flappers and, obviously, Louisa had worked hard to achieve the look.

"Bertie, baby!" Louisa squealed, dancing up to him and throwing her arms around his neck.

Gwen looked at Tom who silently glared at the couple with a look of disgust as they kissed.

"Boy oh boy, baby." Bertie stepped back to admire her.

Smiling, Louisa pirouetted, showing him her new outfit.

"You are one hot tomato!"

Louisa giggled as she pulled out a small compact from her bag and powdered her nose, all the while glancing at Bertie to make sure he was watching. "Where we going, Bertie?" She put her compact away.

"You're not going anywhere," growled a voice from the veranda. "Not with him, anyway." They all turned. Charlie glowered down at them.

Louisa, hands on her hips, glared at her brother. "Charlie Andersson! Who are you to tell me where I can go? You're not my father. I can do whatever I want."

Charlie descended a few steps which brought him face to face with his sister. "Louisa, you don't know anything about this creep. You just see his money and his fast car. You can't see he's not good enough for you. He's nothin' but a small-town thug, and his dad is even worse."

"Hey," Bertie's face grew red, "Just watch who you're calling names, Andersson. I don't see you turning down the money my dad pays you for running his 'errands.' Seems to me, that makes you a small-time thug like the rest of us. You better watch it, or you'll end up in the slammer with your old man." He laughed, turning back to Louisa.

Charlie wasn't finished. He grabbed Bertie's arm and spun him back around to bring them face to face. "Listen to me, you little punk. You get away from my sister and leave her alone. I know your old man had something to do with my dad gettin' arrested, and one day I'll prove it. Unlike you, I'm not stupid."

"Ha," Bertie sneered. "You coulda fooled me. You don't have the slightest idea of what you're dealin' with, Charlie, and if you're as smart as you say you are, then you'd know that. This ain't some small-town operation. Lots of big, important people are involved with this, and my dad's in charge of it all. Louisa couldn't do better'n me even if she went out with the King of England."

Louisa gazed at Bertie with big adoring eyes. It was obvious nothing Charlie could say would convince his sister to stay away from Bertie. Gwen was disgusted.

Bertie looked at the handsome façade of the Andersson house. "And one of these days, *this* will be our castle."

With a snarl, Charlie hurled himself at Bertie, slamming him down to the ground.

"Charlie! No!" Louisa tried to pull her brother off Bertie, but Charlie was unstoppable and pummeled Bertie into the ground.

Open mouthed, Gwen gaped as the two young men fought. The violence scared her and she wanted them to stop. Though she didn't blame Charlie one bit. Louisa acted like a spoiled brat, and Bertie was as creepy as his father. He deserved a good punch in the mouth.

"Charlie Andersson!"

Gwen turned.

Aunt Katherine hurried down the steps, her face white. "You stop that right now!" Joining Louisa, the two of them were finally able to drag Charlie off Bertie.

"You won't ever have this house, you little weasel!" Charlie struggled against his sister and mother. "Haven't you taken enough from us?"

"Charlie!" Aunt Katherine gave him a furious shake. "Stop it! What's wrong with you?"

Charlie, breathing heavily, stopped struggling and glared at Bertie as Louisa helped her beau to his feet.

Bertie's nose was bloodied, and he'd probably have a real shiner. Louisa cooed and comforted Bertie as she helped him brush off his coat and wiped the dirt and blood from his face with her handkerchief.

Charlie furiously shook his mother's hand from his

shoulder and stalked off down the road toward town.

His mother took a step after her son then stopped. Her shoulders slumped in defeat. She turned back to Bertie. "Are you all right, Bertie?"

Her aunt had never sounded so tired.

"No, I'm not," whined Bertie. "Look at me. I'm a mess. Do you have any idea how much this coat cost? He could have ruined it!"

Aunt Katherine sighed. "Come on in the house and let's get you cleaned up. I'm sure with a good brushing your coat will be as good as new."

Grudgingly, Bertie allowed the two women to lead him inside to get cleaned up.

"Wow," Tom looked down the road where his brother had gone. "I've never seen Charlie that mad. I thought he was gonna take Bertie's head right off!"

"He deserved it, too. What a jerk. But Tom, did you hear what Charlie said?" Gwen grabbed her cousin's arm. "He said he was sure Mr. Carmichael had something to do with your dad's arrest! He doesn't really think your dad is guilty. Maybe I should tell him about what I heard in the cave."

Tom shrugged and sat down on the step. "A fat lot of good that'll do. Why would they believe him any more than us?"

Gwen sat down beside him and rested her head on her knees. How could they ever prove Uncle Jonas was innocent?

A short while later the door opened again, and out strutted Bertie, much restored if somewhat battered.

Louisa hung on his arm and gushed about how brave he had been. "Are you sure you're okay, sweetie? I can't believe Charlie would attack you like that."

Bertie straightened his tie and adjusted his hat. "Yeah, baby, he never woulda taken me down like that in a fair fight. I know boxing y'know. Well, he's just a dumb kid. Gotta expect that kinda thing. Glad you're not like that, gorgeous."

Louisa giggled. "Certainly not! So, Bertie, where did you say we were goin' tonight? Some place good?"

Bertie smirked.

Gwen rolled her eyes. *Really, what a jerk.*

"That new joint Jimmy just opened in the fish market." Bertie opened the car door for her. "They only let the best in there and, baby, you're the best."

Louisa laughed as Bertie climbed into the driver's seat and, with a roar and a cloud of dust, they were gone.

"I think I'm gonna be sick." Tom watched them go. "What she sees in that dope is beyond me. If Pop were still here, she wouldn't dare go out lookin' like that."

Gwen suppressed a giggle, wondering what Tom would think of the skimpy outfits and weird hairstyles some of the girls she knew wore on a daily basis. Suddenly her eyes went wide as a thought hit her. "Tom," she stared down the road, "wasn't Bertie wearing a raccoon coat?"

Tom picked up a pebble and threw it across the drive. "Yeah. Isn't that the ugliest thing you ever saw?

He thinks he's some kinda smooth sheik, but if you ask me, he's all wet."

Gwen nodded, but her thoughts were elsewhere. So Bertie had a raccoon coat. He also had a flask. He drank out of it. Her mind now flashed back to the carriage house and the coat they pulled out of the wardrobe; the one with the bullet in the lining. There had been a flask in the pocket of that coat, hadn't there? Could that have been Bertie's coat? There had been some piece of newsprint in there as well. Her father hadn't looked at it, just stuck it back in the pocket when he hung the coat back up in the wardrobe. Now she wished she'd taken a look at it. Maybe it was important.

I wonder if I could somehow prevent Charlie from working for Jimmy Houlihan if that would change history? She paused as she considered this. Maybe he didn't have to die. Then she sighed and shook her head. What would happen to the future? She'd read too many books about time travel to not realize changing something in the past could possibly have serious effects in her own time. What if her parents never met? Would she suddenly disappear? All this made her head ache again. She rubbed her eyes.

"You okay?" Tom looked at her with concern. "Your head hurt? Should I call Ma?"

"No, I'm fine. Just thinking too hard." Gwen was so frustrated of not being able to share her thoughts with Tom, but if she tried to explain she was really from the future, they'd have Dr. Knowlton here in a flash and probably lock her up in the local loony bin.

She glanced over a Tom. "Do you think Bertie will want to marry Louisa?" She had no idea what put that thought in her mind, but she knew the house would eventually end up in the Carmichael family.

Tom scowled and shrugged, pitching more stones. "Beats me, but I wouldn't be surprised. She's really sweet on him, and he doesn't seem to have any trouble gettin' money."

Gwen nodded. Louisa was, without a doubt, a true gold digger.

Tom pitched another rock, grunting with the effort. "Bertie's always comin' around with new clothes or that fancy car of his, flashin' cash. Course, that's to be expected if he's working for Jimmy the Blade." He paused. "I bet if he asked Louisa, she'd say yes." He shook his head in disgust. "She's such a dumb Dora."

Gwen glanced at him, smiling slightly. Some of these '20's expressions sounded so funny.

Later that evening George Carmichael came over, supposedly to talk to Aunt Katherine about the business. As he entered, he seemed to be evaluating the house like a prospective buyer. When his eyes fell on her, Gwen stared back, refusing to look away, but then a chill down ran her spine as a slow, knowing smile spread across his face. Did he realize she'd finally remembered what happened last year?

Gwen fought back an overwhelming urge to go punch him in his fat, self-satisfied face, just as Charlie had done to Bertie. She turned away and stomped around to the back side of the veranda.

Tom joined her a short while later, his face clouded with anger. "Who does he think he is?" He paced across the veranda, unable to keep still.

Gwen's eyes widened.

Tom barely even noticed her. "He wants Ma to sell him this house. Says she can't afford it no more, what with Pop in prison. Says he'd be doing her a *great service.*" He spat this last out in a mocking imitation of Mr. Carmichael. "Great service, my foot. He knows this is one of the best houses in town, and he's too cheap to build his own, especially if he thinks he can get this one for next to nuthin."

"Not to mention it's a perfect location for his smuggling operation." Gwen shook her head.

Tom collapsed on the step next to her and buried his face in his hands. "Ah, jeez, I didn't even think of that. He'll never let up now."

"What did your mother say?"

"She said no. Said Pop built this house, and it's his pride and joy, and she's gonna do everything she can to hold onto it. But, Gwen, if there's not enough money comin' in, you know she'll have to sell it in the end." Tom pulled off his glasses and rubbed his eyes.

"He'll make sure she has no choice to but to sell it to him." Gwen knew Carmichael got it eventually, and knowing there wasn't any way to stop him made it even worse. "I guess that's what Bertie meant when he said this was going to be his castle."

The two sat in a gloomy silence, listening to the roar of the ocean and chirping of crickets.

It was a cool night, but Gwen didn't want to go back in as long as Carmichael was still there. At long last, Aunt Katherine's voice neared the front door as she escorted her husband's business partner out. Quickly, they rose to their feet, tiptoed toward the front of the house and melted into the shadows where they could watch.

"Good night, George," Katherine said coldly. "I'll be sure and give your proposal serious consideration. Thank you so much for coming by." With that, she all but slammed the door shut in his face.

Gwen took great satisfaction as she listened to Carmichael curse softly in the dark. Next to her, Tom bit back a laugh.

Carmichael froze and turned back toward the veranda. "I know you kids are there. You listen and listen good. Your ma is making a big mistake not taking me up on my offer. She can't afford this house anymore and will be out on the streets without a penny to her name when the bank takes it. I suggest you two help her see reason before it's too late."

Gwen's anger flared. Enough was enough. Eyes flashing, Gwen marched out into the light. "Mr. Carmichael, you don't deserve this house." Her fists were clenched at her side. "It's all your fault Aunt Katherine doesn't have any money. You made sure Uncle Jonas ended up in jail so you could use this place for all your smuggling."

"Gwen!" Tom scrambled to stand by her side. "Yeah. You're probably stealing all the money from the business, too."

Carmichael stared in surprise at the two children then threw his head back and laughed. "Oh, boy, you kids are rich. You think you can scare me? The time for that is long past." He took a step toward them, resting his hands on the banister of the veranda steps. His eyes narrowed dangerously. "You kids just keep your nose outta my business, you hear? I get what I want, and you brats aren't gonna get in my way. Right now, every cop in the county jumps when I tell 'em so don't think running to them is gonna make any difference. This is serious business. A lot of money is involved, so just stay out of our way and no one will get hurt." He stepped back with a wolfish grin and tipped his hat to Gwen. He then turned, climbed into his car and, a few minutes later, was gone.

Tom darted down to the drive and flung a rock at the receding taillights.

Gwen shook as she fought back tears of anger. She knew it had been useless, not to mention possibly dangerous, to confront Mr. Carmichael, but she wanted him to know that not everyone was taken in by his act. She suspected Aunt Katherine wasn't blinded either, but her aunt was quickly running out of options.

Over the next couple of weeks, Gwen watched as Aunt Katherine was forced to let go one of the maids and the groundskeeper. Gwen knew soon they'd all be gone, and Aunt Katherine would have no one to help her.

Early one morning, Gwen sat out on the veranda

reading. She looked up as Charlie came trudging up the driveway. He moved like an old man; his shoulders were slumped and every step seemed to be a struggle. "Charlie? Are you okay?"

For a moment she didn't think Charlie was going to reply. He'd hardly said more than a dozen words to any of them since the fight with Bertie. He looked at Gwen now, his sunken eyes reflecting his inner turmoil. He smiled faintly and she could just make out a little of the old Charlie. "Yeah, Gwen, I'm okay. Just another day at work."

"You know, you don't have to work for Jimmy Houlihan." Gwen wanted to reach out to him.

Charlie laughed bitterly. "What choice do I have? No other job is gonna pay me as much. If we don't want to lose the house to that jerk, Carmichael, I've gotta keep working for Jimmy. That's just the way it is."

He turned away and stumbled into the house. Gwen's heart went out to him. He carried the weight of the entire family on his shoulders and in the end he'd pay a heavy price.

CHAPTER SIXTEEN

As the days went by, Gwen fretted she was no closer to finding out what Charlie had done with the money than she'd been from the beginning. She knew he worked for Jimmy Houlihan, but she'd known that from the start. As she pondered the question, it occurred to her no one knew what route Charlie took trying to escape whoever it was Bertie claimed followed them. If she knew that, she could try and retrace his steps and perhaps figure out where he might have stashed the cash.

So, one day when Aunt Katherine was going into town to meet a friend, Gwen asked if she could come, dragging Tom along.

Gwen had been to town a few times with her aunt and always enjoyed the experience. It looked so different from Fishawak eighty years in the future. Downtown was a small but bustling area with a variety of shops, including a hardware store, a mercantile, a barber and other small businesses. The streets were neatly laid out and landscaped with towering oaks. Aunt Katherine dropped them off near the soda shop.

"I'm going to Redmond's." She pointed to a red brick department store down the street. "I'm having lunch with Mrs. Kilroy. I'll pick you up in two hours." Then she was gone.

Before Gwen could say anything, Tom grabbed her

hand and pulled her down the street to where they could see the marina. "Look at all the boats," Tom grinned. He always made Gwen stop at the marina first when they came into town. "You know, most of these bring whiskey down from Canada."

Gwen rolled her eyes. "Yes, I know." He told her this every time.

Tom made a low whistling sound. He grabbed Gwen's arm and pointed. "Look! That's one of them bullet boats!" He hurried closer to the pier. "Those are so fast even the Coast Guard cutters can't catch them. I bet they belong to Jimmy the Blade."

Gwen had to admit the sleek boats did look fast. She imagined they'd be a lot of fun to ride across the harbor, zipping across the waves, but that was assuming, of course, the Coast Guard wasn't on your tail shooting at you.

"Okay, now exactly *why* are we here?" Tom turned away from the boats. Gwen had dragged him away from the model boat he'd been working on, and he'd complained all the way to town.

Gwen was at something of a loss to explain what she wanted to do, so she improvised. "Do you know of any place Charlie would go if he wanted to hide from guys chasing him?"

Tom stared at her like she was crazy. "What are you talking about? What guys are chasing Charlie?"

Gwen wanted to scream. How could she explain this? "Okay, let's just say Charlie had a bunch of money he was supposed to deliver to Jimmy the Blade but some other gangsters were chasing him, so he needed to hide the money. Where would he go do you think?"

Tom just shook his head and jammed his hands into his pockets. "I have *no* idea what you're talkin' about. How should I know where he'd hide money? Depends on where he was at the time. I mean, there are tons of places he could go–on some boat or under the docks in the marina, under a rock someplace, in a river cave, up in the woods, in some building. I mean, who knows? Charlie knows more hidin' places than anybody else in this whole town."

Gwen's shoulders slumped. He was right. There were any number of places Charlie could have hidden the cash. She gazed around the town, watching the boxy black cars rumbling down the dusty roads and people hurrying down the sidewalks. It was a warm sunny day, and everyone seemed to be out and about. If only she had more information about where Charlie and Bertie had come from and where they were going that fateful night. That would certainly help narrow down things a bit but as they stood now, it was hopeless.

"Come on, Gwen." Tom pulled her by the arm. "Ma gave me a little money. Let's go get some ice cream."

With a sigh, Gwen trailed behind as Tom led the way to the soda shop. Gwen was surprised to find it was actually located inside the local pharmacy. As they stepped inside, it occurred to her how little she had seen of the 1920s world she now inhabited.

The soda fountain was a cheery place with a black

and white tiled floor and tall stools covered with red leather lining the front of the counter. Gwen followed Tom to the counter, winding their way around the small tables with their happy occupants devouring ice cream sundaes and sodas. They soon reached the counter where a young man in a white shirt and hat stood smiling at them, awaiting their orders. As Gwen continued to look around, Tom ordered them two strawberry sundaes.

Taking her sundae and heading to an outside table, Gwen hardly noticed the 1920s fashions any longer–the women with their drop-waist skirts, men with stiff collars, ties and jackets even in the warm summer months and everyone wearing hats. As Gwen examined her reflection in the storefront window, she adjusted her own straw hat decorated with pale blue ribbons that matched her dress. She liked the way it framed her face. With a last look, she thought how cool it would be if everyone still wore hats in her time. People in general were more formal here, both in their dress and how they addressed each other. She wasn't sure that was always a good thing, but it was kind of a nice change from her own more casual time.

They sat at a small table outside the drugstore, watching the people and cars go by. Gwen tried not to gawk when the occasional horse-drawn wagon came along. She didn't know people still used horses for pulling wagons in the '20s.

"Sure is a lot more traffic these days." Tom caught the drips from his spoonful of ice cream.

Gwen almost laughed. They'd spotted maybe ten cars the whole time they'd sat there. Back in D.C., they would see that many every ten seconds. Fishawak was a very quiet town compared to anything Gwen had ever experienced. She'd thought the future Fishawak was dead. "I bet it's even busier in the big cities."

"Yeah, probably. I'm not sure I'd ever wanna see that many automobiles in one place, though. Be pretty scary. Can you imagine tryin' to cross the street with that many cars? You'd get run over for sure." He leaned forward as if to convey some awful secret. "Harry O'Connor was run over by one and *killed* right down there." He pointed a little ways down the street. "Everybody wanted to ban automobiles in town after that happened."

Gwen watched as another uniformly black Model-T chugged by. "I'm guessing that didn't work out."

Tom laughed. "Nah. Once people got used to having cars, they didn't wanna go back to horses and buggies."

The two sat by side in a comfortable silence as they finished their ice cream. It was a lovely day. Gwen was both happy and a tad homesick as she closed her eyes and basked in the warm spring sun. She hoped that she was right and little or no time was passing back home so her family wouldn't know she was gone, but she couldn't help but miss them.

When she opened her eyes a few minutes later, Tom stared fixedly at the pedestrians across the street. "What's up?" She tried to figure out what Tom was watching so intently.

"See that tall guy with the straw hat?" Tom pointed. "The one in the gray jacket?"

Gwen followed his gaze then nodded. "Yeah, so?"

"He's one of the goons I saw outside the cave that night."

Gwen now sat up, alert and interested. Yes, she saw the man strolling along the sidewalk as if he didn't have a care in the world. He'd shown no interest in either of them, assuming of course he'd even noticed a couple of kids outside an ice cream parlor.

"I'm amazed he managed to get through the passageway into the cave." Gwen continued to watch him.

Tom chuckled then stood up. "Come on."

"Where are we going?"

Tom turned to her, his eyes bright with excitement. "We're gonna follow him!"

Gwen hesitated then rose to her feet. She looked around as she questioned the wisdom of this course of action but, at the same time, if they followed this guy maybe they could discover the gangster's headquarters. Maybe then she could figure out where Charlie had gone that night.

The two children stayed on their side of the street, mirroring the man's movements. He seemed to be in no hurry. Every now and then he stopped in some shop along the way, talked to the proprietor for a few minutes and then strolled on. Gwen watched the butcher come out of his shop after such an encounter and stare after the man, his cleaver shaking in a tightly clenched fist. For a moment, Gwen worried he might throw it at the thug's back, but then the man seemed to shrink and slowly made his way back into his shop.

Tom stopped to watch the butcher return to his shop. "I bet he's shaking them down."

"Doing what?"

"If he works for Jimmy Houlihan, he'll tell shopkeepers that something bad might happen to them or their shop if they don't pay Jimmy to 'protect' them."

Gwen turned to him in astonishment. "Really? Do they actually pay him? What happens if they don't?"

Tom shrugged. "Charlie told me that at first people wouldn't pay. Then shops would mysteriously catch on fire or deliveries would be ruined or lost. Old Mr. Carson, who ran a tobacco shop on Main Street, 'accidently' fell down some stairs after he said he'd never give money to crooks like Jimmy the Blade. Now everybody pays."

Gwen just shook her head. At twelve, she was fully aware of the wars, terrorist attacks and senseless violence that made up the nightly news in her world, but she figured that was just part of living in the twenty-first century. She'd always believed life was safer in earlier times. Sure, there were gangsters here, but somehow she hadn't pictured them as being as horrible as the bad guys in her time. Obviously, she was wrong.

They followed the man down the street and watched as he continued to extort money from innocent shopkeepers. Gwen's jaw tightened. There was nothing she could do to stop this, especially if the police were all in Jimmy's pocket. Whistling, the man turned down another street and continued on his way.

"He's heading toward the river where Pop's warehouse is," said Tom as they crossed the street, trying not to let the man see them.

Gwen thought hard. "Well, if Mr. Carmichael is running things, then the warehouse might be where they meet."

Tom nodded. "That makes sense."

Gwen continued to think. Where did the money Charlie have come from? Was it money they collected from the shopkeepers for "protection"? Was it money from liquor sales? Was he taking it to or from the warehouse? There were just so many questions.

"Do you know where Jimmy Houlihan is?" She turned to glance at Tom. "I mean, does he have secret headquarters or something?"

Tom laughed. "Not so secret. He owns a fancy restaurant about a mile from here. Everyone knows that's where to find him." He looked around to make sure no one was listening. "They say it's really a speakeasy."

Gwen frowned. It took her a minute to remember a speakeasy was like a secret bar where people could buy illegal liquor. Okay, so did Charlie take money from Uncle Jonas' warehouse to Jimmy's restaurant? Or did he take money from someplace else back to either the warehouse or the restaurant? The familiar rush of frustration swept through Gwen. This was so important, but impossible to find out since it hadn't happened yet. Well, maybe they'd just have to trace possible routes to see what places might be available for Charlie to hide the money.

"Hold up!" hissed Tom, grabbing her arm. Gwen had been so deep in her thoughts she hadn't paid attention to where they were. "We're here."

The man continued his leisurely pace as he crossed the road and headed to the warehouse at the end of the road. The words "Andersson and Carmichael Imports" was stenciled across the top of the building.

A short while later, the man and Mr. Carmichael came out and shook hands. The man got into a car waiting nearby and drove off. Mr. Carmichael went back inside.

"Well, that didn't help." Tom scowled as the car disappeared. "All we know for sure is he works for Mr. Carmichael, and we already figured that."

Gwen ignored her cousin's complaint. She turned her head and surveyed the area. She tried to picture routes Charlie might have traveled.

"If someone was going to take money from here to Jimmy Houlihan's restaurant, which way do you think they'd go?"

Tom rolled his eyes. "I don't understand why you're so stuck on this."

"Tom, please. I know it sounds crazy, but I have to know. If Charlie were taking money from here to the restaurant, how do you think he'd go?"

With a dramatic sigh, Tom turned. "Okay, I think

he'd go down Miller Street here where we are. It's a straight shot to McGrath where you'd turn left. The restaurant is down McGrath. Take you about thirty minutes to walk there from here."

"Okay. Now say someone was chasing him, how do you think he'd go?"

"Gwen!" Tom threw up his hands. "Who knows? He might run down the alleys to the river. He might run down one of the other roads or go into the woods. How many of these imaginary gangsters are we talking about? Do they have him surrounded? Do they have guns? Can they swim? This is so stupid."

"Okay, okay. I'm sorry. I'm just trying to figure out something."

"Yeah?" Tom eyed her suspiciously. "Like what?"

"I…I can't tell you." Gwen looked away.

Tom groaned again. "All right, let's scram. There's nothin' goin' on here, and I don't want creepy Carmichael to spot us. Besides, Ma's probably lookin' for us. It's gettin' late."

Gwen tried to memorize the area as they walked back to the soda shop. She hadn't been in this area in her own time so wasn't sure how much it had changed, but she had a feeling that if he'd hidden the money, Charlie would have done it somewhere along this route. A heavy weight settled in her chest as she thought about his ghost waiting for someone to prove his innocence. If only he could tell her what he'd done with the money. She wondered if he could. He'd only spoken a couple of words to her thus far. Well, she'd figure this out one way or another. She just couldn't let Charlie down.

CHAPTER SEVENTEEN

The following week, William came home to visit. When Aunt Katherine drove up in the family car, Gwen and her cousins came out to the veranda to greet him. His lips pressed tightly together, William smiled at his family as he climbed out of the car. This was the first time Gwen had actually met her oldest cousin. She was curious to see how he differed from his siblings. William was tall and thin, and Gwen was startled to see he strongly resembled her father with his sandy brown hair, aquiline nose and square jaw. It took her a moment to remember this good-looking young man was actually her great-grandfather. Unlike the other Andersson children, William was very serious and formal.

"Hello, Charles." William shook his brother's hand. "Good to see you, Thomas." He placed his hand on Tom's head, ruffling the boy's already unruly hair. He then proceeded to briefly hug Louisa and patted Gwen on the shoulder. "It's good to be home."

Tom and Gwen watched the others as they filed into the house. "Now remember," whispered Tom. "Ma says we're not to say anything to William about the house or anything. She's worried he'll drop outta school, and she wants him to finish more'n anything."

"I know." This must have been at least the tenth time Tom had given her this exact same warning in the past hour. In the end, it didn't really matter since neither of them saw William for the rest of the afternoon.

That night at dinner, Gwen immediately noticed the tension within the family. Charlie looked sullen, William kept glaring at his brother and their mother appeared close to tears. Finally, William slammed down his glass and glared his mother. "Mother, can you please explain to me why you allow young Charles to fraternize with known criminals? I know things are not right here since Father went to prison, but you refuse to talk to me. I am a grown man, and I have a right to know what is going on."

Gwen suddenly wished she was somewhere else.

Aunt Katherine's face went white, her lips pressed into a thin line. "There is nothing you can do, William. Right now, the most important thing is for you to finish your studies and become a physician. As for Charlie, he…" she hesitated, "he works for your father's business partner."

"George Carmichael," William spat. "A well-known associate of that gangster Jimmy Houlihan. Father would *not* approve. Charlie is just a boy and has no business associating with such scum. Do you want him to end up in prison too?"

"What d'you know about it?" snarled Charlie in a low, angry voice. "You're down there safe and sound at Harvard while we're trying to keep a roof over our heads." There was obvious resentment in Charlie's words.

"Charlie!" cried Aunt Katherine in dismay, her eyes

wide.

"No, Ma!" Charlie leaped to his feet. "It's time Mr. High and Mighty knew what's goin' on here." He now turned on his brother. "We've hardly got any money, and we're gonna lose the house. Business is way down since Pop got arrested, and that means we need more cash. Mr. Carmichael might be a slimy snake in cahoots with Jimmy Houlihan, but he's got money, and we need it. What d'you want me to do? Sure, I could sell papers or be a soda jerk but that ain't gonna pay the mortgage or for your fancy school. I'm doin' the only thing I can!"

William's face reddened and eyes were ablaze as he leapt to his feet. .

"How dare you speak to me like that! There is no excuse for consorting with known criminals."

"Yeah, well, tell that to Louisa. She plans on marryin' one. If that's not *consorting,* I don't know what is."

Tom's hand reached for Gwen's under the table. He was trembling

William turned to stare at his sister, frowning in confusion. "Louisa?"

Louisa stared back, refusing to look away. "Bertie Carmichael asked me to marry him, and I said yes. I'm not going to find myself living on the streets or working in a shop just to pay the rent on some dumpy apartment. If I marry Bertie, I can live like a queen."

"Oh, Louisa." Aunt Katherine groaned and buried her face in her hands.

Louisa lifted her chin higher and said nothing.

Open mouthed, Gwen gaped at her cousin. Surely, Louisa would have more sense than to marry Bertie.

Tom's hand gripped hers even harder.

William shook his head in disgust then turned to his mother. "Well, you don't have to worry about my schooling." He glanced at his brother. "I have applied for and won a scholarship that should see me through this coming year. I will get a job on campus and send you what I can, but we must find an honest job for Charles. Ideally, he should return to school in the fall. His education is of the utmost importance."

"I'm not goin' back to school. I'll just be wastin' my time. I need to make some real money, and as long as I work for Mr. Carmichael, we'll do all right."

"Fine. Don't finish school." William resumed his seat, but his face was set. "You cannot continue working for Carmichael. What would happen to Mother if you ended up in prison, or worse? She needs help, Charles, and while Father and I are gone, that makes you the man of the house." He picked up his fork and regarded Charlie with narrowed eyes. "I will make some inquiries tomorrow and try to find you a suitable position. An *honest* position."

Charlie stood stiffly for a few more moments before slumping back into his own seat. "Fine. Whatever you say. You're the boss."

William nodded. Did he purposefully ignore Charlie's sarcasm or did he simply not hear it. William peered down his nose at Louisa. "Now, what is this about you and Bertie? I assume you have not spoken to

Mother or Father to obtain their permission?"

Gwen blinked as she suddenly thought back to her father's description of his grandfather. If this was how he was as a young man, she could see why no one could stand to be around him as an old one. Talk about pompous and obnoxious. She glanced at Tom who looked close to tears. He met her gaze and when Gwen rolled her eyes at William's snooty tone, he gave her a half-hearted smile.

Louisa's cold voice brought them back. "Oh, William, please." Louisa glared at her brother, her eyes hard. "What do you care who I marry? Bertie's got money, and he's going to take over the business one day. We'll be rich. Besides, I'm old enough to decide who I want to marry. I don't need my older brother telling me I need to get permission."

"Father would *not* approve!" snapped William. "I have no doubt the man is a common crook, given who his father is."

"Children, please." Katherine's eyes shone bright with unshed tears. "Louisa," she turned wearily to her petulant daughter. "I will speak to your father about this when I visit next week. I will not have you marrying without his permission."

Louisa rose to her feet, her face dark. "You can't stop me, Mother. I'm old enough to marry without my parents' permission. If I want to marry Bertie Carmichael, I will, no matter what you or Father say." Then with an angry toss of her head, she stalked from the room, leaving a shocked silence behind her.

Gwen's heart broke at the look of despair on her aunt's pale face. William now ignored the others and went about finishing his meal with a kind of grim determination, shoveling in one bite after another. Charlie sat white-faced and glared at his brother.

There was a tug at Gwen's arm. Tom nodded his head toward the door. Without a word, the two slipped from the table and hurried outside.

Gwen's body began to relax once she was out of the house. She hadn't realized how tense she had become. Her head now throbbed and exhaustion threatened to overwhelm her. She sank down onto one of the chairs on the veranda. "Oh, Tom," she whispered, her voice breaking, "That was horrible."

Tom sat down beside her, his face pale and unsmiling. "I've never seen any of them act like that before, Gwen," he said in a small voice.

Gwen glanced at him and suddenly saw him as the young boy he was.

"Everything is falling apart."

Gwen nodded. What could they do?

A few moments later, Charlie stomped out. He looked back toward the house. "If William thinks he can tell me what to do, he's dumber than I thought." Now he looked at Tom and Gwen. "Oh, I'll take whatever so-called honest job he gets me, but there's no way I'm giving up working for Carmichael." He shrugged on a jacket and strode angrily down the drive toward town.

Tom and Gwen exchanged looks and sighed. If only Uncle Jonas were here.

CHAPTER EIGHTEEN

Gwen didn't think January in Maine could possibly be chillier than the atmosphere in the Andersson home during the two weeks William was home. No one spoke to anyone else except when absolutely necessary. When they did, it was in cold, impersonal tones. Aunt Katherine had taken to her rooms, and when they saw her, she looked so pale and drawn, Gwen was sure she was physically ill.

"I wonder if we should tell William to call Dr. Knowlton," she said to Tom one afternoon.

William tried, but Katherine wouldn't see the doctor. She assured them she was well.

Charlie was rarely home. William had secured a job for him in the local hardware store and, true to his word, Charlie went there every day, but Gwen was sure once William left, Charlie would resume his job with Carmichael.

Louisa was like an ice queen. She ignored everyone but Bertie and insisted she was going to marry him no matter what.

Bertie didn't look quite as excited about this as Louisa. However, he did agree they'd be married perhaps around Christmas, as long as it was acceptable to his father.

Gwen and Tom wandered through the house like two lost souls and kept each other company when no one else seemed to notice they were alive. Then Tom fell ill with the measles and sent the family into even further turmoil.

Gwen was bewildered by the concern and worry. Measles in her time was a relatively rare illness since a vaccine was available and, like so many who'd grown up without such diseases, was unaware as to how serious they could be.

Aunt Katherine was roused from her lethargy to spring into action as nurse for her youngest son. Gwen stood anxiously outside Tom's bedroom door waiting for Aunt Katherine and Dr. Knowlton to come out. When they did, they both looked very worried.

"Keep the curtains drawn, Mrs. Andersson, and get him to take as many fluids as you can." Dr. Knowlton paused as his eyes settled on Gwen. He frowned. "You must send Miss Gwen someplace safe. With her delicate constitution, such a serious illness could be devastating."

Gwen interpreted that to mean if she got it, it could kill her. She wasn't actually sure she'd been vaccinated against the disease. She knew her parents had been leery of vaccinations when she was a baby so, as far as Gwen knew, she still might be able to catch the measles.

Katherine wrinkled her brow. "I could send her to my brother's in town."

Gwen turned to look at Katherine. She didn't know her aunt had a brother.

"His wife doesn't care much for children, but I'm sure under the circumstances she'd allow Gwen to come."

Dr. Knowlton nodded. "Good. Then do it immediately. It may already be too late, but perhaps we'll be lucky and she'll avoid infection." He took a few minutes and peered closely at Gwen as he looked for any signs of the measles infection.

Gwen felt a small twinge of fear.

"So far, she appears well, so the sooner she leaves the better."

Aunt Katherine told Gwen to go pack her things while she called her brother.

As Gwen decided what to take, Charlie slipped into her room. Gwen looked up as Charlie closed the door quietly behind him.

"Gwen," he glanced round as if someone might be lurking in the shadows. "Can you keep a secret?"

"Sure. I guess."

Charlie nodded then leaned forward, his words coming out fast and urgent. "OK, listen. I heard you're going to Uncle Frank's. I don't know if you know this, but he works for Pop and Mr. Carmichael. He's the firm accountant. You know what that is?"

"The guy who keeps track of the money."

"Right." Charlie licked his lips. "I haven't said a word of this to anyone, but you might be able to help. I *know* Carmichael had somethin' to do with Pop getting framed for that jewelry heist, and I'm pretty sure he's been stealin' from the company. That's why there's so little money." He paused and gave a cynical laugh. "Although I don't see the Carmichaels hurtin' any.

Anyway, to do that, Carmichael's gotta have Uncle Frank's help since he's the one keepin' track of the dough. Uncle Frank's basically an okay guy but weak, and his wife is a lot like Louisa–always wantin' more and more. I wouldn't be surprised if Aunt Ada is the one who convinced Uncle Frank to work with Carmichael."

Gwen frowned as she considered this. "So you think Uncle Frank is helping Mr. Carmichael steal money from the company, and you want me to keep my eyes and ears open to see if I can get any proof?"

Charlie smiled. "Yeah, that's it. I didn't wanna involve you or Tom in this, but you'll be in a perfect position to keep an eye on Uncle Frank." He put his hand on her arm. "But listen, don't *do* anything. Don't let them know you're watching. I don't want you gettin' hurt or anything. You understand? Just watch and listen."

Gwen nodded. "Okay. I can do that. If it helps prove Uncle Jonas is innocent, I'm in." She would have said more, Aunt Katherine's footsteps approached. When the door opened, Gwen quickly pulled some clothes out of her dresser.

Charlie sat on the chair in the corner and explained how Gwen should behave at the home of their aunt and uncle. "…and don't sit on any of the furniture in the parlor."

Katherine entered.

"Aunt Ada doesn't like people to sit on her furniture. They might get it dirty. Don't talk to the maids. Aunt Ada thinks they're beneath us so we shouldn't even acknowledge them. You have to wear your best clothes to dinner and don't speak unless spoken to…"

"Charlie!" Aunt Katherine put her hands on her hips. "What on earth are you telling Gwen?"

Charlie shrugged. "I'm just warnin' her. Remember, Ma, I spent a couple of weeks there when Gwen had scarlet fever. I'm tryin' to make it easier for her. You know, get her started right. You gotta admit, Aunt Ada isn't the easiest person to live with."

His mother was about to protest further, when she gave a little laugh and, with a shake of her head, went to help Gwen. "I'll admit, Charlie, you do have a point. Aunt Ada can be a bit challenging, but Gwen is a different kettle of fish compared to you. I'm sure she'll get along much better with Ada than you did. I doubt it would even occur to Gwen to shave the cat or see how far a person can get around the house without ever touching the floor. I think it took Ada weeks to get all the footprints off the walls and furniture."

Charlie just grinned and stood up. "Well, Gwen, don't say I didn't warn you. Good luck." Laughing, he walked out of the room while Gwen and her aunt finished packing.

"Is she really that bad?" Gwen fidgeted with the lace on her dress. She sat beside her aunt as they drove into town. This was the first time Gwen had left the house for any length of time, and she was apprehensive. As long as she was in the old house, she felt there was always the chance of getting home through the closet.

After all, it happened once before, but what if she couldn't get back to the house? Would she be trapped here forever? Was there some kind of time limit? Would leaving the house for an extended period change anything? She had no idea, and it worried her.

This Aunt Ada person sounded pretty horrible. Gwen had adapted to life with Tom and his family, but how would she fare living with someone else. People who knew nothing about her. She tugged harder on the lace.

Aunt Katherine glanced down at her niece. "Just be on your best behavior and don't touch anything. Please don't mention your Uncle Jonas to her. She refuses to believe there's the slightest possibility he could be innocent. Only say cheerful things to her. She won't stand for any depressing thoughts unless they come from her." Katherine sighed again. "Well, just do the best you can. It's only for a couple of weeks. You'll be fine."

Gwen looked out the window, her stomach tightening into a knot. Aunt Katherine was hardly encouraging. Then she thought about her mission and some of the tension eased into excitement. Maybe she could discover something to help Uncle Jonas. That provided her with some measure of comfort, at any rate. Just as long as she didn't have to stay for too long; she'd feel a lot better once she was back at the house.

The Callahan home was another large, ornate Victorian even larger than the Anderssons' and certainly nicer than any of the homes around it. The yard and elaborate landscaping had been immaculately trimmed. It was beautiful and, to Gwen, looked more like a park than someone's front yard.

When they pulled up to the front of the house, a butler hurried out to open the car door. Gwen glanced at her aunt, who simply shrugged and gave her a little smile as if to say, "See?" It was obvious Uncle Frank and Aunt Ada liked the finer things in life. The butler took Gwen's small suitcase from the backseat and led them up the stairs of the enormous veranda, through the front door and into the marble tiled foyer.

"Madam is awaiting you in the conservatory." The butler had a distinguished British accent. Gwen was fascinated. It was like being in a movie. He led them farther back into the house until they were in a room entirely encased in glass, similar to a greenhouse. Brightly colored exotic flowers bloomed everywhere. Gwen stared open-mouthed, never having seen such a thing in someone's home.

Gwen swallowed as a tall, thin woman turned to greet them. She had shining platinum blond hair plastered to her skull and was dressed immaculately in a soft blue linen dress. Gwen's stomach clenched again as the small, pale eyes studied her coldly, making Gwen feel like a bug invading this woman's perfect garden.

"Hello, Gwen, dear." The woman's tone was frosty. "I'm so pleased to see you again." Her smile was small and tight, immediately reminding Gwen of the Wicked Witch of the West.

Gwen tried to smile, glancing at Aunt Katherine for

support. "Thank you, Aunt Ada."

Ada stared at her expectantly.

Gwen had the distinct feeling she should curtsey or something, so she awkwardly bent her knees. She felt really stupid. That must have been the worst curtsey in the history of curtsies. Her face burned.

Aunt Ada sniffed in disapproval. "I see, Katherine, this child's education in etiquette and deportment is sadly lacking. Well, never mind. Perhaps we can remedy that while she is here."

Aunt Katherine smiled weakly. "I'm sure she's just nervous, Ada."

"Hmph." Aunt Ada pursed her lips in what Gwen assumed was a smile. Maybe. This was going to be a very long two weeks.

Katherine put her arm around Gwen's shoulders. "Gwen darling, I need to go. Tom needs me. Please be a good girl and do as your aunt and uncle tell you, all right?"

"Yes, Aunt Katherine."

Katherine hugged Gwen tightly for a brief moment, kissed her on the cheek and was gone.

Gwen wished more than anything she was going with her.

"Well," Aunt Ada gave a small shake of her head. "If you must stay here, I will have Mary show you to your room. Dinner is at seven sharp, and I expect you to dress." She paused. "You *do* have some nice frocks with you, do you not?"

"I…I don't know." Gwen's face reddened once

more. She knew she had some dresses, but she had no idea if they would be good enough for Aunt Ada.

Ada pursed her lips and stared down her nose at Gwen. "Well, come along then. I will take you to your room and evaluate your wardrobe. I trust Katherine had enough sense to pack *something* suitable." She turned and led Gwen down the hallway.

"You are not allowed in any of the rooms on this floor except for the kitchen and conservatory. I don't suppose you can get into too much trouble in those rooms." Ada stopped by a small room next to the kitchen and opened the door. It was obviously intended to be a maid's room, but it reminded Gwen unpleasantly of a prison cell. It was very cramped and windowless with just a small cot, a dresser and a bedside table with a small lamp. There wasn't room for anything else. The wooden floor was bare except for a small rag rug.

"This will be your room while you are here," said Ada as if presenting Gwen with a magnificent suite of rooms. "I do not want you wandering around the house. There are a lot of valuable antiques here, and I will not have some irresponsible child dashing about breaking things. I expect you to stay outdoors when the weather is nice and, as I said, you may stay in the kitchen or conservatory when the weather is bad, but please do not bother Cook. Now, let's see what Katherine has packed for you."

Gwen's suitcase was on the bed where the butler must have placed it. Ada quickly opened it. She pulled out Gwen's clothes and dumped them carelessly on the bed or floor after briefly examining each item. Obviously nothing suited her. Gwen knew she shouldn't care what this crazy woman thought, but she hated the way Ada talked about Aunt Katherine.

Ada sighed dramatically and picked up Gwen's best outfit, a navy blue sailor dress. Going over it with a critical eye, Ada finally announced that, for tonight, it would have to do. "Tomorrow, I shall take you to my dressmaker and have a couple of frocks made so you will not embarrass us at dinner. I will send the bill to your aunt, of course."

Gwen swallowed. "But Aunt Katherine can't afford that."

"Well, that's just too bad, isn't it?" Ada glared at her. "Whenever one of you brats gets sick, she expects us to drop everything and take the others in. If we'd wanted children, we would have had them. The least she can do is pay for a couple of suitable dresses. I see no reason why I should allow you to disrupt my routine, and I expect people at my dinner table to be dressed appropriately, not like pauper."

"I...well...I could just eat in the kitchen." This actually sounded like an excellent idea to Gwen.

"And have people say I wouldn't allow my own niece to sit at the table with us?" Ada's eyebrows shot up "I think not!" She put her hands on her hips and stared at her niece. "Mr. Callahan is simply too kindhearted. He should have told Katherine to make space for you in the carriage house. It's summer. You would have been fine, and I told him as much. If he had followed my advice, my schedule would not be thrown into such total disarray."

Gwen's initial fear of this woman faded only to be replaced by anger. What a witch! The way Ada set things up, she wouldn't even see Gwen except at meals and perhaps not even then if they didn't get her some "suitable" dresses. Gwen wondered if Uncle Frank was this big of a snob.

She found out a few hours later when Uncle Frank returned home from work. He was a short, round man with red hair similar to his sister Katherine's. His jowls and droopy eyes reminded Gwen of her old neighbor's basset hound. However, Gwen was relieved to discover that in temperament, he was the complete opposite of his wife. She smiled as she imagined her aunt as of one of those high-strung, yappy poodles.

When he laid eyes on Gwen, he gave her a welcoming smile. "Ah, Gwennie, it's so good to see you. You're looking more and more like your mother every day." His eyes became distant and it took Gwen a moment to remember the other Gwen's mother had been his sister too.

Behind her, Aunt Ada sniffed in disapproval. "Well, I certainly hope she behaves better than that sister of yours. Margaret was a wild troublemaker if ever I saw one."

Uncle Frank just sighed. Obviously, this was an old argument, and Frank wasn't going to get into it. "Ada, my dear," he turned from Gwen. "Gwennie is only here for a couple of weeks until poor little Tommy gets over the measles. It's our Christian duty to care for Gwennie in the meantime so she doesn't get sick. You wouldn't want her ill as well, would you?"

"Why on earth should I care?" Ada stood before the hall mirror and smoothed down her already perfect hair. "If she became ill then we could ship her back to Katherine and get her out of our hair. I have enough to do without worrying about some unruly child." She turned and glared at Gwen.

Gwen's face warmed. This woman got worse every time she opened her mouth. No wonder Charlie had made it his mission to make her life miserable when he'd been here. She smiled at the thought. Gwen suspected that to Ada, having a child in the house was her worst nightmare.

"Ada," Uncle Frank looked at her with a frown. "Surely you don't mean that."

Aunt Ada gave her husband a stiff, chilly smile. "Oh, of course not, dear. You are right. We must do our Christian duty and care for our family, mustn't we?"

Frank smiled happily as if this had resolved the matter.

Gwen sighed. Ada undoubtedly ruled this roost, and Frank just tried to keep the peace.

Dinner was as awful as Gwen imagined it would be. She dressed carefully in her sailor dress, brushed her hair and tied a ribbon around it. Critically eyeing her appearance as best she could in the small dresser mirror, Gwen thought she looked reasonably presentable, or at least as good as it was going to get. With a deep breath, she stepped out of her room and walked down to the dining room. Now she knew how criminals felt on their way to the gallows.

The long cherry dining table dominated the room and could have easily sat a dozen people. Tonight, there were only three. She suddenly pictured her family sitting around this huge table and her throat tightened. *I know I still have to find out what happened to Charlie and that money, but I sure wish I could go home.*

"Here, Gwennie." Uncle Frank pointed to a seat at his end of the table. "Why don't you sit down here by me?" A weight lifted from her shoulders when Gwen saw she wouldn't have to sit near her formidable aunt.

Gwen slipped into her seat. Ada watched with narrowed eyes as if just waiting for Gwen to make a mistake.

Gwen looked at the table and the weight returned. Surrounding her plate were more pieces of silverware than she ever imagined existed. She had absolutely no idea what most of them were for. She glanced again at her aunt, and her stomach clenched at the woman's cold superior smile. *That witch knows I don't know what to do. She hopes I'll fall flat on my face.* Gwen gritted her teeth and studied the silverware again, hoping to find some clue as to what they all were for. It seemed hopeless.

"I hope you're settling in all right, Gwennie," said her uncle as the maid placed bowls of green pea soup before them. He picked up a large spoon and looked at it pointedly.

"Oh yes, sir." Gwen gave her uncle a smile of

gratitude. At least he wasn't being a jerk. She quickly picked up her own soup spoon. "It's been great."

Her uncle winked and began to eat.

Ada looked annoyed.

"Well," Uncle Frank slurped his soup. "Hopefully poor Tom will soon be well and you can return home. Although, it will be nice to have a young person about the house again." He gently shook his head and chuckled. "Your cousin, Charlie, raised quite a ruckus when he was here." He stopped short.

Ada's glare was icy. "That boy is nothing but a young hooligan and practically destroyed this house." Her grating voice quivered. "Considering his father is a convicted felon, I don't wonder his son is running wild. I won't be the least surprised when he follows his father straight into jail."

Gwen dropped her spoon and leaped to her feet. "Charlie is not a hooligan!" She glared at her aunt. "And Uncle Jonas is not a thief!" She was about to say more but quickly bit back her words. She couldn't let Uncle Frank know she suspected he was working with Mr. Carmichael. She'd never find out anything then.

"How dare you speak to me like that!" Ada's eyes flashed with indignation. "You may leave the table and go to your room."

"Ada…" Frank began but retreated back to his soup in the face of her wrath.

Gwen was so angry, she couldn't trust herself to speak and simply turned on her heel and headed for the door. As she left the room, her aunt berated Uncle

Frank, telling him he should have told Katherine they wouldn't take any more of her rude, ungrateful brats. Gwen hurried down the hall and all but ran into her room. She slammed the door to escape the grating sound of that woman's horrible nasally voice. Gwen collapsed on her cot with a sigh and fought back her tears. She was overwhelmed by homesickness and yearned to be back with her own mother and father; people who really knew and loved her. Finally, she gave into her grief as a great sob erupted. She buried her face in her pillow and cried long and hard until there was nothing left.

How am I going to stand living with that horrible witch for two weeks? She turned to her side and stared at the wall. *I promised Charlie I'd help. It might be our only chance to clear Uncle Jonas' name. I just can't let them down.* She took a deep breath and nodded. Charlie depended on her. The heck with Aunt Ada; she wouldn't give up.

CHAPTER NINETEEN

Gwen often wondered what she'd done that was so bad she deserved to be condemned to two weeks with the despicable Aunt Ada. Despite her claims of wanting nothing to do with Gwen, Aunt Ada seemed to make it her mission in life to instruct Gwen on all the rules of etiquette and proper decorum. Yet, as hard as Gwen tried, nothing she did was right. She tried to be patient and, when not being put through her paces by Ada, she kept her eyes open for anything that might provide proof George Carmichael was stealing their money.

Although Mr. Carmichael frequently visited the house, he and Uncle Frank always met behind closed doors, and Aunt Ada felt these were perfect times to teach Gwen the womanly art of flower arranging or how to address formal invitations to a presidential ball. Gwen thought she was going to go insane. She'd been there for a full, frustrating week and thus far had learned absolutely nothing. She was terrified she'd leave without finding anything to help prove what Uncle Frank and Mr. Carmichael were up to. She just couldn't let Charlie down.

The one break in the tedium occurred when Aunt Katherine came by to see her. Katherine gave Gwen a warm hug "Tommy is doing much better. The doctor says his was a relatively mild case, and he should be just fine. I'm thankful Charlie and Louisa have already had them. Oh, and William has returned to Harvard."

"Will I have to stay here much longer?" Gwen knew she needed to find out more information, but she found it more and more difficult to endure Aunt Ada's incessant nagging and criticism.

"At least another week." Katherine showed obvious pity. "Has it really been that awful?"

"Well, would you like me to demonstrate how to curtsey properly to the Duke of York?"

Aunt Katherine laughed and hugged her again. "Oh, darlin', I'm so sorry. Ada really is a piece of work, isn't she? Please be brave just a little while longer." She paused and looked at Gwen with tears in her eyes. "I couldn't bear it if anything happened to you. Margaret and I were very close, and you are all I have left of her. I don't want to take any chances with you catching the measles."

Tears prickled the back of Gwen's eyes as she hugged her aunt. She'd become very close to this woman, and it made Gwen sad to think the day would come when she'd never see her again. "I'll be alright, Aunt Katherine," she sniffed. "It has definitely been interesting. Please tell Tom to get well soon so I can come home."

Aunt Katherine smiled and adjusted her hat as she stood to leave. "I will, sweetheart." She caressed Gwen's cheek. "I know he misses you. He's simply bored to tears and can't wait for you to return. Now, be a good girl, and I expect the next time I see you, you can show me not only the proper curtsey for the Duke of York but how to correctly address a letter to him as well."

Gwen grinned through her tears and waved good-bye as her aunt walked down the steps to the car. The butler opened the car door for her, and then Katherine was gone. Gwen sighed, suddenly depressed and unbearably lonely. Fortunately, Aunt Ada was gone for the day, so Gwen could do as she pleased. Gwen turned and regarded the house for several long moments. Maybe she'd do a little exploring. She wouldn't touch anything, just check things out. She had quickly learned that although the maids feared her aunt, they were more than willing to turn a blind eye to any minor infractions of the rules Gwen might commit.

Gwen quietly entered the house and looked around for Simpson, the butler. He was the one person she had to watch out for. He had no patience with children and would certainly inform her aunt if he caught her snooping around. Today she was just bored. Maybe she could find a book in the library to read. Making sure no one was around, she cautiously tiptoed down the hall and slipped through the door into the library.

It was a marvelous room–full of leather chairs and dark cherry furniture. The walls were lined with floor to ceiling shelves full of all kinds of amazing books. Gwen immediately fell in love with the stately room. She'd never seen Ada in here. Gwen seriously doubted her aunt read anything outside of etiquette books and the social column. With a sigh, she wandered aimlessly through the room, picking up random books, glancing through them then replacing them. She examined the large globe and was interested to see some of the countries looked different from the ones on her dad's back home.

Gwen studied her uncle's desk. It was covered with neat stacks of papers and files. Idly, she sat in the swivel chair and spun around a few times. She then glanced through some of the papers. None of it made any sense to her. The papers appeared to be associated with the company business, but she didn't understand the numbers. She suspected they were important, but, unless she knew how to interpret the information, they were useless to her. She stretched as she stood and resumed wandering. She stood near the tall windows and fingered the blood-red damask draperies, as she absently watched a rabbit hop across the lawn.

With another sigh, she turned and decided that if she wanted a book, she'd better get a move on. Before she could take a step, her uncle's voice sounded just outside the doorway.

"I've got the numbers right here, George."

Gwen's heart leapt into her throat as her eyes darted around searching frantically for a place to hide. Instinctively, she ducked behind the heavy drapes and prayed she was small enough they wouldn't notice her there. No sooner had she hidden then the two men entered the room.

"This is important, Frank." George Carmichael sounded worried. "I'm short two hundred and fifty grand. Houlihan will have my head if I can't come up with the dough and soon."

Gwen heard some papers rustling. "All right, George. Look, I should be able to pull that much from the business. Without Jonas here putting his nose into everything, it's been easy enough to change the numbers. Good thing Katherine doesn't know anything about accounting."

George gave a little laugh. "Well, you're makin' out all right, Frank." He paused a moment. "Don't it bother you, stealing from your sister?"

Frank's laugh was harsh and ugly. "My parents thought the world of her and Margaret. Me? I couldn't do anything right. Oh, sure, they all acted like they cared for me, but from the start, the girls always lorded their rich husbands over me like I was some kind of dumb sap. I showed them. Now I'm richer than either one of them. If Katherine ends up on the street, sure, I'll help her, but I'll make sure she knows who's on top now."

Gwen stuffed her fist into her mouth to keep from crying out. How had she been so fooled by Uncle Frank? She'd thought he was the nice one but, as it turned out, he was as awful as his wife; in fact, worse. He had helped Mr. Carmichael steal the money from the business that was supposed to go to Aunt Katherine.

"I can get you the money by next week." Frank was all business now. "And next time, don't play poker with Houlihan's money. What's the plan?"

"I plan on having Bertie and that idiot, Charlie, take the day's take to Jimmy. I'll have some of my guys ambush 'em and take the money. They're to make sure

Charlie doesn't make it back, and if they fail, I've made sure there's a backup. Then I'll have Bertie tell everyone some guys chased 'em, and when they split up, Charlie never came back. That'll make it look like either Big Billy's boys got him or Charlie took off with the dough. Everyone knows he's a hothead. Either way, I'm in the clear. The money comes back to me, and everything's Jake."

Gwen could hardly breathe as she continued to listen. Carmichael was cold-bloodedly planning Charlie's murder!

"You sure killing Charlie is the only way?" At least Frank had the decency to sound a little unhappy about it. She clenched her teeth tightly to keep from yelling out.

"You know it is."

Frank sighed. "I just don't like the idea of killing a kid, especially my own flesh and blood."

"You got any better ideas? I need that money, and you know it. Charlie would never keep his mouth shut about something like this. He'd love to see Jimmy take me down and, believe me, if I go down, you're comin' with me."

"Well, you've got to get that money back or we could lose the business. We have to make sure Jimmy doesn't come back to you wanting the cash after it disappears."

"If he wants the money, we'll tell Katherine that since it was Charlie who took it, she'd better come up with it." Carmichael paused again. "You know, I might tell her that anyway. I want that house on the bluff, and I'll tell her if she sells it to me along with Jonas' share of the company, then it'll cover the debt owed to Jimmy, which is true. She won't have any choice regardless."

"Sounds like you've got it all planned out." Uncle Frank's chair squeaked. "All right. Let me know the day of the drop, and I'll make sure you have the cash."

George grunted. "I hate usin' real cash but Houlihan has eyes everywhere. If everything ain't kosher, he'll get wind of it. It's all gotta look legit. I gotta admit, Charlie's never let me down on a job, so there's no reason to think he'll screw up this time."

"All right then. That's everything. Here." Papers rustled again. "These are the current figures. Spells it all out. How much liquor has been coming in, where it's been going and how much has sold. Jimmy will want this."

"Great. Well, that's all I need. Walk me out. I wanna talk to you about that new joint Jimmy wants to open."

As soon as the two men left the room, Gwen let her breath out with a soft whoosh. She hadn't even realized she was holding it. She peered out from the curtains, her heart pounding. *I've got to get out of here before Uncle Frank gets back. I can't let him find me or Charlie's dead.* The room was now empty. Tiptoeing across the dark green Persian carpet, she cautiously cracked open the door. The coast was clear. She slipped out and ran as quietly as she could to her room.

Closing the door behind her, she took a deep

breath and collapsed to the floor. Her legs had turned to jelly. Her head spun as she realized the importance of what she'd heard. Uncle Frank and Mr. Carmichael set Charlie up from the start. He was supposed to be killed and the money taken by Carmichael's men. Charlie *was* innocent. What was she going to do? She had to tell Charlie and warn him. She rested her throbbing head against the side of the bed. She suddenly felt so tired it was hard to think. She thought again about what the men had said. It sounded as if it might be a few days before anything happened, so that would give her a chance to get word to Charlie. She rubbed her eyes and shivered.

With a soft moan, she climbed to her feet and flopped down on the bed. *I've got to get a message to Charlie.* She rummaged through her things for some paper then paused. What if Uncle Frank or Mr. Carmichael finds it first? There wasn't any one in this house she could trust to take a deliver a note to her cousin. She frowned. Could she telephone him? Too bad she had no idea what their phone number was, and she didn't think Aunt Ada would let her use the phone anyway. Gwen growled with frustration and began to pace the room. She simply had to get to Charlie and warn him.

At dinner, she picked at her food. She had no appetite and felt thoroughly exhausted. Just lifting her fork was a chore. Her headache was worse than ever, and thoughts whirled as she tried to come up with a plan to warn Charlie. She glanced up and glared at her uncle then ducked her head before he noticed. Now that she knew what Uncle Frank was really up to, she had to be careful not to let her true feelings out. She pushed her potatoes around the plate.

"Gwen?"

"Huh?" Startled, Gwen looked up. Uncle Frank had spoken to her.

"It's not polite to daydream at the table." Ada sipped from her water goblet. "A good guest should always pay attention to what is going on around her at the table."

"Yes, Aunt Ada." Gwen closed her eyes as a shiver ran through her body.

"Gwen," Uncle Frank said again. "Are you not feeling well?"

Gwen blinked at her uncle. "I…I'm fine, sir."

Uncle Frank peered at her closely, leaned over and placed his hand on her forehead. "Ada! This child is burning up. She must have caught the measles after all."

Aunt Ada sighed as she glared at Gwen. "Of course she did. Anything to inconvenience me. Well, we must simply call Katherine and tell her to come fetch the girl. I will not have an invalid in my house. The Ladies' Flower Guild is coming over tomorrow, and all the preparations have been made."

Uncle Frank shook his head and stood. "I'll call Katherine now and let her know I'm bringing Gwen over. That will give her time to call the doctor."

To Gwen, this all sounded as if it were happening far away and had nothing to do with her. She sneezed.

Aunt Ada gave a little cry of disgust.

Gwen smiled briefly then rested her head on her arms on the table. Right now, she didn't care if it was rude or not. She closed her eyes and let the soothing darkness envelope her in its comforting embrace.

CHAPTER TWENTY

Gwen remembered little of the following days. Her uncle had driven her back to Aunt Katherine's, and she vaguely recalled the doctor coming, but her fevered brain made little sense of his words. The room was kept dark, so during the few times Gwen awoke, she had no idea if it was day or night. Her throat was so sore she could barely swallow, and the constant coughing made her chest ache unbearably. Aunt Katherine was always there. She placed a damp cloth on Gwen's burning head or helped her to drink, but Gwen was barely aware of her presence. She was plagued by dreams of men chasing her, and she knew there was something important she needed to tell someone but couldn't remember what it was.

Her eyes snapped open but could see little in the pitch black. What had awoken her? Gwen blinked then coughed hard and long. It was so hard to breathe. She flopped back against her pillows and, through the pain in her head, started thinking of her parents, Robert and Margaret. She froze. Those weren't her parents. Those were the names of the other Gwen's parents, the 1920's Gwen. A stab of fear shot through her as she realized memories that must belong to the other Gwen were coming to the surface. Memories of playing with a small black dog, going sailing on the ocean with her father, the lilac scent of her mother's hair. *No, no, no!* Gwen's heart pounded as she fought to picture her own mother's face or the sound of her brother's voice. Those memories became dimmer and dimmer. What was happening?

She pushed herself up, her body wracked by another deep, painful cough. When the fit had passed, she slowly turned her body, placing her feet on the floor. Her thoughts flew.

Had she stayed too long here? If she stayed longer, would she lose herself entirely? Gwen's eyes flew wildly around the room, trying to decide what to do. Her entire body ached and she found it so difficult to think. Then it hit her, the closet! She had to go back home, and she had to go back *now* before she forgot who she was.

Slowly and painfully, she pushed herself to her feet and clutched the bedpost for support as her legs started to collapse. The room whirled. She closed her eyes and took a few deep breaths as she tried to gather her strength. She lurched forward, reaching for the chair nearby, and used it for support as she shuffled forward, closer to the door. Step by agonizing step, she staggered from her room to the stairs. Her increasing difficulty in remembering her own life spurred her on.

When she finally reached the attic stairs, Gwen collapsed and fought to muffle the deep, rattling cough that threatened to overwhelm her. She groaned softly at the sharp pain in her chest and ribs and rested her burning head against the cool wood of the step. *Dr. Knowlton was right. The measles are going to kill me.* Gwen knew that if she waited any longer, she wouldn't have the strength to make it up the stairs. She wasn't sure how she'd made it this far.

Taking a deep, painful breath, she lifted her head and struggled to her feet once more. She clutched at the banister to drag herself along and up the steep steps to the attic. She panted with exertion, every breath bringing fresh stabs of pain and coughing until she finally crawled the last few steps to the top. She lay on the landing, gasping for air. *Maybe I'll just rest here for a minute.* She closed her eyes and was tempted to just let everything go, but if she did that, who would she be when she awoke? *If* she woke.

No! Her eyes flew open. If she didn't keep going, she might never get home. Gritting her teeth, she struggled to her hands and knees. Since Aunt Katherine had been forced to let all the maids go. There was no one to hear her as she crawled from the landing to the door of the playroom. She tried to pull herself to her feet, but her body refused to cooperate and she crumpled to the floor. She could just make out the shadow of the closet only ten feet away, its door slightly ajar, as if inviting her in. Tears slid down her cheeks.

She rested another minute. *Why am I doing this?* Her thoughts raced. *I'm ill. I should be in bed. What will Aunt Katherine think if she finds me gone? She has been so good to me since Mama and Papa were killed…*Gwen gasped. It was happening again. She had to go *now* before she lost herself entirely.

She refused to give up. *C'mon, Gwen. Get up and get*

moving or you'll be stuck here forever. The thought of never seeing her family again gave her strength. She gritted her teeth and heaved herself to her feet. Stumbling forward, she reached the closet door just as her legs buckled once more. Wheezing, she used her arms to pull herself in through the doorway of the closet. *I've got to get inside. I've got to!* Pushing shoes, toys and other bits of junk out of her way, she reached behind and pulled the door closed enclosing herself into the comforting darkness of the closet. She closed her eyes and knew no more.

"Gwen! Hey, Gwen! Where are you?"

Gwen's eyes flickered open. Where was she? The hard wooden floor beneath her told her she certainly wasn't in bed. It was dark, but she spied a line of light in front of her eyes. She sat up, blinking, and realized she was in the playroom closet. The voice she'd heard belonged to her brother Lance. She struggled to her feet, flung open the door and stepped out into the bright sunshine pouring in through the playroom windows. Her brother stood by the windows staring wide-eyed.

"Gwen!" He stepped closer and looked her up and down. "What the heck are you doing in the closet? Mom's been looking all over for you."

Gwen had never been so glad to see her brother. She wanted to run over and give him a huge hug but fought the impulse. He'd think she was crazy. How to explain why she was sleeping in the closet? "I…I…guess I must have been sleepwalking," she mumbled, looking at the floor.

Lance stared at her even harder, but now he looked concerned. "That's not good. We better tell Mom."

"No, Lance. Really. I'm fine." She suddenly realized she really was. She no longer felt deathly ill; there was no throbbing headache or bone wrenching cough. She was tired, certainly, but that could be explained by sleeping on a hard wooden floor in a closet. Other than being a bit stiff, she was fine. She remembered everything. She gave a small sigh of relief as she followed her brother down the stairs.

"Gwen?" Her mother watched as the two came down from the attic. "Where on earth have you been? I've been looking all over the house for you."

"Mom!" Gwen dashed up to her mother and gave her a big hug.

Mom laughed but looked confused.

"She was asleep in the attic closet," replied Lance. "She said she was sleepwalking."

"Oh?" Mom frowned and placed her hand on Gwen's forehead. "Well, you don't seem to be running a fever or anything. How do you feel?"

Gwen rolled her eyes and tried to suppress a smile. She was just so happy to be home. "I'm fine. I don't know why I went to sleep in that closet, but really, I'm okay."

Her mom studied her a moment longer. "Well, okay. Go get dressed and come on down for breakfast."

"Sure, Mom." Gwen hurried to her room and closed the door. She was home. She twirled around her room, looking over her stuff–all the modern gadgets, her toys and games, her favorite books, all those things that didn't exist eighty years ago. She fell on her bed with a great sigh of relief. It was so good to be back where she belonged.

She closed her eyes for a few minutes to smell the familiar vanilla scent of her sheets and listened to the comforting rumble of the ocean surf. Then she froze, her eyes going wide. Charlie! Oh no! She'd forgotten all about Charlie.

She sat up and leaped to her feet and began to pace her room in dismay. Uncle Frank and Mr. Carmichael were going to kill Charlie, and she could have stopped it. Tears of frustration filled her eyes. She had failed him, just like she'd failed Uncle Jonas. Slowly, she sank into the rocking chair near the window and let the tears fall. Part of her knew it was meant to be. Charlie had died in 1923, and nothing she could have done would have prevented that, but another part wailed at the injustice of it all. If only she hadn't gotten sick. She would have told Charlie, and he would have been saved. It could all have ended different. Why could she go into the past if she couldn't change anything?

She didn't hear anyone come into the room until she noticed Lance's shoes. She looked at him through her tears.

"Gwen?" His eyes creased with worry. "What's wrong?"

Without hesitation, Gwen flung herself into her brother's arms, weeping even harder. "I could have saved him," she sobbed. "He didn't have to die!"

Lance and Gwen had always been close, but this unexpected reaction seemed to take Lance completely by surprise. He stood stiffly for a moment before putting his arms around his younger sister. "Gwen, who didn't have to die?"

Gwen sobbed a little while longer then took a long quivering breath, realizing with dismay what she'd just said. "I…" Wiping her eyes, she stepped back, trying to figure out what to say. Finally, she blurted out, "Charlie Andersson."

"Charlie Andersson?" His frown deepened. "*The* Charlie Andersson? The guy who took off with all the money?"

"He *didn't* take the money! He was murdered. I think he hid the money first. I need to find it to prove he didn't run off with it."

Lance stared at her open-mouthed. "And you know this *how*? The guy's been gone for like eighty years. You'd think if there really was buried treasure in this dinky town, somebody woulda dug it up by now."

"Oh, Lance…" Gwen pushed her hair out of her face. "You wouldn't believe me if I told you. I'm not sure I even believe me." She shook her head. "It was probably some really amazing dream, but it was so real." Presenting the story as a dream might make it seem a bit more believable.

"Uh huh," said Lance slowly. "You wanna tell me about this dream?"

Gwen laughed as she went to her dresser to pull out some clothes. "OK, I dreamed I could go back in time to the 1920s by going into that closet in the playroom. Somehow I took the place of the Gwen that was already there. Her parents were killed, and she was taken in by her aunt and uncle, Katherine and Jonas Andersson." She paused, trying to make sense of all of this. "Lance, it was so real. I mean, I met all kinds of people, and they were just as real as you. There were gangsters and rumrunners, and I found out what happened to Charlie."

Lance tilted his head. "Oh? Exactly what did happen to him?"

Gwen glanced at her brother. She'd gotten his attention. Then she sighed. "He was set-up to look like he stole the money." She then quickly explained what she'd overheard in Uncle Frank's study. "I think he hid the money so he could get to safety. I mean, wouldn't a bag of money be really heavy? Then I think he was going to go back for it later and give it to Jimmy Houlihan."

Lance looked at her and ran his hand through his hair. "Boy, that's some dream. I can't say I've ever had one like that. So, you say Charlie was killed, but what makes you think those guys didn't get the money back like they'd planned?"

Gwen opened her mouth. Then shut it again. That thought had never occurred to her. Could Carmichael have gotten the money back in the end? No. She shook her head. He hadn't. If he had, old Creepy Bob wouldn't still be looking for it. She knew the money had to be out there someplace.

"Hey, if that guy, Carmichael, was stealing money from the company, our great-grandfather's company, that would mean the money would be ours." Then he shook his head with a small laugh. "Well, too bad it was all a dream. We sure could use the money." He looked at her for a moment. "Gwen, remember, you just dreamed all this. Even if that all really happened, there's nothing you could have done to save Charlie Andersson. He's been gone for eighty years." He lightly punched her in the arm and headed for the door before turning back. "Oh, listen. You better get a move on. Mom sent me up here to find out what was takin' you so long. She wants to go into town."

"Okay." Gwen felt oddly deflated. For a few moments she thought Lance might actually believe her but, in the end, he'd decided it was just a dream. *Could it have been?* She shook her head. No. She knew it happened even if she couldn't prove it. She picked up her clothes and started to dress. *I don't know how*, she thought fiercely, *but I will prove Charlie was innocent even if it's the last thing I do.*

CHAPTER TWENTY-ONE

Gwen made her way downstairs and ate her cereal without really tasting it. Her mother kept looking at her oddly and asked several times if Gwen felt all right. "Okay," said Mom after Gwen assured her yet again she was fine. "Well, we need to go into town to run a few errands. You can see if Molly is at the historical society with her grandmother. Maybe she can come back with us."

That cheered Gwen up immensely. She hadn't seen Molly in a while and realized she missed her friend. Again, she felt that feeling of disorientation of trying to reconcile having spent the last several weeks in the 1920s with her life here in the present where apparently no time had passed. Gwen had to consider carefully what she said so she didn't sound crazy.

After a couple of stops at the grocery store and gas station, they headed to the downtown area. Mom parked the car, and the two of them strolled over to the historical society. To Gwen's delight, Molly sat at the desk playing with a small handheld video game. She looked totally bored.

Molly looked up and with a whoop of joy and jumped over to give Gwen a big hug. "Gwen! Thank god you're here. I've been *so* bored. The Internet's down so I can't even get online. I swear this must be worse than prison." She grinned then a small frown pulled at her brow. "You look different somehow." Molly studied Gwen.

Gwen shrugged a little uncomfortably. "I'm the same as I've ever been." Her mother was talking to Molly's grandmother. "Mom said you can come home with us if your grandma says it's okay."

"That would great." Molly put her game in her pocket. "I have got to get out of here before I go nuts."

"Molly," called Mrs. Berger. "I have some things I want to show Gwen's mother, so why don't you two go over to the ice cream parlor and get some ice cream. Here's some money."

Molly scooped up the cash, and the two girls hurried from the shop to the ice cream parlor nearby. Gwen realized it was in the same place as the soda shop she and Tom visited. Again she had that feeling of disorientation.

It was a warm day, so the girls sat outside to eat their ice cream. Gwen enjoyed the feeling of normalcy when Molly jabbed her in the ribs with her elbow. "Don't look now," Molly hissed, "but Creepy Carmichael just walked by. He keeps looking at us."

A shiver ran down Gwen's back. She tried to look around without being too obvious. Yes, there he was. Bob Carmichael stood about fifty yards away, looking toward a shop window, but Gwen noticed him stealing glances at her and Molly. When he caught her looking at him, he gave her a wink. Gwen's head whipped back around, a tight knot forming in her stomach. That guy really was so weird, and he scared her.

"Come on." Gwen got to her feet. "Let's go." She turned to head back to the historical society then stopped abruptly. Frowning, she studied the downtown pedestrian mall laid out before her. It took her a few moments to understand the large building in front of her, not far from the water's edge, had been her uncle's old warehouse. It had been turned into a shopping mall with all sorts of little boutiques and specialty shops.

She quickly realized that most of the buildings along this street were present eighty years ago. There was the old hardware store, the current jewelry shop had been a tobacconist's, and the clothing boutique, the butcher shop. *This* could have been Charlie's route. She turned her gaze toward the river. It flowed through town just beyond the hardware store. A greenbelt park had been constructed, and much of it had been allowed to return to its natural state with a trail along the river's edge.

Molly tugged at her sleeve. "Come on. He's still staring at us. It's seriously creeping me out."

Gwen nodded, frustrated she still had no clue as to where Charlie might have hidden the money.

When they reentered the historical society building, Gwen told her mother about Bob Carmichael watching them. Mom and Mrs. Berger moved to the front windows and looked out, but there was no sign of the man.

"Well, I don't see him now," said Mom. "He does have a right to be in town. Just let me know if you see him again. It could just be a coincidence. Anyway, we're done here. You girls ready?"

As they drove back to the Andersson house, the girls discussed their plans for finishing setting up the hideout. Knowing that Creepy Carmichael was in town made them feel a little safer.

Mom went to pack the girls a picnic lunch while Gwen and Molly headed to the carriage house to retrieve the items they'd failed to take down before. Molly looked around to see if there was anything else they should take. Gwen was drawn once more toward the big wardrobe. She started thinking about the raccoon coat and its mysterious bullet. When she reached the wardrobe, she pulled open the heavy door, lifted the canvas bag and studied the old coat for a few moments. She clearly remembered Bertie wore a coat just like this one. Could this be his? What were the chances of there being two of these hideous coats?

Gwen reached in first one pocket and then the other before finding the small silver flask and the old newspaper clipping. Gwen peered down at the yellowed scrap of brittle newsprint. It was dated June 23, 1923, but only a fragment of it remained. Carefully, she began to read:

BODY OF YOUTH FOUND OFF SHORE

The body of an unidentified youth was discovered by local lobstermen on Friday evening. The youth had been dead several days, apparently from multiple gunshot wounds. He is believed to have been killed during a gun battle between government agents and unknown rumrunners off the coast of Little Deer Island last Monday night. Commander Burns of the Coast Guard cutter...

That was all there was. Gwen stared hard at the item. Could that unknown youth have been Charlie? That could explain why Bertie had the clipping and the body was discovered not long after Charlie disappeared.

"Whatcha lookin' at?" Molly came over with some books. "Hey, isn't that the paper that was in that raccoon coat?"

"Yeah. Look." Gwen handed her the scrap of paper.

Molly read over it and shrugged. "So?"

"I'm wondering if this could have been Charlie Andersson."

Molly frowned and looked at the paper again. "Charlie Andersson? What would he be doing in the ocean? The article says it was some kid killed in a battle with rumrunners."

Gwen nodded slowly as she tried to put the pieces together. "What if it *was* Charlie and not some kid killed by the Coast Guard? What if he really was killed by some other gang for the money? Think. How could he end up in the ocean?"

Molly thought a moment. "Well, he coulda been on a boat, I guess, and fell off. Or he could have fallen into the river and been carried to the ocean or maybe been killed someplace else and dumped there."

Gwen began pacing. She was sure Charlie wanted her to find that coat. The whole reason she had looked in the wardrobe to begin with was it had seemed to glow. If the coat belonged to Bertie and there was an article about some dead kid, could that mean Bertie had known something about the murder?

"C'mon." Molly handed the paper back to Gwen. "I don't have a lot of time. If we're going to work on the cave, we better get going."

Gwen hated to give up just when she knew she was close to some answers, but she gave Molly a nod then slipped the paper into her pocket. She would add this piece to her puzzle and hope she could eventually make some sense of it all. She still needed more information to figure this out.

The girls spent the afternoon taking the last few items down to the cave and organizing it into a cozy den. They spread the old carpets across the sandy floor, arranged the books on the little bookshelf they'd brought, set up the card table Gwen's mother had let them take and covered it with a tablecloth. They arranged the old rocking chair and beanbag chair around the bookshelves. They set various little knickknacks into some of the small niches in the rock to make the walls look less bare. They were also able to rest an old curtain rod across a couple of rocks and the curtains created an extra space they used to store things they weren't sure what to do with. All in all, it was a fantastic place. They sat at the card table with the glow of the electric lantern pushing back the darkness. Finally, they pulled out the lunch Gwen's mother had packed.

"I think I'll see if Dad will let me take a couple more of these lanterns." Molly's mouth was full of tuna fish. "We definitely need more light in here. We should bring some extra batteries too. Just in case." She sighed. "Too bad we can't hook up a TV or the Internet in here. Wouldn't that be awesome?"

Gwen nodded but then smiled a little wistfully, thinking had she and Tom turned this cave into a hideout back in the '20s, it wouldn't have been much different than it was now. That was comforting somehow.

"So, have you seen that ghost again?" Molly looked through the cooler for some more chips.

"No." Would she? "I just wish I could prove he was innocent."

Molly shook her head. "You're nuts, you know. I guess if you did find that money, it would at least prove he didn't actually run off with it."

"If he hid it that would fit the story of the guys chasing him. It would be hard to run with a heavy bag of money." Gwen furrowed her brow in thought. "If he hadn't been killed, he would have gone back for it, right?"

"I would."

"I don't think he would have stolen the money." Gwen stood up and began to pace. "I think he would have been worried about his family. You know, what would the gangsters do to them if he ran off with all that cash?" The only reason Charlie worked for Houlihan in the first place was to help Aunt Katherine. "My guess is Charlie hid the money so he could escape and planned on coming back later when it was safe. Then he could take the money to Houlihan like he was supposed to."

Molly shrugged. "I guess. Be hard to prove that, even if you found the money."

"Yeah, but at least it would show everyone he hadn't run off with it."

It wasn't long afterwards that Molly needed to go home. The girls made arrangements for Molly to come back the next day.

That night, as Gwen got ready for bed, she thought of everything that had happened to her. She again wondered if any of this was real or if she'd dreamt it all. She stretched out on her bed, facing the ceiling with her arms behind her head.

What about Charlie? Could he give her any kind of clue as to where to look? Did she dare go upstairs and see if he was still there? She shivered thinking of the ghostly form she'd seen in the past, but why should she be scared? She knew Charlie. She knew he wasn't a criminal. He certainly wouldn't hurt her; he wanted her help.

Well, I'll just wait till everyone goes to bed, then I'll go see if he's there. She pulled out a book and, making herself comfortable, began to read.

When she awoke, her light was still on and, at first, she wasn't sure where she was. She blinked at her clock.

It was 3:15 in the morning. It took her a moment to remember her plan to look for Charlie. She hesitated. Did she really want to go up there again in the middle of the night? She took a deep breath, got to her feet and put on her robe. She had to. For Charlie's sake.

Everyone would certainly be asleep now. Her heart pounded as she silently padded down the hallway from her room to the attic steps. She paused to peer through the darkness. She tried to swallow, but her mouth was dry. In the background a clock ticked away the seconds. *Come on, Gwen. There's nothing to be afraid of. It's just Charlie.* She squared her shoulders, took a deep breath and marched up the stairs and into the playroom.

It was like a stab to her heart to see it so empty and desolate. She glanced around. No sign of Charlie. She wandered to the closet and shone her little light on the dates. Yes, there they all were: Tom, Charlie, Louisa, William and even Gwen. Gwen gave a little smile and gently ran her finger along the marks as she pictured each face.

The hair on the back of her neck prickled as she noticed the growing chill in the room. She turned. The faint glowing figure stood near the doorway. A tightness in her chest made it difficult to breathe.

"Gwen." It sounded as if it came from a great distance.

Gwen gasped for air, trying to will her heart to slow. She closed her eyes, her body shook and there was a rushing in her ears. *It's okay. It's okay.* At last she calmed down enough to allow herself to peek at the figure.

"Charlie," she whispered. "Is…is it really you?" Her heart gave a little flip of joy as Charlie grinned the old, cocky grin Gwen remembered so well.

"Oh, Charlie!" Gwen stopped, a hard lump in her throat. "I'm so sorry. It's all my fault. I heard Uncle Frank and Mr. Carmichael. You were supposed to be killed by Mr. Carmichael's men. I wanted to warn you, but…I got sick." She wiped away the tears that freely flowed down her face. "I'm so sorry," she whispered miserably.

Charlie continued to smile, but now his eyes were full of sympathy and sadness.

Gwen swallowed and looked away. Suddenly, she was no longer afraid.

"Charlie," she gripped her hands together. "Do you know who killed you? Do you remember?"

Scowling, Charlie held up a small, silver bullet. Gwen bit her lip in confusion. It looked like one they'd found in the old raccoon coat. She knew he'd been shot, but did the bullet mean something else? Maybe ghosts couldn't remember how they died.

"Do you remember what you did with the money?"

Charlie looked away helplessly and didn't respond.

Gwen growled then thought hard. "Okay, maybe you can still help me. I think someone was chasing you that night and you ran to the river to get away, but someone shot you and you fell into the river. Some lobstermen found a body in the ocean right after you disappeared. Anyway, if you were going to hide the money near the river, where would you hide it?"

Charlie's brow furrowed, then his ghostly face darkened with anger. He began to silently pace about the room. Gwen shivered as the temperature dropped even further. Abruptly Charlie came to a halt and faced her, frowning in concentration.

Gwen had decided that at least for *this* ghost, talking wasn't something easily accomplished. She waited patiently until finally the words came out, soft and just barely discernible:

Cave…bridge.

Gwen gave a little cry of triumph only to find Charlie fading away as if the effort of giving her that message had used up all his energy.

"Don't worry, Charlie," Gwen said to the empty room. "If the money's still there, I'll find it. I'll prove to everyone you were innocent."

CHAPTER TWENTY-TWO

Early the next morning, Mrs. Berger dropped Molly off on her way to the historical society.

"How come you're always with your grandmother?" asked Gwen as the two girls headed down to their hideout.

Molly shrugged. "Mom and Dad both work, so during the summer I hang out with Grandma. I don't mind. She's more fun than they are and lets me do a lot more interesting stuff. Like come over here."

Gwen laughed.

When they reached the cave, they checked to make sure nothing had been touched. Gwen wouldn't put it past Lance to come sneaking around. It all looked pretty much the same. Molly had managed to find a couple more electric lanterns which brightened the cave, making it even more welcoming than before. The girls pulled out one of the games they'd stashed away on the shelves, but Gwen was restless. She wondered if she dare tell Molly about her encounter with Charlie's ghost the night before. He'd given her a hint after all, and maybe her friend could help her figure it out.

"I saw the ghost again," she finally said in a small voice. "He gave me a hint, I think."

Molly was immediately alert. "Really? What did he say?" She leaned in closer.

Gwen stared at her game piece for a moment.

"Well, first I asked him if he knew who killed him, and he showed me a bullet." Her eyes met Molly's. "I mean, we already figured out he was shot, so what good does that do us? Anyway, when I asked him where he might have hidden the money, he said just two words–cave and bridge. That's it."

"Cave and bridge." Molly's eyes widened. "Then he must have hidden the money in a cave near a bridge on the river!" She stopped and frowned. "But which bridge? There are the two big ones that cars use, but there are also a bunch of footbridges. Even back in the twenties there must have been a bunch of them."

Gwen rested her chin on her hand. "I wish I had a map from back then. If we could study it, and if we assumed he fell into the river, we might be able to figure out where he could have hidden the money."

"I think we might have a map." Molly jumped up and scurried over to the bookshelf. "I found this book about the history of Fishawak in all those books in the carriage house. I thought it might be interesting to look through. Working with Grandma has always got me looking for stuff like that." She pulled the book from the shelf and laid it on the table. Gwen positioned the lantern so they could get a better look.

It had been published in 1950 and was full of photographs, maps and charts. They pored through the table of contents and were rewarded with a reference to several area maps, one of which showed the downtown area sometime around 1930.

"I bet we'd have more luck on the Internet," said

Molly as they tried to study the small image, "but I guess this will do for now."

"Okay." Gwen peered at the map, "Jonas Andersson's warehouse was right there, and if we assume Charlie was going from there to Jimmy Houlihan's restaurant over…" she adjusted the light to try and read the street names better, "here, then the most direct route would be along Miller Street."

Molly frowned. "How d'you know Charlie was going from the warehouse to Houlihan's restaurant?"

Gwen hesitated then shrugged, "It's just a guess. We have to start someplace."

Molly stared at her a moment longer then nodded as she looked back at the map. "So, if somebody showed up on Miller Street to rob him, where would he go to escape?" Molly leaned in closer, squinting at the map. "If he went down toward the river, he coulda hid in the weeds or crossed over someplace."

"The two big bridges that cross the river would probably be too far away."

Molly nodded. "So, it must have been one of the footbridges. This map doesn't show any of those."

"Plus, we don't know which of the bridges that are here now were around back then." Gwen's frustration was growing. "We'll just have to check them all."

Molly twirled a lock of her red hair around her finger. "I know the Chamber of Commerce has maps of the park areas. It would have all the footbridges across the river. I think we might even have some at the historical society."

"Do you think your grandmother could bring one when she comes to get you?"

Molly nodded. "Sure. I'll call her when we go back up to your house."

"Great." Gwen looked back at the old map. "Now, he said 'cave.' Are there caves along the riverbank someplace? That could narrow down our search."

Molly shrugged. "I wouldn't call them caves exactly, but Grandma told me once there are hollows all along the river where the rock has been worn away. I guess there might be a few big enough to be called caves. We're talking eighty years ago, though. The river has flooded a bunch of times and a lot of hollows get buried or filled up with mud and sand."

Gwen frowned at Molly. "If they're all filled with mud, how can we find them?"

Molly opened her mouth, shut it then sank back into her chair. "Great." she scowled, crossing her arms across her chest. "I really thought we had it."

"I still think we do, and I think we should start searching for that bridge and check the riverbank. If there's a cave, it couldn't be too far from the bridge. We can bring some shovels. The question now is, how do we get there? I don't think our parents will let us go wandering around the river digging things up. At least I know mine won't."

"Won't what?"

The girls jumped and gasped with fright as Lance emerged from the entrance, flicking off his flashlight and grinning at the girls.

"Lance!" Gwen glared at her brother. "What are you doing here? Mom said this was our place."

"Oh, take it easy. I'm just looking." Lance gave her a dismissive wave of his hand as he gazed around the small space. "Wow, this is so cool!" He picked up one of the old liquor bottles Molly had stuck on a small ledge. "So, it really was used by rumrunners, huh? How'd you girls ever find this place? It took me awhile, and I knew about where it was supposed to be."

"I'm psychic." Gwen had her hands on her hips. "Okay, you've seen it. Now go!"

"Hold on. Hold on." Lance gave her one of his infuriating grins and continued to examine the cave and its contents. "So, what won't Mom and Dad let you do?"

The girls looked at each other but said nothing.

Lance rolled his eyes with a deep sigh. "C'mon, Gwennie, you know I won't tell them anything."

Gwen glanced again at Molly, who gave her a little shrug. Gwen sighed. "We think we've figured out where Charlie Andersson might have hidden the money."

Lance laughed. "Are you *still* stuck on that? C'mon, Gwen. Get real! It's just a story."

"No, it's not." Gwen's eyes sparked with anger. "I *know* it all happened. I think Charlie was murdered, and his body fell into the river. Then some lobstermen found it in the ocean." She thrust the newspaper clipping into his hand.

Lance blinked then stared down at the paper in his hand.

"Anyway, he was killed, and I think he hid the money in a cave near the river. Look!" She thrust her finger at the map. "I think he was ambushed along this road and ran to the river, here, hoping to get across by a footbridge. He knew the bad guys were catching up, so I think he hid the money someplace near a bridge. Trouble is, we don't know which bridge. Molly's grandmother said there used to be caves along there, so we want to go look."

Lance was silent now as his eyes met Gwen's.

She stared at him defiantly. She knew him well enough to know when he was getting hooked. Even Lance, who thought he was too cool to hang around with two twelve year olds, would find it hard to dismiss the possibility of finding buried treasure.

"Okay." Lance dropped his gaze to the map and leaned closer. "If he got ambushed here, then you're right, running to the river was probably the best idea, especially if he knew the area and the other guys didn't. I don't know why you think he was ambushed there instead of someplace else, but I'll take your word for it. You say there's a footbridge someplace?"

Molly nodded. "Several. There's a map that shows where the bridges are now, but we don't know which ones were around back then. We're just gonna have to check out all of them."

"How are we going to get over there to go dig? That's what we were trying to figure out." Gwen sighed.

Lance tapped his fingers on the table for few moments then grinned. "Fishing!"

CHAPTER TWENTY-THREE

Gwen had to admit it, when her brother put his mind to something, he usually came up with some good ideas.

"Listen," he'd said. "I saw some old fishing poles in the carriage house. I'll tell Mom we wanna go try them out at the river. I know she wouldn't let you girls go by yourselves, but she'll let you go if I come. We'll take some shovels and tell Mom it's so we can dig for worms."

That was exactly how it had worked out. Gwen's mother called Molly's grandmother and got permission for her to go along. The plan was Faye would take her siblings into town the next day, pick up Molly and drop them off at a one of the local parks.

"It's the perfect cover." Molly grinned. "River Run Park has a fishing pond. Nobody can really fish in the river this close to the ocean, the cliffs are too high, but if we say we're going to River Run, Grandma will assume we're gonna go fish in the pond."

The next morning, as they drove toward town, Faye peered at her brother, her eyes narrowed. "Okay, Lance, since when have you been interested in fishing, especially with a couple of twelve-year-old girls?"

Gwen leaned closer, interested to hear exactly how Lance would explain it. Faye was no fool.

Lance laughed and brushed his hair from his eyes.

"Hey, if it gets me out of scrapin' paint off the walls, I'm all for it." Then he shrugged. "I just thought it might be fun to go fishing, and the girls asked if they could come."

"Mmm hmm." Faye raised an eyebrow. "Right. Next you're going tell me you're interested in taking senior citizens duck hunting."

"Hey, that might be fun." Lance grinned. Faye just shook her head and sighed. Gwen sat back with a smile. Good old, Lance. After picking up Molly, it took only ten minutes before they pulled into the little park near the river. Lance and the girls piled out of the car.

Faye looked at her brother. "Okay, Lance, how long do you think you'll be? I need to go to the craft store to get more paint for my mural, but if you guys think you'll be awhile, I can always go clothes shopping."

"We should be here for a few hours at least." Lance pulled a couple of shovels out of the back of the car while Gwen and Molly gathered the fishing gear. He glanced at his watch. "Why don't you pick us up around three?"

Faye nodded then looked up at the sky with a frown. "They said we could have thunder storms later today. You guys better keep an eye on the weather. If it starts to rain, I'll pick you up here." Then with a wave, she was off.

Gwen gazed around the small park and wiped sweat from her face. It was hot today. There were a few picnic tables and a small playground. If she looked behind her, she could make out the old hardware store farther up the hill. The park was empty except for the three of them, and the air felt heavy and oppressive with the impending storm. "Okay, Molly, where's the map?"

Molly pulled out a colorful map diagramming the greenbelt with all the parks, trails and bridges along the river. "There are three bridges." She pointed to the marks on the map. "One not too far from here, one nearer where the old restaurant would have been, and one closer to the ocean."

Lance nodded. "Okay, if we start at the one farthest up river first and work our way back toward the ocean that should work since we don't know how far he got. He might have made it almost to the restaurant for all we know." He folded up the map. "Okay, twerps." He grinned as he shouldered the shovels. "I hope you're prepared to do some hiking."

Gwen studied the river as they hiked along the trail. It was a good ten to fifteen feet below them; the banks little more than rocky cliffs containing the rapidly flowing water between them. Gwen shuddered to think of poor Charlie's body falling into that.

It took them about thirty minutes to reach the first bridge. It was made of redwood and spanned the river where the edges of the bluff came within twenty feet of each other. It didn't look particularly old. Gwen peered over the edge of the bluff and gulped when she realized how far down the river really was. How would they climb down this?

Lance joined her, frowning. "I dunno, Gwen." He

leaned on the shovels. "You really think he would have hidden the money here?" He turned and studied the trees behind them. "Maybe he hid it in the woods."

Gwen shook her head, her mouth set. "No, I'm sure he would have hid it in a cave near the bridge."

Lance shrugged as if he'd given up trying to figure out his sister. "Okay, you and Molly stay here, and I'll go down and look."

"Oh, no you don't!" Gwen grabbed her brother's arm.

"Yeah, this was our idea." Molly stepped up beside her. "We're going too!"

"No." Lance shook his head. "It's really dangerous here, and I don't want you two getting hurt. Listen, I'll just go down and take a look. If I see anything, I'll call you down." Before the two girls could protest any further, Lance began his descent, carefully examining the cliff face as he went.

"I knew he'd just mess things up." Gwen folded her arms across her chest.

Molly nodded as they watched Lance slowly work his way down toward the river.

The girls quickly grew bored. Gwen was hot and sticky, and the ravenous mosquitoes wouldn't leave her alone. As far as she could see, Lance wasn't making much progress in the search, and he continued to refuse to let them join him, much to her growing irritation. *I never should have told him about this.* She threw stones at a tree. *He always has to take over everything.* Gwen was about to climb down and start looking when Molly grabbed her arm.

"Did you see that?" Molly stared out into the woods, a wary expression on her face.

"See what?" Gwen followed her friend's gaze. "I don't see anything.

Molly frowned. "I could have sworn I saw somebody walking around out there."

Gwen stood still and peered out into the forest, but all she saw were trees. In the background was the occasional clang of Lance's shovel against rock, just audible above the roar of the river. She shook her head. "Well, I don't see anything now."

"Hmm." Molly stared a while longer then turned back to Gwen. "Let's find out if Lance is almost done. This place is kinda creepy."

Gwen agreed. The dense woods grew darker as the heavy rainclouds muted the sunlight to a dismal gray.

"Lance!" Gwen looked over the side. "Any luck?"

Lance made no reply but appeared over the edge of the cliff a few moments, later covered in dirt and sweat. He shook his head. "Nothing here but solid rock." He wiped his face with the bottom of his soiled T-shirt. "I guess I could go check the other side, but it looks pretty much the same."

"Maybe we better just move on to the next bridge." Molly glanced back into the woods.

Lance looked a little surprised when Gwen agreed, but he simply shrugged, picked up his shovel and started down the trail to the next bridge.

The humidity grew even more oppressive as they

moved on. Gwen felt as if someone had dumped a bucket of water on her head, while the mosquitoes used her as their own private smorgasbord. She had applied bug repellant before they left, but apparently no one had informed the mosquitoes.

The second bridge was just past River Run Park and like the first one, was made of redwood to blend into its surroundings. Gwen had to admit they really were very pretty, but it bothered her they looked so new. "Do you know when these bridges were built?" Gwen asked Molly as they got closer to the bridge.

Molly shook her head. "I'd bet it was more recent than nineteen twenty."

"Maybe they replaced old bridges with these new ones."

Molly shrugged. "Let's hope so, or we're back to where we started."

Lance examined the cliff face looking for a safe way down. "I can't believe you guys talked me into this."

Gwen studied the terrain. The slope wasn't quite as steep here. It would be an easier climb.

"Okay, you guys, wait here." Lance shouldered his shovel and started his descent.

"Oh no you don't!" Gwen snatched up her shovel. "We are not sitting around up here waiting for you. I don't care what you say. We're coming."

Lance opened his mouth to protest then sighed in defeat. "Well, then be careful. These rocks are slippery."

Gwen studied the steep slope as she carefully descended, trying not to slip on any loose stones. She looked for any kind of opening that might be hiding the treasure.

"Here's something!"

Gwen looked up. Molly excitedly peered in the side of the hill. Her heart thumping, Gwen scrambled across the rocks to join her friend.

CHAPTER TWENTY-FOUR

"Look!" Molly pointed to a small gap between two stones. "Could this be it?"

Gwen looked for Lance and spotted him farther down the slope. He was examining another pile of rocks. She turned her attention back to the opening Molly had discovered. It was maybe three feet high but only a couple of feet wide. She pulled her flashlight off her belt and tried to see farther in.

"I don't know." Gwen twisted her mouth. "It's awfully small. Charlie certainly couldn't have crawled in there."

Molly leaned forward and thrust in her arm as deeply as she could, feeling around inside. She pulled back with a frown. "It's empty. I could feel the back wall. There's nothing in there."

"Well, at least that proves there are spaces where Charlie could have hidden the money." Gwen turned and resumed her descent. She studied the landscape for any other openings. Secretly, she was pleased Molly hadn't found the cave. She was convinced this was something she would have to do.

The steep bank was riddled with small hollows, and Gwen's initial excitement began to fade into discouragement. After examining her fifth or sixth such hole, she collapsed onto a rock and leaned against the bank to rest. She closed her eyes as a blanket of exhaustion settled over her. Startled by a deep rumble of thunder, her eyes snapped open. Looking upward into the sky, her attention was captured by a furtive movement near the edge of the cliff. Gwen frowned and turned around to peer up the hill. There was nothing beyond the shrubs and plants.

Lance frowned at the sky. "Maybe we better go check the last bridge before the storm really hits. If we don't find anything on this side of the river, we can come back and check the other side later." His voice was just audible over the river.

Gwen waved to let him know she'd heard as she continued to watch the bluff's edge. When they reached the top, she almost expected to see someone waiting for them. The path was deserted.

"Something wrong?" Molly looked around.

"I thought I saw something move up here a few minutes ago." Gwen peered into the murky forest. "I don't see anything now though."

Molly shivered. "I hope no one's following us." The girls exchanged glances: Creepy Carmichael.

Quickly, Gwen and Molly picked up their fishing gear and followed Lance down the trail to the last bridge about half a mile farther on. Gwen was disappointed to find this bridge appeared to be more recent like the others. Again, she hoped they'd just replaced the old bridge with a new one. There was another rumble of thunder, closer this time.

"Okay." Lance studied the ominous dark clouds overhead. "We gotta make this quick. We'll probably get soaked, but I want to be of out here before it gets really bad."

This part of the cliff was even rockier than the sections they'd already searched. They found few openings big enough to hide a bag full of money but they were empty.

The wind picked up dramatically. Choppy waves rose above the surface of the dark river. Their time was up when the first fat drops of rain plopped onto the rocks beside her. Abruptly, the sky opened up, releasing a deluge of rain so heavy it was hard to even breathe. Trying to wipe the water from her eyes, Gwen spotted Lance as he pointed up to the top. She nodded and began to follow her brother back up the cliff.

Gwen struggled against the blinding rain and buffeting wind to reach the top of the bluff. She collapsed as soon as she reached level ground, shaking from cold and exertion. She was soaked. Suddenly, she heard a scream. She raised her head and gasped. Her heart began to race.

A few feet away, Molly was held tight in the grip of some man. She shook the water from her eyes. Bob Carmichael. Struggling to her feet, she looked for her brother.

"Lance!" Her brother's body lay in the middle of the path behind the struggling pair.

Gwen stood momentarily stunned. She was shocked back to her situation by the sound of Carmichael's angry yell. Gwen's head snapped up just in time. Molly slipped from the cursing man's grasp. With a glance back at Gwen, Molly took off down the path toward the park as fast as she could run. Gwen could only hope she was going to get help.

Carmichael turned and glared furiously at Gwen and, with surprising speed for a man so large, lunged forward and grabbed her by the arm. "Where is it?" He yanked her closer. "Tell me where the money is, or I'll throw you off this cliff!"

With a cry of pain, Gwen struggled against his iron grip. "I don't know where the money is!" she shouted over roar of the pounding of the rain. "I wouldn't tell you if I did!" A sudden flash of lightning was followed by a crash of thunder so enormous the ground trembled with its fury. Carmichael was startled just enough to loosen his hold on Gwen's arm. As wet as she was, Gwen slithered loose and started running up the path. Her heart skipped a beat as she realized she was headed away from the park where Molly had gone to find help. There was nothing to be done about it now.

Carmichael roared furiously as he lumbered after her.

She fought to keep her balance on the slippery rock. With a stab of terror, Gwen realized Carmichael was almost upon her, his heavy ham-like hand reaching out to grab her. With a burst of speed, she darted forward. She stumbled as her feet slipped on the wet, muddy rock. There was nothing below her but thin air. She screamed as she tumbled off the cliff toward the raging river below.

The slope of the cliff saved her. Gwen hit a rock about halfway down the cliff. It proved just big enough to stop her wild descent. She moaned as white hot agony shot up her side. The rain continued unabated and Gwen shivered even harder now, lightheaded.

Panting, she craned her head and peered through the dense curtain of rain, trying to spot Carmichael. She could just make out his bulbous head peering over the edge. The pain in her side echoed the rapid beating of her heart.

Gwen gasped as the rock supporting her began to shift. A torrent of water raced down the hillside and loosened her precarious perch from the cliff. She glanced down and inhaled sharply. The river was now several feet closer to her.

Gwen clutched a clump of nearby grass, as her eyes swept the rock face. She had to find someplace safer. There! A small ledge maybe eight feet over and a couple of feet up the cliff. If she could make it up there, then she'd be safe. At least for the moment. She prayed Molly returned soon with help.

The rock shifted again. It now tilted dangerously toward the water. Gwen had to move and fast. She took a deep breath and, biting back a cry of pain, struggled to her feet. It was all she could do to keep her balance against the howling wind and constant downpour. The slick rock made her footing unsteady. As she inched forward, her foot slipped. She plastered her face against the rock face, its cold metallic smell filling her nose. She panted against the throbbing pain in her side that threatened to overwhelm her. Gwen gritted her teeth and began to move. Step by agonizing step, she made her way laboriously across the stony cliff, gradually closing in on the little ledge.

Gwen's feet slid out from beneath her again. She fell hard, black spots dancing across her vision. She shook her head and her blood turned to ice as she slid closer to the churning water. Now her breathing came in short gasps as she fought against panic. Desperate, Gwen reached out and scrabbled for a handhold. Her hand struck something hard protruding from the rocks. She grabbed onto it, praying it wouldn't slip from her grasp. Groaning, she pulled herself upward and managed to get her feet anchored against a boulder. She looked down. An old pillar of wood had stopped her descent.

Another deafening crash of thunder brought her back. She had to get out of this weather. Her side throbbed, she shook with cold and there was a lunatic after her. She struggled to her feet and winced. *I've got to keep moving.* Gwen swung around trying to spot her pursuer then resumed her ascent to the ledge.

CHAPTER TWENTY-FIVE

It seemed an eternity before Gwen finally crawled up onto the ledge with a great sigh of relief. An overhang protected her from the worst of the rain. She shrank back as far under the protective rock as she could. She shivered so violently, she was sure Carmichael would hear her teeth chattering.

She looked around her little sanctuary. The ledge was about four feet deep, ending against the face of the cliff. Gwen frowned and gently touched the stone in front of her. Instead of solid rock, there was a number of smaller stones neatly piled one on top of the other. Several had become dislodged, revealing a space beyond. With trembling hands, she pulled at one then another and soon looked down a short passageway. She glanced back over her shoulder. The farther away she could get from the open, the safer she'd feel. Maybe this was the perfect hiding place.

Gwen pulled her flashlight off her belt and shone it down the passageway. It was several feet long and opened into a larger chamber. It wasn't perfect, but she could hide here. She crawled forward and shone the light around the small space, hoping it went farther in. Then she stopped. Her eyes went wide as a chill ran down her spine. A few feet away, in a small alcove, stood what appeared to be an old suitcase. Her breathing came faster as Gwen stared at the case. Her mind struggled to make sense of what she saw. Could this actually be what she'd been searching for? Could this be the missing gangster's gold?

Gwen's head swam. Her heartbeat pounded in her ears. She leaned back against the damp wall of the niche, clutching her painful side. Then she laughed, her dangerous situation momentarily forgotten.

She'd found it! There was no doubt in her mind. She, Gwen Andersson, found the infamous gangster's gold. She glanced back down the short, narrow tunnel. No adult could fit through that space. Gwen imagined Charlie had just been small enough to push the bag all the way in.

She carefully dragged herself closer and stared at the old bag. It was made of brown leather heavily discolored by mold and mildew. Its musty smell strong in the small space. It opened along the center with a lock and had a pair of handles at the top. Straps encircled the bag at either end, fastened with buckles of tarnished brass. There was no doubt the bag had been here a very long time.

Shining her light across the bag, Gwen intently studied the center clasp and buckles. She pushed the clasp, but it didn't budge. She yearned to open the bag this very minute, but she knew Carmichael was still out there. Now was not the time. She'd just sit tight and wait for help to come. She closed her eyes and prayed he'd lost her. She wasn't so lucky.

"Well, well. Look what we have here." Carmichael leered at her through the mouth of the tunnel, the light from his flashlight blinding her. "Looks like you knew where the treasure was after all, huh, missy?"

"Get away from me!" Gwen recoiled against the back wall of the chamber. "Leave me alone."

Carmichael laughed. The sound made Gwen's stomach turn. He appeared even more pig-like with his dripping hair plastered against his fat pink face. "I don't think so. You have something there that belongs to me, and I'd appreciate you handing it over."

"This money doesn't belong to you. It was stolen by George Carmichael from Jonas Andersson back in the twenties. George killed Charlie because of this money. You have no right to it." Gwen snapped her mouth shut as rage darkened Carmichael's face. She couldn't believe she'd said all that. Then her anger surged again. It was all true, and this Carmichael was as bad as the rest of them. No way were they going to win again.

With a roar of fury, Carmichael lunged forward, his long, beefy arm extended the length of the passage. Gwen's heart stopped. He would just be able to reach her legs. She kicked and pulled her legs up as close to her body as possible, but Carmichael kept coming. He grunted as her foot connected with his elbow. Gwen cried out as his massive hand locked around her ankle. Gwen was dragged slowly but surely toward the cave mouth.

"Let me go!" Gwen frantically struggled to pull away. Her free foot searched for an anchor, but the man was simply too strong. She was trapped.

Once her legs were free of the tunnel, Gwen ignored the sharp pain from her ribs and kicked wildly, hoping to break her captor's iron hold. Despite her resistance, Carmichael hauled her out as easily as a cat pulling a mouse from its hole. Gwen continued to scream and struggle until the sharp point of a knife pressed against her throat. She froze. Her body went cold as Carmichael pulled her close, one arm across her chest, the other pressing a hunting knife to her throat. Gwen could smell his rank odor like that of a mangy dog.

"Awright, Miss Know-it-all," Carmichael snarled over the combined roar of the rain and river. "I want you to crawl back in there an' bring out that bag, y'hear? If you don't, just remember, I got your brother up there. Be a real shame if sumthin' was to happen to him, huh?"

Gwen gasped as the tip of the knife pricked the delicate skin of her throat. She swallowed and closed her eyes against the tears of pain. She refused to let this creep see her cry.

"Do I make myself clear?" He pulled the tip farther across her neck. It felt like a line of fire burning across her throat.

"Yes," whispered Gwen faintly. She trembled so hard she was afraid the knife would cut her even more deeply.

"Good." Carmichael roughly thrust her back toward the cave.

Gwen reached for her throat. She bit back a cry.

Her fingers were stained with red. Her gaze snapped back to Carmichael, and she knew in that moment she was dead. Once she brought out the bag he'd kill her. All he had to do was push her in the river and claim she slipped. The rocks were so wet, who could say it didn't happen that way? Her breath came in short gasps, as her mind struggled to figure a way out. She was on the ledge with Carmichael's bulk between her and an escape. There was no way she could get around him

"Get moving, kid." Carmichael gave her another shove. "And remember, no funny stuff, or your brother becomes a tragic drowning victim."

Gwen nodded as she fought back tears. She turned and began to crawl back into the chamber, her hands raw from the rough stone. The bag was exactly as she'd left it. She gently ran her fingers along its damp surface. She was reluctant to move it from where it had been safely hidden for so many years.

Carmichael yelled at her to hurry up.

She closed her eyes and sighed. She seized the leather-bound handles and heaved the bag toward her. It was surprisingly heavy. Struggling to breathe, she wrestled the bag down the tunnel and to the ledge. As soon as she was almost clear, Carmichael grabbed her by the back of her shirt and held her tightly as he hauled the bag out the rest of the way. His eyes were bright with excitement.

"Finally!" He gazed at the locked bag. He gave a short, harsh laugh as he turned toward Gwen. "Well, missy, I gotta thank you for helpin' me find what's rightfully mine." His ugly face contorted with what Gwen supposed was a smile. "Too bad you ain't gonna be around to help me spend it." Without warning, he flung Gwen away from him and off the ledge.

Gwen screamed as she hit the raging floodwaters below. The river's powerful current dragged her beneath the churning water. Her head popped up above the wild surface of the river for just a moment. She gulped a great lungful of air before she was yanked back under. Again and again she struggled to rise above the water only to be pulled back into the murky depths, freezing water filling her nose and mouth. She tried to swim to the shore where she might find something to grab onto, but the throbbing in her ribs, the numbing cold and the strong current of the river quickly sapped her flagging strength.

Gwen was exhausted, her arms and legs like lead. She was too tired to fight any longer. It was then she spied a pair of moss-covered boulders rising above the water a few feet away. *I don't want to die!* Gwen gathered her strength for one last effort and lunged toward the boulders. Her fingertips brushed the slippery surface of the nearest boulder then slid off. "No! "The last of her strength was gone.

In that final moment it felt as if someone gave her a strong push, and Gwen grabbed onto one of the boulders, wedging herself between them. Her wild tumbling trip down the river had come to a stop.

Gwen panted in pain, her ribs screaming in protest. Stiffly, she wrapped her numb arms around the nearest rock and held on, breathless and choking on the swallowed river water. She rested her face against the cold, wet stone, shivering violently as she tried to regain some of her dwindling strength. Where was Carmichael? Had he hurt Lance? Fear for her brother's safety brought a surge of unexpected energy. She had to find Lance.

Gwen whipped her head around trying to get her bearings. She was about fifty yards down river from the bridge. She frowned in confusion as she peered through the curtain of rain. The bridge looked different, older somehow. *It seems kind of blurry. Almost like it's covered in mist.* Maybe it was the effect of the rain?

As she stared, a tingling rushed through her body. A young man appeared at one end of the bridge. She inhaled sharply. It was Charlie! He seemed a little blurred, just like the bridge. Charlie hesitated and looked back the way he'd come. He then turned and sprinted across the bridge. He was halfway when a second figure appeared. Gwen's eyes went wide as she recognized the bulky raccoon coat.

Bertie Carmichael!

Bertie thrust out his arm, a gun in his hand and fired. Gwen saw the flash but there was no sound. It was like watching television with the volume on mute. Charlie staggered, turned and fired his own pistol. Bertie took a step back then fired again. Charlie clutched his chest and stumbled against the railing. The wood gave way beneath his weight, and Charlie tumbled over the edge into the river. In an instant, he was gone.

Bertie hurried over and looked down. Then he raised his eyes and met Gwen's; it was if he saw her despite the distance. Gwen couldn't breathe, could barely think. There was no doubt, it *was* Bertie. He stared at her for the briefest of moments and then he too vanished.

Gwen's mind whirled as she gasped for air. Had that been the end of Charlie's life, played out just as it had happened eighty years ago? Bertie *had* killed Charlie. As she tried to come to grips with what she'd just witnessed, a movement caught her eye. Carmichael's massive form lumbered along the top of the bluff toward the bridge. The heavy bag was clutched firmly in his arms.

"No!" she cried against the roar of the river. "He can't win. It's not fair."

Carmichael stepped onto the wooden bridge and began to cross. Suddenly another figure materialized on the far side of the bridge. It stood facing Carmichael. At first, Carmichael didn't seem to notice. Gwen blinked, trying to clear the water from her eyes.

Carmichael, nearly to the far side now, slowed and came to a stop as he finally noticed the image before him. The large man stood frozen for several long moments then took a few stumbling steps back as the figure approached. It was then Gwen really got a good look at the mysterious figure and almost cheered. It was Charlie Andersson. He had returned. She blinked and rubbed her eyes. This time he looked as real and solid as Carmichael.

Charlie advanced, his head low, ready to fight. He thrust out his hand. Carmichael clutched the bag to his chest and firmly shook his head.

Gwen was mesmerized by the scene. Forgotten were her pain, her fear and her desperate situation.

Charlie demanded justice for all the sins committed against him and his family.

She prayed he got it.

His head wildly swinging back and forth, searching for an escape, Carmichael continued to back away. Step by step, Charlie pushed forward until he was but a foot or two away from his quarry. Pushed against the bridge railing, Carmichael froze, yet still he refused to release his death-grip on the satchel. Charlie stared at him for several long moments. Then Charlie reached forward, grabbed the bag and yanked it roughly from Carmichael's grasp. Once the bag was his possession, Charlie stepped back , gave Carmichael a mocking salute then simply vanished.

Gwen's eyes went wide as a second later the bridge began to fade until it too blinked out of existence. Gwen buried her face against the rock as Carmichael's terrified screams reached her. Then it was silent. Gwen lifted her head and scanned the river for any sign of Bob Carmichael, but it was if he'd never existed. He was gone. And so, too, was the money.

CHAPTER TWENTY-SIX

Gwen quickly became aware once more of her precarious situation. She was so tired, her body numb. She could barely feel the rocks beneath her. All she wanted was sleep. She shook herself and looked around. She saw no way of escape. The bluff was at least twenty feet away. She didn't have the strength to fight the water even over that short distance. If she let go of the rocks she was dead. She shivered uncontrollably. She closed her eyes, praying for deliverance.

"Gwen!" She stirred. "*Gwen!* Where are you?" Gwen's eyes slowly slid open. She'd almost dozed off. Had someone called her? She listened carefully trying to hear anything over the roar of the river around her.

"*Gwen!*" The voice sounded scared and desperate.

Gwen frowned, trying to get her muddled mind to work. Then it hit her–Molly!

Gwen opened her mouth to reply, but all that came out was a hoarse croak. She swallowed and tried again. It was no better. Now she heard more voices. *Great.* Her weariness was overtaking her. *Molly brought friends.* The voices seemed to be getting closer.

"There she is," someone shouted.

It all seemed like a dream. She was so tired of holding onto this cold rock. Maybe she should just let go so she could take a nap.

No! Hold on! Help is coming. Gwen's eyes fluttered open. Who said that? It sounded like Charlie. She peered around. Someone spoke above her. She looked up.

"Hang on, Gwen!" Her sister Faye was white-faced with terror. "The police rescue team is on its way to get you!"

Gwen nodded and tried to embrace the rock more firmly. Her arms were so numb she knew it was only a matter of time before she lost her grip entirely. The water had risen farther and was now up to her neck. She coughed violently as she swallowed a mouthful of the brown water. Her ribs screamed in pain. With a gasp, she slipped farther into the water.

"Gwen!" This voice was male, deep and reassuring. "I'm Office McPherson. I'm on my way down. Don't let go! Do you understand me? *Do…not…let…go*!"

"Okay," Gwen whispered. She heard noises above as the policeman was lowered down on a rope. She wanted to watch, but it just seemed like too much effort. It was *all* too much effort. She was so cold, so weary. She closed her eyes. None of it seemed to matter. As darkness began to embrace her, her hold on the rock loosened. As she began to sink under the dark surface of the water, a tight grip grabbed on her arm and then nothing.

Gwen lay warm and snug in her bed. *What weird dreams I have these days.* She fought the urge to wake up. She just wanted to sleep. She couldn't remember the last time she'd felt this tired.

"Gwen? Gwennie, honey, can you hear me?"

Gwen finally forced her eyes open and met the worried ones of her mother. Gwen blinked and slowly made out the room. She frowned. She seemed to be in a hospital bed.

"Mom?" Why was she in a hospital bed? Had she been in an accident? Gwen's head spun.

Her mother smiled, tears shimmering in her eyes. "Yes, sweetheart, it's me. How do you feel?"

Gwen considered this question. Her entire body ached as if someone had pounded on her with a baseball bat. She tried to sit up and gasped at the pain in her ribs.

"Oh be careful, Gwennie!" Her mother took her hand. "You cracked a few ribs. The doctor said you should be just fine, although you'll be pretty sore for a while."

Gwen frowned as she tried to remember what had happened to her. Her eyes went wide as all the memories came flooding back. "Carmichael… He tried to kill us! Lance!" The image of her brother's inert body brought a stab of fear. "Lance--he hurt Lance."

"It's okay," soothed her mother gently. "Lance is fine. He has a mild concussion. He'll have to take it easy for a few days, but he's okay."

With a long sigh of relief, Gwen sank back against her pillows. Lance was okay. Hurt maybe, but still okay. "What happened?" She looked to her mother. "I mean, how did I get here?"

Her mother pressed her lips together and looked away for a moment, brushing away her tears. Then she attempted a weak smile. "We almost lost you, Gwennie," Her voice broke. "The police just managed to grab you as you lost your grip. When they pulled you out, you were suffering from hypothermia and a few cracked ribs. You wouldn't have lasted much longer in that cold water." She paused and reached over to hug her daughter. "Oh, Gwennie, we were so scared! When the police called yesterday afternoon and said they were taking you and Lance to the hospital, it was all so confusing. We really weren't sure what happened."

Gwen hugged her back, trying not to think of those horrifying moments in the river. She shivered. "Did they find Bob Carmichael?"

Mom shook her head. "We know he was there since Molly said he attacked her, but the police don't know where he went."

"He fell into the river," replied Gwen, her voice flat. "He tried to kill me. Then…" she paused. There was no way she could tell her mother Carmichael met up with the ghost of Charlie Andersson on a bridge that no longer existed. She wasn't sure she believed it herself. "He…he slipped and fell into the river. He never came back up." That wasn't really a lie, and at least it sounded a lot more plausible than claiming he fell off a ghostly bridge.

"Oh, Gwen!" her mother's eyes opened wide. "What did he want? Why on earth would he try to kill you?"

"Because of the gangster's gold." Gwen sighed wearily. "We figured out where it might be and went looking for it. He must have been following us and thought we'd found it." She gave a bitter laugh. "Thing is, I didn't find it until after he started chasing me."

Gwen's mom gaped at her. "Wait. You...*found* the missing money? Where? How?"

"We figured he hid it along the river in a cave near a bridge." Gwen absently played with the edge of the blanket. "So, we started checking the three bridges between the old Andersson warehouse and Jimmy Houlihan's restaurant. Thing is, all those bridges were new. Anyway, when I was trying to get away from that creep, I climbed up onto this ledge and found a little cave. That's where the bag was."

Her mother was silent for several long moments. "What happened to it?"

Gwen took a deep breath. "Mr. Carmichael made me drag it out. Then he took it and...and pushed me into the water. I don't know what happened to it after that." She paused as the memories of that awful moment came rushing back. "I guess it fell into the water with him."

Her mother hugged her again and gently brushed the hair from her face. "I just thank God none of you were seriously hurt. You kids could have been killed. What on earth were you thinking climbing around on those steep cliffs?"

Gwen secretly smiled. Obviously her mother had passed from the "Thank God, you're all right" phase into the "Whose stupid idea was this in the first place?" stage. She knew everything would be all right.

Later that day, after Gwen had told her story to the police, both Lance and Molly came to visit.

"I can't believe that jerk hit me in the head." Lance rubbed the back of his head. "I never even saw him."

"Thanks for saving us, Molly." Gwen gripped her friend's hand tightly. "I'd be dead now if you hadn't brought help."

Molly ducked her head. "I was so afraid you'd think I'd abandoned you," she replied in a low voice. "I ran to the park as fast as I could and found Faye. She called for help. When the police got there, I showed them where you were."

Molly glanced at Lance. "We found Lance right away, but I got so scared when we couldn't find you or Creepy Carmichael. Then when we saw you in the river, I thought you were a goner." She looked at Gwen as tears threatened to overflow.

"If you'd been any later, I would have been." Gwen shuddered and tried very hard *not* to think about how close she'd come to drowning. They all sat in silence for a few minutes.

"It's too bad we never found the money," sighed Molly sadly. "That would have been so awesome."

Gwen hesitated then leaned forward and with a smile and whispered, "I did."

Lance and Molly gaped at her open-mouthed.

"What?" Lance grabbed her by the hand. "You really found it? Where is it?"

Gwen grimaced and shrugged. "I don't know. In the river, I guess. I found it in a little cave when I was trying to escape from Carmichael. There were some rocks piled in the entrance so you wouldn't know there was an opening unless you were really looking. When I pulled away the rocks, trying to find a place to hide, I found the bag." She frowned. "I never got a chance to open it though. Carmichael showed up and made me give it to him."

"Well, that's that then." Lance slumped in his seat. "Carmichael got away with all the cash, and we got nothing."

"He didn't get away." Gwen pictured that last scene on the spectral bridge. "He fell in the river and disappeared. I'm not sure if he had the bag or not. It was…kind of hard to see." It would be even harder to explain that a ghost took it.

Lance brightened immediately. "Then maybe it's still around there someplace."

Gwen shrugged. "I think it probably fell into the river with Carmichael." She was sure she'd seen the bag disappear with Charlie before Carmichael fell into the water, but had she really? It felt like a dream now. She hadn't exactly been in her right mind at that point, so who knew what really happened?

"Well, I still wanna go back and look." Lance's jaw was set.

Gwen gave a little laugh. "I don't think Mom will ever let us go 'fishing' again."

CHAPTER TWENTY-SEVEN

Gwen was allowed to go home the next day, but her mother refused to let either her or Lance out of the house.

"After what you two pulled?" Her face was red. "No way! You guys can just stay here. The doctor said you both were to take it easy, so you can do just that."

"Don't worry," said Lance as they settled into lounge chairs on the veranda. "Give her a few days and we'll be fine. I really do want you to show me where you found the money, even if it isn't still there. I just wanna see what we were looking for."

Gwen nodded, wincing at the pain in her ribs as she tried to get comfortable. "Yeah, I'd like to go back, too. It all seemed so unreal. Maybe going back will make it seem more like it actually happened."

Lance grinned. "Well, there you go. We just need to convince Mom to let us go back so you can work this all out in your mind. You know, like therapy. She's so worried you've been totally traumatized by all of this, she's been talkin' about finding you a therapist."

Gwen gaped at him, appalled at the thought. She didn't need a therapist. "That's just stupid." She folded her arms across chest and rolled her eyes. "Carmichael is gone for good. I saw him fall into the river. Sure it was scary, but I'm okay. I know he can't hurt me again."

"I know that." Lance leaned back into the cushions. "But Mom and Dad don't. Besides, maybe it really will be therapeutic. You did have a pretty rough time."

Gwen stared off toward the horizon as her hand unconsciously traced the thin red line etched across her throat. A sailboat was off in the distance. "Yeah, I'll admit I was really scared, but it happened so fast. A lot of it seems more like a dream, or like it happened to somebody else."

"Well, we'll give Mom a few days then see what happens." Lance closed his eyes and basked in the warm summer sun. "We'll get there eventually."

Gwen nodded, but her mind was elsewhere. Had Charlie really saved her again? Had he pushed her to the rocks? She hadn't felt his presence since she'd gotten home, but she was sure he hadn't left. He'd certainly gotten his revenge against the Carmichael family, but his innocence still hadn't been proven. Gwen believed he wouldn't leave until she could show everyone he hadn't taken the cash. That would only happen if she could find the bag of money. She leaned back against the lounge chair, staring up at the brilliant blue sky enjoying the cool breeze caressing her skin. She had no idea how to find the bag now. As far as she knew, it was at the bottom of the river. She sighed. It was hopeless.

Suddenly, a thought occurred to her. Now that she knew where the money had been hidden, couldn't she go back in time again and find it? She sat up as her heart began to race. If she could find the money back in the nineteen twenties, then the family would know Charlie hadn't run off with it! They could return it to Jimmy Houlihan, and maybe everything would be okay.

Gwen could barely sit still as she pictured the

doorframe in the attic. There was one more date with Gwen's name on it. She was sure of it. That should mean she could go back one more time. She'd have to go check it out, but Gwen was certain the date was in August, just a few weeks away. How wonderful it would be if she could prove Charlie's innocence in his own time, when it really mattered. She smiled and paused. Would it somehow change the future? Well, so what? It'd be worth it. Then Charlie would truly be free.

For several days, Gwen thought of little else but how she was going to find the money and save Charlie. It was going to be the most important thing she'd ever done, and it needed a lot of planning. She couldn't wait for August 12, the final date. She wasn't sure how she was going to last until then. Her mother solved that problem.

"Gwen," said her mother one morning. "Molly's mother called. The family is going to their cabin up in the mountains, and they want to invite you to come along. Molly gets really bored being there by herself and would love to have a friend come along. I told them you would."

At first Gwen was going to protest. She'd been looking forward to some peace and quiet, her pile of books and, of course, working on her plans to help Charlie, but then she hesitated. Was that what she really wanted? It'd be nice to get away from the construction for a couple of weeks. Her books weren't going anywhere, and she'd be back well before August 12. She wasn't too sure about this camping stuff, but if nothing else, it'd make the time go by faster. "Okay, Mom." Spending two weeks with Molly might actually be fun, even it was in the middle of the woods. "That'll be great."

"Lance," their dad went over the list of the day's chores. "We think it would be good for you to get away for a while, too. We talked to Matt's parents back in D.C. They said Matt is driving them nuts asking when you can come back to visit, so we thought now would be a good time. A couple of weeks away from here would be good for you. Faye just got a part-time job working at the local theater here, so she's going to be busy too. We feel bad a lot of your summer has involved working on the house. What do you think?"

Gwen knew Lance really missed his best friend. He and Matt chatted online every night.

"That'll be really great Dad." Lance grinned. "Matt told me about a new skate park that just opened near him, and it sounds awesome." That quickly, it was all settled.

Gwen called Molly right after breakfast, and the two girls excitedly planned their trip. Molly's mother had also kept Molly close to home after the incident at the river, so Gwen hadn't seen much of her lately. Starting the next day, they'd spend two whole weeks together. Gwen spent most of the day packing and repacking as she tried to decide exactly what to bring. She'd never been camping before and wasn't sure what she'd need.

When Gwen arrived at the lake cabin with Molly

and her family, she checked out her new surroundings uncertainly. It seemed so…rustic. As Molly's dad outlined the list of activities he'd planned, her stomach knotted. Kayaking? Hiking in the mountains? Camping in a tent? Man, this really didn't sound like something she would have agreed to. But, she smiled politely and tried to act excited. *Gwen,* she scolded herself as she got ready for bed that night. *After what you've been through, hiking through bear country should be a piece of cake. Quit being such a baby.* After that, she vowed to quit whining and have fun.

One evening as she and Molly sat outside by the fire pit roasting hotdogs on sticks, Gwen decided the time had come to tell Molly the full story of what happened with Carmichael. She quickly ran through the entire story, including seeing Charlie's demise at the hands of Bertie.

"You really saw Bertie shoot Charlie on a ghost bridge?" Molly's eyes narrowed. "Then after Charlie took the money from Carmichael, the bridge disappeared, and Carmichael fell into the river? *That's* what you saw?"

Gwen nodded with a shrug. It did sound pretty far-fetched, but no worse than anything else that had happened to her so far this summer. "That's what I saw. I know you don't believe me, but that's what happened."

"Well," Molly frowned at her smoking hotdog, "you gotta admit it sounds pretty weird. However, I'm not surprised a Carmichael did him in. If that Bertie was anything like our current creep, it makes sense." She paused and cocked her head. "You said Charlie shot at Bertie, right? We found a hole and a bullet in that raccoon coat. I think that proves Bertie was the killer."

Gwen nodded. "That's what I think. It all fits." She paused. "Molly, there's more, but I'm afraid if you didn't think I was nuts before, you will now."

Molly looked up and tilted her head. "I'm not sure anything could be crazier than what you've told me so far. Go ahead. I promise I won't have you locked away someplace."

Gwen bit her lip, took a deep breath and plunged ahead. "I've actually been able to go back in time to the nineteen twenties. I've met Charlie in real life and his whole family. I can go back on the dates written on the closet door. If I go into the closet on one of those dates, I end up in the past. I…uh…"

Molly had a look of stark disbelief.

"You…go…back…in time," said Molly slowly, as if trying to translate this information into something that made sense. "Back to the nineteen twenties, and you do it by going through a…a *closet*? What kind of time machine is *that*?"

Gwen sat silent, regretting having said anything.

Molly stared at her for a few minutes. "You're serious, aren't you? You really think you've gone back in time?"

Gwen looked at her now smoldering hot dog. "I don't *think*, I *know*. I know it sounds crazy, Molly, but I've really met all these people. I heard George

Carmichael plotting to have Charlie ambushed and killed for that money."

Now Molly was speechless. "Wow. Um, so why didn't you tell Charlie and warn him?"

"I got sick." Gwen sighed miserably. "Then I started forgetting who I was, and the other Gwen's memories seemed to be taking over. I was afraid I'd lose myself completely, so I went back to the closet and came back home. I think I can go back one more time. August twelfth, nineteen twenty-four. I know Charlie was dead by then, but at least I could get the money back and prove to everyone he didn't leave town with it. Maybe the business wouldn't go bankrupt and Uncle Jonas wouldn't lose everything."

Molly was silent for a long time. "You know, I actually believe you." She laughed. "Maybe I'm as crazy as you are. That is so amazing! What would happen if you do go back, get the money and prove Charlie is innocent? I mean, would it affect things in the future?"

Gwen shrugged. "I don't know, but I have to try. Why else have I been able to do any of this? I think I'm supposed to prove he's innocent, and this is the only way I know how."

The rest of their camping trip sped by, and soon it was time to go home. Gwen found it more and more difficult to sleep knowing she'd soon be going back to see Tom and Aunt Katherine again. She missed them, and knowing this would be the last time she could see them made her impending trip bittersweet.

When Molly's father dropped her off, Gwen waved

good-bye then ran into the house to see Faye and her parents. Lance wouldn't be home until the following day. "Mom!" She dumped her stuff in the front hall. "I'm home! Where are you?"

There were noises above her.

Gwen ran upstairs. The noise came from the attic. She paused for a moment then ran up the stairs as fast as she could. She reached the landing, her heart pounding, and stared into the playroom with growing alarm.

Her father looked up from the debris of what had once been the playroom. The walls had been stripped down to their studs. "Gwennie!" He grinned, wiping sawdust from his brow. "You're home! How was your trip?"

Gwen stood speechless as she stared at the remains of the closet. Like the rest of the walls, it had been stripped and there was nothing left of the original doorframe or the height marks. She felt sick. Finally, she turned to her father "What are you *doing?*" Her voice broke as she fought back the tears. "What have you done?"

Dad blinked and looked around the attic in confusion. "I'm taking down the old wallboards."

"But why are you doing it *now?*" Tears trailed down Gwen's cheeks.

Her father frowned and raised his hands as he took a step toward her. "Why not now? I decided to get a head start while I wait for some of the supplies I need for downstairs. Gwennie, what's wrong? What have I done?"

Gwen stopped. How could she explain how important the marks on the woodwork had been to her? Her father couldn't possibly understand.

He stood staring at her, an anxious look on his face.

"Nothing, Dad. Nothing at all." Gwen whirled and pounded back down the stairs and out of the house, tears flowing freely as she ran down to the beach to the hideout. There she collapsed into one of the beanbag chairs as violent sobs wracked her body. It was all ruined now. She could never go back and prove Charlie's innocence. She could never save him.

She wept long and hard, pouring out all her anger and disappointment. She knew it wasn't really her father's fault. He didn't know, but if only he could have waited another week to start his remodeling. If only. Finally, when she'd exhausted all her tears, Gwen lay wearily in the gentle embrace of the old beanbag chair. She sat up and felt around in the dim light provided by her small flashlight for one of the electric lanterns. A soft light pushed back the gloom. She climbed to her feet and sat at the little table. It felt cold and lonely in the hideout now.

"Gwen?" Her mother called her name, but she sat silently, not wanting to talk to anyone. "Gwen?" The voice was closer now. Gwen realized her mother was making her way up the tunnel into the hideout. A moment later she was there.

Gwen sat cradling her head in the semi-darkness,

still not saying a word.

Her mother approached quietly and took a seat in the opposite chair. She reached out and gently took Gwen's hand.

"Honey," she said softly. "What's wrong? Dad said you took one look at the attic and ran off in tears. Was there something up there you wanted?"

Oh, how could she possibly explain? How could she explain she wanted to travel back in time to find some hidden money and prove the innocence of a long dead boy? There was no way her parents would understand that. They'd think it was some dream or fantasy game.

Gwen wiped her tears. She knew she had to give some kind of answer. She sniffed miserably. "There were measuring marks on the closet doorframe." She looked at the table. "They were from when Dad's grandfather was a kid. They were really special to me, and now they're gone forever."

Her mother frowned. "Measuring marks? On the closet doorframe?"

Gwen nodded and looked at her mom, tears filling her eyes once more. "Mom, it made it seem like those people were real! Well, I know they were real, but real to me. Now they're gone. It's like they never existed."

Mom's shoulders slumped as she squeezed Gwen's hand. "Oh, wow. I had no idea. I know your dad didn't either. That would have meant a lot to him, too. What a shame."

Gwen could tell her mother really felt bad about it,

but what good would that do? The damage was done. The money was gone, and now her plans for going back and proving Charlie's innocence had been destroyed. She felt as if she'd been cheated.

Her mom gently wiped a tear from Gwen's cheek. "C'mon, sweetie. Let's go explain what happened to your dad. He's really worried about you."

Gwen nodded again and forlornly trailed her mother back to the house.

Dad stood on the front porch. He ran down the steps when Gwen and her mother arrived. "Gwen," his brow furrowed, "are you okay?" He placed his hand on her shoulder.

Gwen's mother quickly explained about the measuring marks.

Dad's face fell. "Oh no!" He looked at Gwen. "I had no idea they were there. I would have at least tried to save them. Oh, Gwen, I'm so sorry." He reached out and drew his daughter into a big hug.

Gwen hugged him. It was hard to stay angry with her dad for very long even if her heart had been broken.

CHAPTER TWENTY-EIGHT

Lance came home the following day. Five minutes later he pounded up the stairs and burst into her room with a big grin.

"Hey, ugly, what's goin' on?"

Gwen gave him a wan smile. "Nothing much." She paused a moment. "Mom said we could go back to the river once you got back. Then I can show you where the money was." Somehow, it just didn't seem that important any more.

"Cool! I told Matt all about what happened. He can't believe all that went down in some Podunk little town in the middle of nowhere. He wants to know when he can come up. Guess he figures next we'll go hunting for pirate treasure."

A moment later he was gone, and Gwen was left to her own unhappy thoughts. She still hadn't seen Charlie, although she felt he was still around. She sensed he wanted to tell her something. *I'm so sorry I failed you, Charlie.* There was a lump in her throat as she fought back the tears that constantly threatened to overflow.

That evening Lance brought up the subject of going back to the river to see the cave. After some initial hesitation, Dad agreed to take them the following day. Gwen called Molly to invite her along.

"It's all good," replied Molly a few minutes later. "Mom said I could go to the river with you as long as your dad goes. I want to see that mysterious cave. After all we went through it's the least I deserve." She hesitated. "I'm really sorry you couldn't go back again and help Charlie."

Gwen took a deep breath and wiped away an errant tear. "Thanks, Molly. I'll see you tomorrow."

The following afternoon, Gwen's dad picked Molly up on the way to the park.

Gwen greeted her with a smile but was still depressed and out of sorts. Going back to the cave would just remind her of her failure to save Charlie.

When they arrived at the park, Lance led the way toward the last bridge. Silently they stood and stared at the area where so much had happened. It was a quiet summer afternoon. A soft breezed ruffled Gwen's hair. The river was much lower and calmer than it had been the day they were attacked by Bob Carmichael. Gwen ambled along the trail, half-heartedly studying the slope of the bluff down to the river as she looked for the old post that had prevented her from sliding into the river. Not that it mattered now.

Then she saw it: a large wooden pylon maybe two feet tall embedded in the rock a few feet from the river's edge. Suddenly, Gwen's heartbeat quickened. An unexpected urge to find the cave became almost overwhelming. Nimbly, she scrambled down the slope, afraid her father would stop her, but he said nothing.

Gwen climbed over the rocks and brush down to the support. She turned and looked back up the slope. There! The small ledge was above her. Taking a deep breath, she began the ascent. Her sense of urgency grew as if the cave physically pulled her in. Panting a little from the exertion, she finally struggled onto the ledge and looked around. With a shudder, she clearly recalled the bulk of Bob Carmichael looming above her. She could still hear his menacing voice demanding she get the bag or he'd hurt Lance. She shivered and rubbed her arms. *It's okay. Carmichael's gone for good.* Her mother had told her the night before that they had finally found Carmichael's body near the mouth of the river. He could never hurt her again.

Gwen now turned and peered into the short tunnel then dropped to her hands and knees and made her way into the small cave. It was chilly in there. Her nose filled with the earthy smell of wet stone.

Oh, Charlie! Her throat tightened as she settled against the back wall. She had been *so* close to retrieving the bag, only to have it snatched away at the last moment by that jerk, Carmichael. She wanted to scream in frustration as she pounded her fist against the damp rock. Tears streamed down her cheeks. Why? Why did all this happen if she wasn't going to be able to help? What was the point? She sniffled miserably and closed her eyes. She frowned. There was another odor here. It had kind of a musty animal smell. She'd smelled it before but couldn't quite place it.

She opened her eyes and pulled out her small penlight. She flashed it around the cave and froze. She rubbed her eyes and blinked. It was there. Sitting exactly where she'd originally seen it was the old, mildewed leather bag.

Mouth open, Gwen stared stupidly at the bag, trying to make sense of it. She *knew* she'd pulled it out. In fact, she could still see the drag marks from when she pulled it along behind her. It had disappeared on the bridge. So how could it have possibly gotten back in the cave? Shivering, she became aware of a drop in the temperature. She turned and there, a few feet away from her, Charlie grinned happily.

"Charlie!" she gasped. "You! You put it back, didn't you?"

Charlie nodded, still smiling. Then his grin faded, and Gwen heard a faint voice. *Tell my brother, Gwen. Tell him I didn't take it.*

"I will, Charlie." Gwen reached out to him, "I'll tell them all. This proves your innocence. They'll all know you didn't steal it."

Charlie smiled again a little sadly this time. *Good-bye, Gwen. Thank you.*

Fresh tears prickled the backs of her eyes. "Good-bye, Charlie. I…I'll miss you."

He nodded then grinned and gave her wink. He lifted his hand in farewell and slowly faded away. Gwen stared at the place where he'd been and wiped away her tears. "I *will* tell them, Charlie!" She grabbed hold of the bag and began dragging it out behind her.

She reached the ledge just as the others appeared. "Hey, Gwen!" Lance climbed up onto the ledge. "Where are you?"

"I found it! The bag with the money--it was here

after all!"

The others gathered around her as she dragged the heavy bag onto the ledge. They stared at it unable to speak.

"Well, I'll be…" Dad shook his head as examined the cracked leather. "It sure looks like it could be the real thing!" He gently touched the lock then pulled his hand back. He looked at the others. "C'mon. Let's get it up to the car. I know your mom and Faye will definitely want to see this."

Gwen's thoughts whirled. She couldn't believe what had just happened. Charlie put the money back, and now they could prove he was innocent! She grinned as she clambered back up the hill. She felt so light she could almost fly. She practically skipped down the trail back to the car where Dad stowed the bag in the trunk.

"I can't believe we found the missing gangster's gold!" Molly bounced up and down in her seat. "This is *so* awesome. Grandma's gonna have a heart attack when she hears."

"Well, hold on," Dad glanced at the group. "We don't know for sure this *is* the missing money. It could be somebody's lost laundry for all we know. But here," he handed Molly his cell phone, "go ahead and call your grandmother. See if she wants to meet us at the house for the grand opening."

To Gwen it was the longest twenty minutes of her life. She thought they'd never get home.

Dad hauled the bag out of the trunk and dropped it on the porch table. Faye and Mom soon joined them, open- mouthed as they gaped at the old bag.

Molly's grandmother pulled in a few minutes later. "I don't think I've ever driven so fast in my life." She laughed as she joined them on the veranda. "Oh my, this really looks like it could be it, doesn't it?"

Everyone gathered around. Gwen chewed her lip as her dad first unbuckled the two straps at either end then tried the lock in the center. It wouldn't give. "We may have to break it. I doubt we could even pick the thing. It's probably full of rust."

Lance ran into the house and came back with his father's toolbox.

Dad took a screwdriver and inserted the tip into the keyhole then struck it hard with a hammer. The lock snapped open.

Unable to breathe, Gwen watched as her father carefully pulled open the wide mouth of the suitcase to reveal a layer of black oilcloth. Bit by bit, he pulled away the oilcloth to reveal the contents. He stepped back so Gwen could get a better look.

A wave of dizziness washed over her. She couldn't catch her breath. The bag was filled with stacks and stacks of neatly bound cash.

In silence, they all stared at the fortune before them.

Suddenly, Lance let loose a wild whoop of victory. "We *found* it!" He danced around joyfully punching the air. "We're rich!"

A second later, Molly, Faye and Gwen joined him, dancing and screaming, while the three adults stood by with huge grins.

"You know what this means, don't you?" Mrs. Berger carefully examined a stack of bills. "This proves without a doubt Charlie Andersson did *not* run off with the money."

Mom felt deeper into the bag and brought out what looked like an old black ledger buried beneath the stacks of cash. "What's this?"

Dad took it and briefly studied the contents. "I'm no expert, but to me, it looks like an old account book from my great-grandfather's company."

"I bet it proves this money was stolen from Jonas Andersson!" Gwen stood nearby. "That would make it ours."

Dad ran a hand through his hair. "Why, you could be right. We'll need to get an accountant to look into this and see what they think. There's an awful lot of money here."

"There should be about two hundred fifty thousand dollars." Molly's grandmother looked into the bag. "Or at least that's what the story always claimed."

"Well, even after taxes, that money would go a long way to fixing up this house." Dad grinned. "We really need to find out." He paused, his face dropping. "Actually, it wouldn't belong to us. It would belong to my grandfather, William Andersson."

Mrs. Berger looked at him, eyebrows raised. "Your grandfather is still alive?"

Dad nodded as he tossed a stack of bills back into the bag. "Yeah, he lives in a retirement home in New

York." His face brightened. "Well, the news that old Uncle Charlie wasn't the scumbag Grandpa always said he was might make him happier, but," he paused with a wry grin. "I doubt it."

The following week was a quiet one for Gwen; no visits from dead relatives, no journeys into the past and definitely no hairbreadth escapes from crazy nutjobs. Life began to settle down into a normal, quiet routine.

One morning as she sat reading the comics in the newspaper, her dad came and sat down beside her.

Gwen looked up.

"Gwen, you and I are going on a little trip."

Gwen frowned. "Trip? Where?"

"We're going to drive down to New York to visit Grandpa Bill. Since you're the one who found the money, I feel it's only fitting you be the one to tell him about it. And Charlie." Dad laid the scrap of newspaper about the dead youth on the table. Gwen had shown it to him earlier. "And I've got to agree with you. I think this was Charlie they found. I also wouldn't doubt that it was George Carmichael who had him killed, although I guess we'll never be able to prove that."

"I think Charlie would want his brother to know he didn't steal that money, and I bet he's the one that put that ledger in the bag so he could prove Carmichael was stealing the money from the company."

"You may be right, honey." Her dad smiled. "Well, pack your stuff. We'll be driving down to New York, and I'd like to leave this afternoon. We'll just be gone a couple of days."

Gwen wasn't sure how she felt as they made the long drive to her great-grandfather's retirement home. She remembered William as being rather stuck-up and full of himself. According to her father, it didn't sound like he'd changed much over the years, but still, she was determined he know the truth about Charlie.

Oak Hills Retirement Center was a lovely establishment set on a wooded estate in Utica, New York. There was a small lake surrounded by a large central building and a number of smaller homes and condos. Gwen's father explained the houses and condos were for older people who could live on their own, while in the main building were small apartments for those who needed more help. Her great-grandfather, now well into his nineties, lived in the main building.

"Does he know we're coming?" Gwen twisted a lock of her hair as they climbed the stone steps to the entry hall and lobby.

"Yes. I called the staff this morning to let them know we were coming." Dad carried the old leather bag.

A receptionist greeted them at the front desk and smiled warmly. "You must be Mr. Andersson's family. I know his caregiver, Jenny, told him you were coming." She hesitated.

Dad laughed. "Don't tell me, he was less than thrilled."

"Well, some of our residents are more excited about visitors than others." She made a call and a few minutes later, a short black woman with sparkling eyes and a ready smile came to meet them.

"Hello!" She grinned and shook their hands. "I'm Jenny, Mr. Andersson's primary caregiver. You must be Michael and Gwen."

"Yep. I know Grandpa doesn't have much use for family, but we have something really important to tell him. We drove all way down from Maine to see him. We'll try to keep it short."

"Mr. Andersson, your grandfather is one stubborn old goat. Not many can work with him, but him and me, we got an understanding and get along just fine. I know deep down, he's excited you came to see him, but believe me, he won't show it."

Dad nodded and together, he and Gwen followed Jenny down a series of hallways before they stopped outside a door near the end of the last hall. Jenny knocked then opened the door. "Mr. Andersson?" she stepped in. "You've got visitors."

The room was dimly lit by a small table lamp. All the drapes had been tightly drawn and Gwen could just make out a man sitting stiffly at a small table in the corner of the room.

"Well, come in if you're coming."

Gwen gave a little gasp. Even now, she readily recognized William Andersson's deep voice and the sharp edges to his words.

Dad gave her a little push, and they entered the room.

Jenny gave them an encouraging smile and disappeared as she closed the door behind them.

"Grandpa?" began Dad a little hesitantly. "It's me,

Michael, and my daughter, Gwen."

"Gwen?" the voice suddenly sounded very old and confused.

Gwen looked to her father, who looked as bewildered as she felt.

"Come here, girl," grumbled the old man. "Let me get a better look at you."

Gwen stepped closer to her great-grandfather and peered through the shadows to try and get a better look at him. He sat ramrod straight and was still as thin as he'd been as a young man. His bright blue eyes stared hard at her for several moments. "No, I was wrong. You're not Gwen."

Gwen took a step closer. "What happened to Gwen?" She was afraid of the answer.

William's eyes went blank as he stared far into the distance, or perhaps into the past. "She died." His voice was barely above a whisper. "Twelve years old and pneumonia took her. She never was strong after the scarlet fever almost killed her. Got so the family couldn't even afford a doctor and so… she died." He shook himself and brought himself back to the present and scowled at her. "So, what d'you want? Couldn't be bothered to visit me before, so why now?"

Gwen stood frozen. The other Gwen had *died*? She shivered, lightheaded for a moment. It was as if part of her had died. She'd figured Gwen had passed away by this time, but not as a child. She blinked away the unexpected tears and returned her attention to her great-grandfather, who glared at her impatiently.

"I…I came to give you something," said Gwen quietly. She turned to her father, who handed her the heavy bag. With some effort, Gwen lifted the bag and dropped it heavily on the table before William. "I think this belongs to you."

William stared at the bag as if it might bite him. He glanced over at Gwen and Dad then slowly, tentatively he opened the bag. With a gasp, his eyes wide, the old man gazed at the stacks of cash still in their original wrappings. "What is the meaning of this?" His eyes were glued to the money.

"It's the missing money." Gwen's words tumbled out. "The money everyone thought Charlie stole. I found it. He never took the money. He hid it in a cave along the river. George Carmichael and Uncle Frank stole the money from the company. They planned to kill Charlie then tell Houlihan Charlie had run off with the cash and keep it themselves. Bertie Carmichael shot Charlie and he fell into the river. But nobody knew what happened to the money, so Mr. Carmichael let everyone think Charlie ran off with it." She paused and turned to look at her grandfather. "Charlie was innocent."

William Andersson looked up again and stared hard at Gwen, his eyes wide. "Gwen," he whispered, his voice quavering. Gwen knew he wasn't seeing her but the Gwen long gone. He looked back down at the bag. Slowly, he reached in and brought out a packet of money, staring at it as if he didn't know what it was. Suddenly his shoulders sagged, and he buried his face in his hand. "Oh my God, Charlie! I am so sorry!" His body shook with deep sobs now.

Dad blinked in confusion, glued to the spot.

Gwen moved closer and gently placed her hand on the old man's shoulder.

"It's all right, William." She didn't see him as her aged great-grandfather, but as her young cousin trying to figure out how to keep a family from falling apart. "Charlie only wanted to help the family. I think he stole the company ledger to prove Carmichael and Uncle Frank were stealing the money. We found it in the bag with the money. Charlie was good. He didn't want to work for Carmichael. He only did it to help the family. He never would have stolen that money and left the family to suffer if he could help it."

"I know." William sobbed, not looking at her. "I was just so *angry*! It was easier to believe he ran off and was alive somewhere than the alternative." The old man eventually brought his emotions under control. He sat back in his chair, wiping his eyes and nose with an old handkerchief. He studied Gwen again.

"Little Gwennie was a great kid. Some ways you look a lot like her, but I can see you're not her. She was such a shy little thing..." He gave a hoarse laugh. "You sure talk like her. I'm sorry she never got the chance to grow up."

Gwen took a deep breath. "What happened to Louisa and…and Tom?"

Again, William seemed to not notice Gwen referred to his siblings as if she'd known them. "Louisa married that idiot Bertie, but he had a wandering eye and it wasn't long before she left and took their son with her. She married again a few years later. Nice guy. He was a lawyer. Had a couple more kids. Haven't heard anything from any of them in years. Tom," he paused and looked sad again, "was killed in the war. World War II that is. He was a pilot and his plane was shot down over Germany. He never came home."

Gwen bit back a cry of dismay. Not Tom! Maybe he'd been dead for over sixty years, but the news was as painful to her as if it had just happened. Tears began to trickle down her cheeks as she fought down a sob.

William silently handed her a Kleenex, never questioning her response. "I miss him every day," he whispered.

"He was the best," replied Gwen tearfully.

William looked at her then reached out with one arm and hugged her. "He was that." William cleared his throat and returned his attention to the bag of money. "So, you said this money was stolen from my father's business?"

Now Dad stepped forward. "Yes. I had an accountant go over the ledger, and he said it was obvious the company accountant had been covering up the fact Carmichael embezzled funds. There was probably a second set of books that made everything look legit. This money rightfully belongs to you."

William stared at the cash.

Gwen was sure he was thinking about how a simple bag of money had caused so much pain and suffering.

"I don't want it. I want you to have it." He looked

at Dad. "You can use it to send your kids to school or whatever you need it for."

"Oddly enough, Bertie Carmichael left me the old house. I'm fixing it up so we can use it as a bed and breakfast. It's a great place."

William was silent for a moment then nodded. "Guess Bertie was trying to make up for what his family did. Glad to hear it's back in the family. Good. Then use the money to make the old place look good again. It was Father's love. I know he'd be overjoyed to see it restored and have Anderssons living in it again."

"Thank you, Grandpa!" Gwen threw her arms around him and hugged him tightly.

William's eyes widened and then he gave a little pleased smile before he harrumphed and gently disengaged himself.

"Thank you, Grandpa," echoed Dad, smiling warmly at the old man who now fixedly polished his glasses.

"I expect you to send me photos when you get that white elephant all fixed up," William said sternly. "And," he hesitated, "perhaps some photos of your family."

"I'll be happy to."

"I'll write you letters!" exclaimed Gwen. "Or do you have e-mail?"

For the first time, William laughed. "Believe it or not, young lady, I do know my way around a computer. E-mail is fine if you prefer. I'd just like to hear from you from time to time. I've isolated myself for far too long."

They stayed a while longer before Jenny came back and said it was time for William's physical therapy. They bid each other farewell. Both Gwen and Dad promised to stay in touch with him. Gwen gave her great-grandfather one last hug. As they headed back to the car, Jenny called them. They waited for her to catch up.

Smiling broadly, she beamed at them. "I don't know what you told that old goat, but I've never seen him so happy in all the years I've worked with him. I just wanted to thank you for giving him a new lease on life."

Gwen and Dad exchanged glances and smiled back. "Jenny, thank you for taking care of my grandfather. I can't tell you how glad we are we came. We will definitely be staying in touch."

The rest of the summer sped by like any normal summer. The work on the house progressed rapidly, and her father declared that, with the help of the money, they could hire more workmen. He hoped the house would be ready for its first guests the following summer.

Gwen spent many long, lazy afternoons with Molly in the hideout talking about their adventures, as well as the upcoming school year. All too soon, the summer came to an end.

The night before school was due to start, Gwen stood outside on the veranda gazing at the ocean. There was a nip in the evening air, warning of colder weather to come.

This has been the most unbelievable summer of my life. Gwen had a deep sense of wonder. So much had happened. Had she really managed to go back in time or find buried treasure? Had she actually cleared Charlie's name, thus solving Fishawak's oldest mystery? It was like something she read in one of her books. Things like that didn't really happen to real people and yet, here she was with hundreds of thousands of dollars of missing gangster money. Sadness settled over her as she thought of Charlie. Had she really seen his ghost? She shook her head. None of her old friends in D.C. would ever believe any of this crazy tale. Thankfully, she now had Molly and well, okay, Lance as well, to share all of this with.

She walked along the veranda, pushing her hair from her face. She remembered spending time here with Tom playing checkers with the sound of the surf behind them. Her throat tightened. Poor Tom, who died sixty years ago in an airplane over Germany, would always be ten to her. She missed him terribly. And Gwen. The girl she'd never known but whose life had allowed her to embark on a wild ride through time. Again, she felt a pang of sadness thinking of how young the other Gwen had been when she died. All because of the missing money. She shook her head in regret. Such a waste.

A door opened and her mother called her. She paused a moment and considered the coming day. It was the start of a new school year in a new town with tons of new kids. Gwen smiled. The summer might be over, but her adventures in Maine were just beginning.

THE END

ACKNOWLEDGMENTS

There are many people I wish to thank who helped me on my journey to getting this book published. I would first like to thank my brother, Brian Van Korn, who was my biggest supporter. Whenever I doubted myself, he was the first to reassure me and gave me the confidence to go forward.

Thanks to my friends, Margie Faraday, Jacintha Mezzetti, and Reta Geer as well as my sister, Karyn Prine, all who read early versions of the book and gave me invaluable feedback. A big thank you to Dawn Dowdle who took me on as a client and taught me so much about writing. I also want to thank my online critique group who also helped me polish out the rough spots on my first novel attempt.

I want to especially thank all the children who read this and gave me their invaluable feedback, with special thanks to Kayla Burbee and Spencer Keane.

This book was a long time coming and I'm sure there are people who I have forgotten to mention who helped me over the years. I apologize if you are one of them, but it definitely took a village to get this book off the ground.

Ellen H. Reed

Finally, thanks to all of my family, who supported me along the way.

ABOUT THE AUTHOR

Ellen Reed grew up in New Jersey but moved around a good deal with husband, living in such places as Eagle River, Alaska and Jakarta, Indonesia. The mother of four children and grandmother to two, it was always her dream to write books for children. While spending a summer in Norway, she wrote and illustrated several books for her young daughter when they ran out of English language books to read. It took National Novel Writing Month in 2009 for her to finally get up the nerve to try writing an actual novel. A creative person by nature, Ellen has been involved in numerous theater groups, quilting groups and writing groups. This is her first, but hopefully not last, novel for children.

Visit Ellen's website at www.EllenHReed.com

Made in the USA
Middletown, DE
26 March 2019